Wolf Mate Surprise

Wolf Mate Surprise

Highland Shifters Book 3

Caroline S. Hilliard

Copyright © 2022 by Cathrine T. Sletta (aka Caroline S. Hilliard)

All rights reserved.

This publication is the sole property of the author, and may not be reproduced, as a whole or in portions, without the express written permission of the author. This publication may not be stored in a retrieval system or uploaded for distribution to others. Thank you for respecting the amount of work that has gone into creating this book.

Produced in Norway.

This book is a work of fiction and the product of the author's imagination. Names, characters, organizations, locations, and events are either the product of the author's imagination or used fictitiously. Any resemblance to actual persons, living or dead, organizations, events or locations is purely coincidental.

ISBN: 979-8-4353-4657-2

Copy edited by Lia Fairchild

Cover design by Munch + Nano
Thank you for creating such a beautiful cover for my story.

CONTENTS

About this book	i
Chapter 1	1
Chapter 2	11
Chapter 3	25
Chapter 4	39
Chapter 5	55
Chapter 6	70
Chapter 7	87
Chapter 8	98
Chapter 9	111
Chapter 10	123
Chapter 11	144
Chapter 12	154
Chapter 13	164
Chapter 14	178
Chapter 15	190
Chapter 16	205

Chapter 17	223
Chapter 18	235
Chapter 19	249
Epilogue	263
Books by Caroline S. Hilliard	272
About the author	273

ABOUT THIS BOOK

There's no second chance at love for a shifter. Or so he thought.

Julianne is instantly attracted to the gorgeous man at the pub. But he's gone before she can pluck up her courage to talk to him. She has all but given up hope of ever seeing him again when he comes to her rescue.

Being cornered by her possessive ex leads to the revelation of a world she never knew existed. One where shifters and witches are real and living among the unsuspecting humans. And the amazing man she's falling for is one of them. But would he have told her if he didn't have to?

Duncan can't forget the wild-haired beauty from the pub. If he didn't know better, he might have thought that she's his true mate. But she can't be. He already met his mate years ago, and she rejected him.

Somehow Julianne dulls the pain of his mate's rejection, and he's pulled to her like a bee to a succulent flower. Even knowing she can never replace his true mate, and that their fling might be short-lived, he cannot resist her. But can he live with the knowledge that she can never truly be his? And is it fair to her?

This work is intended for mature audiences. It contains explicit sexual situations and violence that some readers may find disturbing.

CHAPTER 1

Duncan sighed. He needed a distraction. Badly. The old pain and disappointment surfacing had taken him by surprise and rendered him close to catatonic for the last twenty-four hours. He had thought the worst was over. Finally starting to enjoy life again, he had foolishly let his guard down. Well, that wasn't entirely true. The wild-haired beauty at the pub had taken him completely by surprise.

Desperate to pee, she had begged him to let her go ahead of him, and while he stood there behind her waiting for whoever was in the toilet to finish, his body had decided it wanted her. Seriously fucking wanted her. *Fucking* being the operative word. Her looks, her voice, her scent. Everything about her appealed to him, and he hadn't been able to control his body's reaction.

A few minutes later, Duncan had walked out of the pub with an erection as solid as a steel bar in his pants. Walking around the pub with his dick throbbing and ready for action wasn't an option, so he had walked back to his hotel room.

But that wasn't the source of his pain. That surfaced later when he couldn't get the wild-haired beauty out of his head no matter what he did.

A shifter like him might interpret his reaction to this woman as a sign that she was his mate, his true mate. And for a werewolf like him that might have been true, if not for the fact that he had already found his mate years ago, and she had rejected him.

There was no such thing as two true mates for one werewolf, so that was it. Duncan had already found his mate, and he wouldn't get another chance.

Losing your true mate was always devastating for a shifter, and there were quite a few examples of shifters going insane or dying as a result of losing their mate. Duncan could understand why. Although in his case, it wasn't really losing his chance with Sarah, his true mate, that was the cause of his lingering pain. It was the knowledge that his opportunity for a truly happy mating was lost. He wanted a mate and pups, but the knowledge that he would have to settle for second best scared him away from commitment.

He sighed again. It was time to bury the old pain, and Duncan knew the best cure. A woman. A short, no-strings fling with a beautiful woman. Someone with the beauty, voice, and scent to set a man's blood on fire. The wild-haired beauty had been the cause of his recent dive into painful thoughts, but she would also be his cure. A night or two with her and he would get the fantasy of her out of his mind and be back to his usual uncomplicated existence in no time.

After a quick shower, he dressed and exited his

some of the locals. Just for a chat and a laugh, though—nothing else."

"Then go for it." Sabrina gave her a small smile. "And perhaps you can pick up someone for me while you're at it. You know I'm no good at that sort of thing. I tend to scare men not attract them."

"And by pick someone up for you, you mean…" Julianne knew perfectly well what her friend meant, but she couldn't help teasing her. Sabrina was probably the most prudent and correct person Julianne knew, and even though she pretended not to be, her friend was a bit shy around men. And not shy in the sense of a cute type of coy. Instead, Sabrina tended to be stern and standoffish when men approached her. She had a tendency to confuse men and make them keep their distance. Julianne had watched it happen many times. A man would approach Sabrina, drawn in by her big blue eyes and long blond hair, and try to strike up a conversation, only to have his hopes dashed by her friend's curt nods and one-syllable responses.

A slight red tinge crept over Sabrina's face and neck. "You know what I mean. Just someone I can talk to while you're busy charming the local produce."

Julianne grinned at her friend and nodded. "I know. Just checking. You want something to drink?"

"Just another black soda, please."

Julianne nodded and left her seat to head for the bar. Sabrina didn't drink much. The occasional glass of wine. That was all.

Julianne eyed the clientele hanging around the bar before approaching. There were a couple of men who were worthy of more than a casual glance, and Julianne aimed for them. They were both decent-looking and been more or less continuously since she had met him. Tall, probably about six foot four, with a seriously muscular body. Short and curly brown hair and dark-brown eyes. The truth was that she couldn't get him out of her head, and it was kind of distracting. If she hadn't been so desperate to pee at the time, Julianne probably would have tried to strike up more of a conversation. And after she had been to the toilet, he was next, so there was no time for a chat then either. Instead, she had gone back to the table she was sharing with Sabrina. After gushing about the man to her friend for fifteen minutes, Julianne had plucked up the courage to go talk to him. But by then he was nowhere to be found.

"You're thinking about him again." Sabrina had an uncanny ability to guess what was on Julianne's mind.

"Yeah, but I'm going to stop. No point regretting a lost opportunity. I've only seen him the one time. Most likely he's a tourist like us and has probably left this town by now. I'm never going to lay eyes on him again." Which was a shame because she wanted to look into those warm dark-brown eyes again. Or perhaps they were black. Julianne hadn't been able to decide. Was there such a thing as black eyes?

Sabrina shrugged. "I'm sure there are other men in this town worthy of your attention. But you have to give them a chance, even if they don't catch your eye the first time you look at them. Some jewels have to be dug out and polished before they can shine."

Chuckling with amusement, Julianne swung her gaze from scanning the people in the pub back to her friend. "You and your proverbs." She sighed. "But I know you're right. And it would be nice to get to know sitting across the table from her. They were back at the pub in Fort William for dinner, as they had been every night while staying in the Scottish town.

"I mean it. You should find yourself a nice Scot to bump pelvises with while we're here. It would do you a wealth of good." Sabrina stared at her, looking completely serious.

Julianne smiled as she shook her head at her friend. "Sabrina, I'm not a one-night stand kind of woman. You know that." But her thoughts immediately went to the perfect specimen of a man she had spoken to three days earlier. "Although, if I ever see Mr. Tall, Built, and Chivalrous again, I might reconsider."

Her friend's serious expression softened into a gentle smile. "That's what I'm talking about. Someone like that would boost your confidence and take your mind off Mr. Stupid, Cheating Asshole."

"My ex isn't really occupying much of my mind anymore, you know. I'm done with him. But I'm not ready to get out there yet. The whole dating scene feels a bit overwhelming." Julianne sighed before narrowing her eyes in mock indignation at Sabrina. "You, on the other hand, need to get laid. Badly. What has it been? Two years? My three months of singlehood is nothing compared to that."

Lifting an eyebrow in response, Sabrina clearly wasn't ready to get into that discussion. "Nice try in turning this around on me. But no. This is about you, getting over your idiot of an ex once and for all."

Julianne just laughed and shook her head slowly. "Let's just focus on enjoying our holiday. Whatever happens, happens." The image of the gorgeous man from three days ago was clear in her mind, as it had bedroom. The kitchen was empty, and he breathed out a sigh of relief. Duncan usually wasn't one to mope around in his room, so there were sure to be questions from the others living in the large house. But he really wasn't in the mood to placate Trevor and Jennie's concerns at the moment.

Trevor was the owner of the estate where Duncan was living, and a fellow werewolf. He had recently found his mate, a human woman from America called Jennie.

Duncan and Trevor had been friends for a long time. The estate in Fearolc in Scotland was Trevor's property, but since he spent most of his time in America, Duncan ran the estate on a daily basis. Which suited him fine. It was remote, Fearolc being a small village on the west coast, but not too far from Fort William to be able to go there for a night at the pub or a couple of hours of bed play with a pretty barmaid or tourist. Usually he opted for both.

Duncan set about making himself a quick omelet. He needed some food in his belly before setting off to the pub. But he didn't want to spend too long preparing a meal before leaving, or he would risk being late for a possible reunion with the wild-haired beauty. At least he hoped she would be there. He realized it was a long shot, since she was obviously a tourist, but it was worth a try. And if she wasn't there, he would have to find another woman to spend the night with. But he really hoped it didn't come to that.

∞∞∞∞

Julianne laughed as she looked at her friend Sabrina

had what she thought looked like kind faces. Sidling up to the counter right next to them, she waited her turn to be served.

One of the guys she had selected turned his head and looked at her, and she returned his gaze with a smile.

"What would you like?" His voice was steady as he stared at her.

Julianne kept smiling at him. "A beer would we nice. Something local. And a black soda for my friend over there." She pointed at Sabrina, who nodded in response with a soft smile on her face.

The guy turned and let his gaze linger on Sabrina for several seconds before returning it to Julianne. "Sure. Coming right up."

He ordered before turning back to her. "I'm Connor and this is Sebastian." Connor indicated his friend, who nodded at Julianne in greeting.

"I'm Julianne, and my friend's name is Sabrina."

Their drinks were placed on the counter in front of them. The guys had both ordered beers. Connor handed her the beer she had ordered, before taking his own beer and Sabrina's soda, and headed toward the table where Sabrina was sitting.

It was obvious he was intending to hit on Sabrina, and Julianne had to clamp her mouth shut not to laugh. She gave him fifteen minutes tops. By that time his self-esteem would have taken so many hits he would either be in tears, or he would be leaving in anger. And Julianne was betting on the second outcome.

Reaching the table, Connor introduced himself to Sabrina, who eyed him suspiciously before quietly uttering her name. Julianne would have liked to keep observing the exchange between Connor and Sabrina, but instead she chose to focus her attention on Sebastian, who had sat down beside her. Her first impression was that he was the silent one of the two guys, but she had been wrong before.

Looking at Sebastian, she smiled. "So, do you live around here?"

He returned her smile, but it didn't quite reach his eyes. "No, I'm from Glasgow. Just here for a few days."

She snuck a glance at Sabrina and almost burst out laughing. Her friend had a barely concealed look of disgust on her face and was leaning a little away from Connor, who was in the middle of an animated tale by the looks of it.

Swinging her gaze back to Sebastian, Julianne was taken aback at the hungry expression on his face as he blatantly stared at her breasts. Noticing she had turned back to him, Sebastian raised his gaze to her face and gave her a bland smile. There was no look of embarrassment or shame on his face.

Julianne felt the need to say something sharp, but she didn't want to make a scene. The only thing he was guilty of was staring at her body, and even though it was rude, it wasn't a crime.

She looked over at Sabrina. Connor was leaning in a bit more, and her friend was starting to look pissed off. By the looks of things, it was only a matter of time before Sabrina would tell him in no uncertain terms to get lost.

A hand on her thigh made her jerk and snap her gaze to Sebastian. He was leering at her with a sly expression on his face. So much for thinking these guys had kind faces.

"Move your hand." Julianne stared at Sebastian, letting him see her anger at him taking liberties like this.

"Sure. I'd be happy to." His nasty grin broadened as he slid his hand between her legs.

Gasping, she tried to move away from him, but he put an arm around her waist and pulled her closer to him on the bench seat.

"I think the lady was quite clear. Move!"

Julianne shivered at the force of the command. The voice was deep with a bit of a growl to it, and she felt an urge to obey, even though the command clearly wasn't directed at her.

Sebastian's grip on her loosened a bit, but he didn't let her go. "Find someone else. This one is taken."

Fury shot through her. *This one.* Like she was a toy that could be owned. Well, she had been around the block a time or two, and she had learned to defend herself. Before Sebastian realized what she was planning, Julianne shoved her hand between his legs and squeezed hard. A high thin squeal came out of his mouth as his face contorted in surprised agony. His hands disappeared from her body as he crumpled forward in his seat, moaning as his bruised testicles were giving him hell.

As soon as Sebastian let her go, she shot out of her seat to get away from him. Only to crash headfirst into a massive chest. A large hand landed on her shoulder steadying her.

"Easy. I think you took care of him beautifully." There was amusement in the deep voice. "He'll probably think twice before bothering you again."

She raised her eyes, her gaze locking with warm dark-brown orbs. And she grinned when recognition sang through her. *Him.* It was him. And he had come to her rescue when she needed him.

CHAPTER 2

Duncan felt his beast relax as he stared into the wild-haired beauty's sparkling green eyes. She was safe. The asshole who had touched her had paid for what he'd done. He could still hear the bastard moaning in pain. *Good.* Otherwise, Duncan would have had to sort the idiot out himself.

"Thank you for helping me. Again."

Duncan grinned at her. Her words proved she remembered him. At least he had made some kind of impression last time they'd met, even though he had been speechless by her strong effect on him at the time.

She was more beautiful than he remembered. Dark lashes framed her green eyes. A nice contrast to her pale complexion. Freckles like a sprinkle of cocoa powder covered the smooth skin across her straight nose and high cheekbones. And surrounding her beautiful face were wild thick auburn tresses reaching down past her shoulders. Her scent of chocolate and spice surrounded him and made his cock twitch, but keeping in mind what she had done to the asshole touching her without her consent helped him to tamp down his desire.

"Anytime, but I think your actions were more effective than mine. Good to know you can protect yourself."

She sighed and looked away from him. "I wish I didn't have to, but some guys…"

Duncan felt himself frowning. "You mean you experience this kind of behavior often?" The idea had his hackles rising, and an urge to be there and protect her rose in him.

She looked up at him and shook her head. "No, not often. But it has happened before."

The need to protect her and prevent something like this from happening to her again made him stare at her. "I'll protect you."

As soon as the words were out of his mouth, he inwardly cringed. What had made him say something like that? Duncan didn't have any intention of following her around all the time. He would like to spend a couple of nights with her, that was all.

Her face broke into a huge smile. "I believe you, but I can't actually afford a bodyguard."

Duncan smiled back, thankful she had taken his statement as a joke.

"Julianne, will you introduce me to your new friend?"

Duncan looked up as a female put her hand on the wild-haired beauty's arm. The woman was pretty in a polished way. Too polished for his liking, with big blue eyes and a refined face. Long, straight, and glossy blond hair fell down her back.

"Um." Julianne looked up at him, a slight blush creeping over her face.

He smiled down at her. "Duncan. My name is Duncan."

"Julianne." She turned and indicated her friend. "And this is my friend Sabrina."

"Nice to meet you both." He nodded in greeting to Sabrina, who was studying him in a way that made him feel like she could see right through him. All his thoughts, all his shortcomings.

"Shall we try to find another table here or would you like to go somewhere else? There is another pub up the road. Looks a bit rougher than this one, but it's actually quite nice. I know the manager, so—"

"We'll go there." Julianne cut him off abruptly. "I've had enough of this place."

"Okay." Duncan swung his gaze to Sabrina, and she gave him a small nod.

Exiting the pub, they walked three abreast up the street with Julianne in the middle.

"So, I guess you live around here then?" Julianne gave him a quick glance before looking ahead.

"Yes. Well. Not here in Fort William but in a small village not far from here, toward the west coast."

"Really? We were actually talking about going further west to see more of the coast. It's supposed to be beautiful."

Duncan could feel her eyes on him as she was talking, but he resisted meeting her gaze. He wanted her to be able to look at him uninterrupted, and hopefully she liked what she saw. Some people were intimidated by his size, but she didn't seem to be.

"It is." The coast was beautiful and wild. Like her, with her beautiful face and wild hair. "I can show you some nice places if you want. Not the typical tourist spots."

"Oh. That would be perfect."

Her happy voice made him turn his head and look at her. The brilliant smile on her face did something to him. Like a ray of light shining directly at his chest, heating his body. And not just by desire.

Duncan moved his gaze to Sabrina, where she was walking on the other side of Julianne. "If you both would like that, of course."

A small smile formed on her face, before she glanced his way and gave him a quick nod. "Thank you. That would be nice."

"Okay. You just tell me when you'd like to go then."

They reached the other pub, and Duncan let the two women enter ahead of him.

He nodded at Brian, the manager. Brian was tending the bar himself this evening, and he grinned as Duncan approached the counter with the women. True to his nature as a bear shifter, Brian was a big, burly fellow. Happily mated, with two teenage daughters. The pub was a favorite among the shifters in the area, but it was also frequented by other locals and tourists.

"Duncan. What can I get you and the beautiful ladies with you?"

Turning his head toward Julianne and Sabrina, Duncan raised one eyebrow in a silent question.

Julianne smiled her beautiful smile. "A beer, please. Anything you recommend."

Brian nodded and turned his gaze to Sabrina. "And for you?"

"Just an ice water, please."

Her expression was unreadable as she carefully studied the people in the pub, and Duncan got the same feeling he had earlier. That Sabrina was somehow reading people, gaining more information about each one than could possibly be picked up by a normal person.

"I think there's still some tables available in the back." Brian put their drinks on the counter and nodded at Duncan.

Duncan nodded back. "Thanks."

Leading the way, Duncan walked down a short corridor to the back of the pub. It was filling up, but there was still a couple of free tables. Letting the women slide into the small, curved bench seat, he took the only chair.

"Is there a toilet in this place?" Julianne stood.

Duncan couldn't help the grin spreading across his face, remembering the way they had met three days ago. "Yeah. Go back to the bar and up the stairs. You can't miss it."

Julianne had just disappeared from sight when he was startled by Sabrina's blunt question. "So, who are you really?"

His eyes snapped to hers to see her staring at him. "What?" There could be several reasons for her asking. She might be trying to protect her friend from another guy like the one Julianne had just fended off. Or it could be a deeper question concerning his nature as a shifter.

Sabrina sighed in apparent exasperation, like he was

being difficult or deliberately stupid. Which he supposed was close to the truth.

"Who are you?" She narrowed her eyes. "Or shall I say what? You project an unusual amount of energy. I've encountered similar before, but nothing quite on the scale of what you did earlier when coming to Julianne's rescue. Are you a warlock of some kind?"

He was shocked. It was only a couple of days ago that he realized witches were real. Not just creatures popular in folklore and fairy tales. But this woman obviously knew about witches. And warlocks. Duncan had never heard about warlocks in real life, but it wasn't a stretch to assume they were the male equivalent of witches.

"Not exactly." Debating what to tell her, he landed on something close to the truth. "But you're right that I'm a bit more than human. What do you know about warlocks?"

Sabrina studied him for several seconds before responding. "Are you going to tell me what you are? I would like an answer before I tell you what I know."

Duncan sighed and stared into his pint. This wasn't something he should be discussing with a stranger. Walking away would be the best thing to do. But just the thought of never seeing Julianne again made his stomach tense up. He had come to Fort William to find her, and he couldn't let her go until he had at least talked to her some more.

Lifting his gaze to meet her blue one, he made a decision. Sabrina already knew about witches. And that might not be all she knew of the supernatural world. Even if she didn't know about shifters yet, she would most likely find out soon with the way she observed and analyzed people around her. It was only a matter of time.

"I'm a shifter. A wolf shifter." Duncan studied her face as he let the information sink in, but there was no shock or surprise to detect.

She seemed to consider his words for a few seconds. "A werewolf." It was more of a statement than a question.

He nodded. "We're called that too."

"So how does that work? You change into a wolf when the moon is full?"

"Yes and no. I change into a wolf, but not just at a full moon. I can change anytime I want."

Nodding, she seemed to accept his words without any trepidation or surprise.

"So, what are you?" He might as well be as blunt as she was. No point in dragging this out. Julianne would be back soon, and he would like to know as much as possible by then.

"I guess the most common term is witch, and I'd appreciate it if you didn't tell Julianne. She doesn't know what I am." Sabrina didn't appear concerned about telling him. Most likely because he had already told her something about himself that she could use against him as leverage if necessary.

Duncan frowned, remembering his experience with witches in the last couple of days. Apparently, they could heal people, but they could also take over someone's mind and even flay someone alive just by using a burst of their power.

"Am I interrupting something?" Julianne's voice had him snap out of his thoughts about witches.

Raising his gaze to her, Duncan smiled and shook

his head. "Your friend is just watching out for you, is all."

"Oh no." Julianne turned to her friend. "Sabrina, have you interrogated him?" She looked shocked and horrified.

Duncan chuckled and answered before Sabrina could. "Don't worry. She's been gentle. Nothing I can't handle."

Sabrina lifted an eyebrow at him but didn't correct him.

"Leaving you alone with him was a mistake, it seems." Julianne narrowed her eyes at her friend, but the corners of her mouth were quivering a little with amusement. "Don't scare my gorgeous savior away. I might need him again sometime."

He snorted at her unexpected words, and she turned to him with a brilliant smile and green orbs shining with amusement. Duncan hoped she meant what she said about him being gorgeous. That it wasn't just something she uttered to be funny and cute. A weird kind of tingling sensation spread through his chest, unlike anything he had ever felt before.

***

Julianne watched the surprise on Duncan's face at her words. Like he hadn't expected her to think he was gorgeous. Which was absurd. There was no way he didn't know how amazing he looked. Tall and dark with the thickly muscled body of a god. And a pleasant and caring personality. That he wasn't already taken was a miracle, and she was quite sure he wasn't. Unless he liked to prey on women like her, pretending to be considerate and protective to draw them in. But she didn't think so. Her gut was telling her that Duncan was a genuinely nice guy.

"So, when can you give us a guided tour of the west coast?" She decided to pick up their conversation from earlier to get back to a safe topic. Duncan had a bit of a funny expression on his face, and she didn't want him to decide to leave because of the sudden awkwardness between them.

Looking relieved at the change of subject, he looked up from his perusal of his pint. "Anytime. Whenever you want."

"Are you on holiday at the moment?" Sabrina's question made Julianne cringe. It sounded like she didn't believe Duncan had a job.

Chuckling, he looked at Sabrina. "My work is flexible. I'm taking care of a large estate with everything that entails, but I plan my own workdays. Whether I choose to work in the evening, weekend, or the middle of the day doesn't really matter, unless there is something urgent that needs taking care of."

Julianne swallowed down her embarrassment at her friend's invasive question. "Tomorrow. Is tomorrow okay? The weather is supposed to be good for another couple of days. After that it gets dicey."

"Tomorrow is good." Duncan's smile drew her gaze to his face. Strong jaw and high cheekbones, skin covered in a becoming five o'clock shadow. All male and extremely attractive. And those lips. Masculine yet soft-looking. Julianne had a sudden impulse to lean forward and kiss him.

Realizing she had been staring at his lips for several seconds, she quickly looked away in embarrassment and tried to remember what they had been talking about. *Right, west coast tomorrow.*

"Good. Tomorrow then." She forced herself to look at him.

As he nodded at her slowly, Julianne could see the corner of Duncan's mouth twitch with amusement. He had obviously noticed the way she had been staring at his lips.

"Your accent is a bit hard to place," Duncan said. "It seems to be a mix from several places. Where are you from?"

Julianne inwardly sighed in relief at Duncan's question. Perhaps he had picked up on her mortification and decided to rescue her again. It appeared to be something he was particularly good at. "New Jersey originally, but I've lived in London for the last six years. I guess my American accent has withered a bit over the years."

"And you, Sabrina?" Duncan swung his gaze to her friend. "I can't place your accent, either, although it's not the same as Julianne's."

Sabrina let the corners of her lips pull up into something resembling a smile. "I grew up in South Africa. We moved to Edinburgh when I was fourteen and on to London at seventeen."

"Makes sense, then, that I wasn't able to guess where either of you are from. I'm Scottish, but I lived in America for many years before moving back here a couple of years ago."

"Many." Julianne looked at him, giving him a small smile. "It can't be that many years since you can't be much older than I am. Or, did you move to America as a boy?"

Duncan shook his head, and his eyes darted to Sabrina. "No. I was an adult by the time I moved across the Atlantic. Maybe it just felt longer than it really was. I had a good time, but it was nice to come home."

Julianne was a bit confused by the look Duncan gave her friend. Like Sabrina knew something about Duncan that Julianne didn't. A feeling like she was being kept out of a big secret crept over her, and she took a sip of her beer to try to hide how that made her feel.

"Your perception of time depends on how you spend it."

Sabrina's voice interrupted her thoughts and suddenly Julianne understood. Duncan and Sabrina had been talking while she had been to the toilet. They had, of course, already talked about his time in America.

Smiling, she looked at Sabrina before she swung her gaze to Duncan. "Proverbs. It's her specialty."

Duncan smiled at Sabrina. "Good to know."

Julianne launched into a series of questions about the west coast of Scotland, and Duncan answered whatever he could, which was most of them. Until Sabrina called a halt to their evening.

"I think it's time we got some sleep. It sounds like it'll be a busy day tomorrow." After glancing at Julianne, Sabrina turned to Duncan. "Thank you, Duncan. We've had a pleasant evening."

"No problem. And so have I. Thank you." Duncan rose from his seat. "Can I give you a ride somewhere?"

Julianne got up and let her gaze glide over his tall, muscular form as she tipped her head back to meet his eyes. "We're only staying about a mile away, so we'll be fine walking. But it's nice of you to offer."

"Are you sure? It's no trouble at all, and then I'll know that you're safe."

So protective. This guy wasn't merely one-night stand material; he was boyfriend material. Perhaps even more than that. Julianne felt her cheeks heating at the thought and quickly looked away. "Okay. Since you put it that way."

"Let's go then." Duncan started walking.

Sabrina raised an eyebrow at her while they were following Duncan out of the pub, but Julianne just shook her head. This wasn't the time to express her thoughts or explain them.

Exiting the pub, they followed him up a side street to a small parking lot. A sleek blue sportscar responded with a beep as they approached it.

After getting in, Duncan started the car. The engine purred to life, and Julianne sighed in contentment at the sound. She had always been partial to the solid rumble of a powerful engine, and this most definitely was one of those.

Duncan turned his head toward her and stared at her with an odd look on his face. "You like cars?"

She gave him a huge smile. It was funny how he resembled Sabrina in that he somehow knew what was on Julianne's mind. "Yes, I love a powerful, well-maintained engine and the art of engineering that goes into making it."

Chuckling, he maneuvered the car out of the cramped parking lot. "A woman after my own heart. Where to?"

"North."

"Okay. You just give me directions as we go then. I'll do whatever you tell me to."

Julianne's lower belly tingled at his words. That would sound even better if repeated in another setting.

Duncan steered the car expertly through the narrow streets until they got to the main road. She indicated to continue north, and they drove for about a minute.

"Just up here on the right." She used the opportunity to rest her eyes on his face for a few seconds. He really was one of the most gorgeous men she had ever met. And his pleasant and caring nature just added to his attractiveness.

Parking the car at the side of the road, he turned to her, but she didn't turn away in embarrassment this time. Julianne wanted him to know she was interested.

Sabrina opened the door and got out of the backseat, but Julianne couldn't seem to make herself move just yet. "I'd invite you in, but…"

His lips stretched into a slow smile. "But we have an early start in the morning if you want to see a little of the west coast. There's always tomorrow night."

Tomorrow night. There was tomorrow night. Heat started pulsing in her lower belly. Duncan's smile amped up to a huge grin, and she realized her jaw had dropped at the implications of his words. Heat suffused her face, and she quickly turned away and scrambled for the handle to open the car door.

"Here, let me." The door slid open, and she realized that he had pressed a button to open the electric door for her.

"Thank you." She almost shouted the words as she shot out of the car. Then, she checked herself and turned around, but she didn't dare to look at his face. "Thank you, Duncan, for taking us home."

"My pleasure. Pick you up at eight?"

"Yes, eight is great."

"Sleep tight." The door slid closed, and the car pulled away and sped down the road.

"Are you all right?" Sabrina's voice behind her snapped her out of her shock.

"Yes, just shell-shocked."

A small chuckle from her friend had Julianne turn around to look at her. "Are you laughing at me?"

Sabrina nodded. "You really like this guy. Your admiration practically wafts off you."

She groaned. "Oh no. That's embarrassing. He probably thinks I resemble a gawking schoolgirl."

Smiling, her friend shook her head. "No, Duncan likes you. And he's a nice guy. You'd do well with him."

Julianne frowned at her friend. She couldn't remember Sabrina giving a man this kind of praise before. Ever. Not even the man Sabrina herself had been dating for a year had received this kind of approval. "Wow. I've never heard you say anything like that about a man before."

Sabrina smiled before turning around and heading for the small bed and breakfast they were staying at. "Let's get to bed. We have to get up early tomorrow."

Tomorrow, yeah. Julianne couldn't wait.

CHAPTER 3

The car handled perfectly as Duncan drove much too fast on the winding road toward Fearolc. He needed to get home, get some sleep, and be back by eight o'clock in the morning. To see her. Julianne. He couldn't remember being this excited to spend time with a woman. Not since... No, he wasn't going to let his past get in the way of this. Whatever this was, he was going to enjoy it. Enjoy her.

His thoughts went to her expression at his mention of them spending the night together. The heat in her eyes and the deep blush that crept over her face had his cock take notice. He had so carefully stayed in control of his mind all evening, not wanting a repeat of what had happened the first time they'd met.

At least she saw him as a possible bedpartner. And if he played his cards right, perhaps as soon as the next night. Then again, he wanted it to feel right. If Julianne showed any kind of reluctance, he wouldn't push her. It would have to be her choice. He could wait, but he wanted her in his bed. Hopefully, it wouldn't take too long before she was ready. Just the thought of pushing into her wet channel and hearing her moan, had his cock throbbing in no time.

The drive didn't take long at the speed he was going. He soon turned off the main road and followed the dirt road up to the estate. Parking in front of the large house, he noticed there were still lights on in the kitchen. One or more of the occupants had yet to go to bed.

He adjusted his shirt to hide the thick ridge in his jeans as he approached the entrance. Either it was Trevor and Jennie—his landlord and landlady, so to speak—who had decided to have a late snack, or it was Michael and his mate, Stephanie.

Michael and Stephanie had mated just two days ago, shortly after being rescued from a local panther clan. Jack Malcolm Williams, the alpha of the panther clan, had kidnapped Stephanie in order to mate her in a special ceremony. Ambrosia, an evil witch and Jack's co-conspirator, was going to use their mating bond to increase Jack's power to a much higher level than a normal alpha, and thereby making him the king of the panthers around the globe. But that wasn't the only, or even main, reason Ambrosia had intended to increase Jack's power. The witch would gain something from the ritual as well. They hadn't been able to discover what she would gain exactly, but it would have to be something significant for her to let someone else obtain as much power as she had been intending to give Jack.

Thankfully, they had been able to rescue Michael and Stephanie and stop Jack's mating ceremony.

Trevor, Jennie, and Duncan, as well as Michael and Jennie's friends, had all been a part of the mission to save Michael and Stephanie from the panther's clutches. It had all turned out well, except for the small matter of a missing evil witch. In all the chaos, Ambrosia had managed to escape, and they were all worried she would plan a similar stunt with another alpha.

Entering the kitchen, Duncan grinned at the sight that met him. Thankfully, the thought of the evil witch had quickly taken care of his hard cock, and he felt comfortable stepping into the room, where his friend Trevor was swearing as he pulled something flat and black out of the oven.

"Trying to impress Jennie with your cooking skills again, are you?" Duncan couldn't help poking at his friend's pride. Trevor wasn't actually a bad cook.

"Not impressed." Jennie's amused voice from the living room had Duncan burst out laughing.

"Like this wasn't just as much your fault." Trevor's reply was obviously for Jennie, and Duncan had a feeling he knew what had happened.

"New mates." Duncan couldn't stop grinning. Someone had obviously gotten a bit carried away while waiting for their pizza to cook.

"Yes. And loving it." Jennie walked into the kitchen, smiling. "We only need to get better at setting an alarm to remind us of important things, like a pizza in the oven."

Laughing, Duncan turned to head for his bedroom. He needed sleep before playing guide to Julianne in the morning. And her friend, of course. But it was the wild-haired beauty who was his primary focus.

"Not so fast there, mister." Jennie's voice was serious, and he turned around with a smile.

"Sounds like I'm in trouble." Duncan watched as Jennie's face softened into a smile.

"Not so much. It's nice to see you smiling and laughing again. You had us worried there for a while. Are you all good now, or is there anything we can do to help?"

Their concern for him was touching, but he didn't really want to explain the reason for his somber mood the last few days. Duncan had never shared his failure with anyone, and he intended to keep it that way. "I'm fine. You don't need to worry about me."

Jennie didn't look convinced, but she let it go. At least for the time being.

"We're going north for a few days." Trevor walked up beside Jennie, his arm snaking around her waist and pulling her close. "Visiting Leith. We'll leave in the morning."

"If you can get out of bed you mean." Duncan grinned. As newly mated Trevor and Jennie couldn't stay away from each other. Constantly touching when among other people, and often holed up in their bedroom for hours during the day. Duncan had wanted a mate for a long time, but even he thought their focus on each other was excessive. Having a mate would be great, but being attached at the hip like Trevor and Jennie, and come to think of it, Michael and Stephanie, was a bit much.

"Okay, maybe not the morning. But at least some time during the day." Jennie was looking up at Trevor with a heat in her eyes that made Duncan feel like he was a voyeur, watching something that should be private.

"Um, I think I'll go to bed."

"Before you go." Trevor's words stopped him before he had taken one step. "We'll talk to Leith about Ambrosia and what happened with the panthers. He knows a lot of shifters and might be able to help us figure out which packs or clans to watch more closely. Maybe he knows whether there are any unmated alphas in the north and can help us warn them."

"Sounds good. Just tell me if there's anything I can do. I don't know of any unmated alphas, but I'll talk to a few people and see what I can find out."

"Thank you, Duncan. We'll be back in less than a week. Any news, just call."

Duncan nodded. "You too. Enjoy your trip to Loch Ness and say hello to Leith from me. I haven't seen him in months."

Trevor smiled and nodded back. "Will do."

Making his way up to his room, Duncan thought about his friend Leith. The man was one of the most perceptive people he knew, and always willing to help someone out. He could come across as broody but that was probably because of his solemn expression. Duncan had seldom seen the man laugh. Leith was a rare kind of shifter, and it had to be difficult not to have any of your kind around you to share experiences with. There were a few others like Leith around the world, but no more than about twenty, and none of them were living close to each other.

Stepping into his bedroom, Duncan undressed and went into the bathroom. After brushing his teeth, he crawled into his large bed. It was a bigger bed than he needed, since he always slept in it alone. Enjoying the company of a couple of women a week wasn't unusual for him, but he never brought any of them back to the estate. At least he hadn't so far. For some reason he didn't feel the usual reluctance when thinking about bringing Julianne into his personal space.

∞∞∞

Julianne woke early and got into the shower. Her sleep had been broken and restless, but she still felt ready for a new day. Excited even. To experience the west coast. And to see Duncan again. The man was as gorgeous as a Greek god, but that was only one part of what drew her to him. His always-protective, always-caring personality was the other part. He was unlike most other guys she had met, who were primarily interested in what she could give them and not so much the other way around.

Sabrina was up by the time Julianne got out of the shower. Usually her friend was the early riser of the two of them.

"Eager to see him again?" Sabrina lifted an eyebrow at her.

Julianne smiled and shook her head in mock exasperation. "This is turning out exactly the way you wanted it to, isn't it? To find a Scot to bump pelvises with, as you so eloquently put it. Duncan might be willing to do that, but I'm still not sure it's a good idea."

"You need the confidence boost. Just roll with it." Sabrina gathered some fresh clothes and headed for the bathroom.

Julianne burst out laughing. "Just roll with it. Where

did that come from? You don't usually speak like that. You're all about control."

"Perhaps I'm changing. Trying to be more modern. Your suggestion, remember?" After throwing her a quick glance, Sabrina disappeared into the bathroom and closed the door behind her.

They had breakfast, and each of them made a packed lunch. Duncan hadn't elaborated on where he was taking them, but he had mentioned places that weren't typical tourist spots. A clear indication that buying lunch might be out of the question, and a packed lunch was the safest bet.

After packing some extra clothes, food, and water in their backpacks, they went out to the road to wait. It was still ten minutes until Duncan had said he would pick them up, but it was a nice morning, and they might as well wait outside in case he was early.

A big black SUV pulled up to the curb in front of them, and Duncan jumped out of the vehicle. He rounded the car with a huge smile on his face. "Good morning. Did you sleep well?"

Sabrina answered affirmatively, but all Julianne could do was nod. Wearing shorts and a fitted tee, Duncan was even more mouthwateringly handsome than he had been the night before. And that was saying something. His sculpted torso and arms were thick with muscles that she would like nothing more than to run her hands over. And his powerful legs could have belonged to a professional athlete. Her eyes rose to his tanned face and met his laughing black eyes. They looked black in the sun.

"Did you remember to pack your swimsuits?" Duncan's dark voice sent a shiver down her back.

"Julianne?"

She felt herself blushing with embarrassment, as she realized that she had been staring at him for several seconds and hadn't been paying attention to what he was saying.

"What was that? I'm sorry I…" She didn't know how to explain her completely malfunctioning brain. This didn't usually happen to her. Normally she was levelheaded and not easily embarrassed, but around this man she acted like a blushing schoolgirl with a crush.

"I was asking whether you remembered to pack your swimsuits. There's this small, secluded beach I was planning to take you to."

"We've got our swimsuits, but we forgot to bring our towels. I'll go fetch them." Sabrina had already turned around and was heading for the entrance by the time Julianne turned to her.

"Thank you, Sabrina." She smiled at her friend's retreating back before turning back to Duncan.

"You look beautiful today." There was a hint of desire in Duncan's gaze as he stared into her eyes. "I mean, you did yesterday as well, but the sun on your face…" He suddenly looked away like he didn't know how to continue the sentence and became a bit shy.

"Thank you, Duncan." Somehow his sudden shyness gave his compliment a higher value, and it warmed her. "You look really good yourself. I guess you probably realized that from my drooling just now."

"Drooling, huh?" There was a huge grin on his face when he swung his gaze back on her. "Then I guess you won't mind if I do this."

Duncan suddenly closed the distance between them, and she felt his hands on her shoulders. He leaned down and gave her a kiss on her cheekbone, right below her eye. Smiling, he stepped back. "Yeah, chocolate. That's what I thought."

Confused by his actions and words, Julianne stared at him. "What?" The place his lips had touched her seemed to pulse with heat, and she relished the feeling, but it had an addling effect on her brain.

"Your cute freckles look like a light sprinkle of chocolate powder. I have been wanting to test my theory ever since I first met you. And I was right. You do taste like chocolate."

Julianne burst out laughing. How could she not? She had never been fond of her freckles growing up, but she had learned to accept them. Duncan's unusual compliment was by far the best she had ever been given.

Opening the passenger side door, Duncan indicated for her to get in. "Shall we? I'm sure Sabrina will be along any minute." Then he frowned as he studied her face. "Have you put on sunscreen? With your complexion you will get burnt today if—"

Walking over to him, she interrupted his concerned speech with a smile before he could finish. "I've put on sunscreen. High factor. I know I can't be out in the sun without it. The bottle is in my backpack, so I can reapply it often."

"Good." He smiled down at her and held out his hand. "Give me your pack and I'll put it in the back."

Sabrina returned just as Julianne was getting into the vehicle. Duncan put their packs in the back, and they all got in and fastened their seatbelts.

***

The scent of Julianne lingered in his nostrils, and the feel of her soft skin against his lips had him fighting his body's reaction to her. No woman had ever had this profound effect on him before, and he liked it. Duncan knew it wouldn't last, but it was exhilarating all the same. The excitement of just being around her caused him to forget all about his pain for a while, and it was such a relief he actually felt more relaxed than he had in a long time. Excited and relaxed at the same time. It didn't seem possible, but that was how he felt.

"Do you have a lot of cars or just the two we have seen so far?" Julianne's amused voice snapped him out of his reverie. "I was expecting the Maserati you drove yesterday, so I didn't even realize it was you until you stepped out of the car."

Duncan chuckled. "This SUV is my friend Trevor's car. I'm just borrowing it, since it's a bit more suitable for where we're going today. The Maserati is my only car. I like the way it handles."

He glanced over at Julianne to see her nodding.

"Are you comfortable back there, Sabrina?" Their eyes met in the rearview mirror, and she nodded.

"Yes, thank you."

Duncan would have liked to spend a little more time talking to Sabrina alone. The fact that she was a witch intrigued him. She seemed like a nice person, if a bit too overprotective of Julianne. If only he knew that he could trust her, he would have told her about Ambrosia and asked her advice. They could use all the help they could get in trying to stop the evil witch.

"How long are you staying in Fort William?"

Duncan hoped they were staying for at least a few more days.

"Another week." He could feel Julianne's eyes on him, but he kept his eyes on the road. "The day after tomorrow we're going for a daytrip to the Isle of Sky. It's supposed to be raining that day, but hopefully it'll turn out better than the forecast."

"Are you going there by yourselves or are you joining a guided tour?"

"A guided tour. We thought that was probably the best way to see as much as possible in just one day. There won't be much time to explore on our own, but at least we'll get to see some of the well-known places."

"Anything else planned, or are you just playing it by ear?"

"Well..." Julianne turned to look at Sabrina in the backseat before continuing. "We were talking about taking the train to Mallaig to have a look around the fishing port. Perhaps have lunch at one of the seafood restaurants."

Duncan smiled and nodded. "It's a nice place. We might have time to go there today. It's not too far away from where we're going. Have you noticed the train tracks following the road?"

"Yeah. Those are the tracks going to Mallaig?"

"They are."

"I didn't realize. Makes sense, though, since we're going west from Fort William."

The conversation changed as they neared the west coast. The women gushed at the scenery and pointed out various features of the landscape to each other as Duncan focused on where they were going.

He finally slowed and turned off the main road, onto a small dirt track winding its way up into the hills. After about ten minutes, he stopped the car and turned to the ladies.

"There's a nice spot up here with a magnificent view. It's only about ten minutes' walk, so we can leave everything in the car."

"Okay. Sounds good." Julianne nodded enthusiastically and gave him a brilliant smile.

They exited the vehicle, and Duncan led the way up a small rocky path curving around toward the western side of the hill. After walking a few minutes, a strong scent had him come to a sudden stop and turn around to tell the women to stay quiet. The next thing he knew, Julianne's head collided with his chest, and just like in a cartoon, she bounced off his body. Quickly grabbing her waist, he managed to prevent her from falling on her ass.

"Sorry." He kept his voice low and looked down into her astonished face. "It wasn't my intention to stop so suddenly and make you crash into me. But there's a red deer nearby. If we stay quiet, we might be able to get close enough to see it."

Her lips stretched into a big smile as she nodded vigorously.

Duncan looked behind Julianne to Sabrina, who was standing right behind her friend, nodding.

Letting go of Julianne, he turned around and moved silently ahead on the path. Judging by the strength of its scent, the deer wasn't far away, unless they had already managed to scare it away. Although, Duncan doubted that. He hadn't been listening for wildlife, but he would have picked up the sound of a deer running. The stags could weigh upward of five hundred pounds, so they weren't silent when moving quickly.

There was a rocky outspring ahead, and Duncan slowed as he reached it. Based on the strong scent, the deer should be just around the bend. He inched forward until he spotted it calmly grazing just twenty yards from the path. They were downwind of the large stag, which was working in their favor.

Duncan took a step to the side and indicated for the two women to come forward. Their expressions as they spotted the deer were priceless, and he took the opportunity to study Julianne while the women were captivated by the sight of a prime specimen of Scottish wildlife.

The feel of Julianne's narrow waist beneath his hands was etched into his mind, and Duncan wanted to reach out and touch her again. Only this time he would like to let his hands explore above and below her waist as well.

His cock twitching in response to his thoughts had him averting his eyes. Focusing on the stag, he tried to clear his mind of his desire for the wild-haired beauty beside him.

The animal's head suddenly lifted, and it stared directly at them. It only lasted a second before the red deer bolted away from them and out of sight on the rocky hillside.

"Wow." Julianne's voice was filled with awe. "I never thought we would get to see one in the wild." She turned to him. "Thank you. But how did you know that it was there? I mean, it was still hidden behind the bend when you told us it was nearby."

Duncan didn't meet her eyes but kept his gaze on the place where the deer had been standing. He didn't want to lie to Julianne, so he would stick to the truth as much as possible. "They have a distinctive kind of grunting sound that they use to communicate with other deer." That wasn't a lie, just not how he had known about the stag.

"You've obviously met deer in the wild before. Have you ever been this close to one?"

He turned to her and smiled, looking into her beautiful green eyes. "Yes, a few times. It's possible if you move in from downwind of the animal." He had even killed a few of them in his wolf form, but he couldn't tell her that.

"Wow again. But it was something else you were going to show us up here, wasn't it?"

He chuckled. "Yes, it was. Just another few minutes of walking and we'll be at our destination."

CHAPTER 4

After a short climb, they emerged onto a natural platform shaped by the elements. Julianne was still in awe after seeing the large red deer. It was a magnificent animal with huge antlers and a beautiful reddish-brown coat.

But there was another living creature that had made just as big an impression on her. Maybe more. Walking behind Duncan had left her a bit breathless, and not so much from the short climb. His body was a work of art, moving with the grace and power of a large predator. Julianne didn't know why she made that association, but for some reason it just fit.

Staring at his muscular ass had almost made her stumble more than once. And the thought of seeing his hard body without any clothes to conceal it, had her all hot and bothered. The possibility of spending a night in his arms was teasing her mind and making her both excited and a bit anxious. Duncan was the very image of a male model, while she was just a normal woman. It was enough to make her freak out a little at the thought of being intimate with him.

It took her a couple of seconds before she understood they had reached their destination. The view that met her when she managed to rip her gaze away from Duncan's ass had her speechless. The panorama of the rugged coastline spread out before her in all its magnificence—she could only stare. Scanning the horizon, she counted several islands off the coast.

"That's the Isle of Skye." Julianne turned to see Duncan pointing in a northwesterly direction. "And that's Eigg. Behind it is Rhum, but it's not easy telling the two apart from here."

"And to the south?" She had finally managed to find her voice again.

"That's the Ardnamurchan peninsula. Not an island."

"Wow. I feel like I'm saying that a lot today, but I really mean it. Scotland is a beautiful country and this…" She trailed off, not finding words strong enough to describe what she was seeing and the impression it made on her.

"Is wow?"

Julianne turned to see Duncan grinning at her, and she burst out laughing. "Yeah, that about covers it. I guess the fact that I'm not a poet has become quite obvious by now."

"Well, don't be too hard on yourself. Wow is a powerful word. I understood what you meant, and that's the point of communication, isn't it?" Amusement was shining in his eyes while he was teasing her.

Smiling and shaking her head slowly at his words, she couldn't take her eyes off his face. Wow was right. The Scottish scenery was taking her breath away. Particularly the gorgeous creature she was resting her eyes upon at the moment.

"Is Mallaig north of here then?"

Sabrina's question made Duncan turn to her friend, and Julianne took a slow, deep breath to find her center. This guy was playing havoc with her mind. Or body. Or more accurately, both. In any case she was having trouble thinking straight around him.

"Yes. We can go there later today if you want. Shall we, ladies?" Duncan started walking toward the path down the way they had come.

Sabrina took a few steps to follow Duncan, before hesitating and raising an eyebrow at Julianne in a silent question. Julianne shook her head with a smile and indicated for her friend to go ahead. Then she fell in behind Sabrina. It might be for the best that her friend was between herself and the hunk of a man. Perhaps Julianne would be able to focus on something other than his muscular behind on the way back to the car.

About ten minutes later, they got into the car, and Duncan somehow managed to turn the car around on the narrow dirt track. Shortly after, they were on their way back down the hill toward the main road.

They didn't talk much. The landscape outside the car windows was enough to keep them riveted while Duncan was driving. They finally came to a stop in a forested area at the end of another dirt track.

"Okay, this is it. We have to walk from here." Duncan glanced at Julianne and Sabrina with a smile on his face before exiting the car.

Duncan got their backpacks out of the back of the vehicle and handed them over before he put on his own pack.

"It's about an hour's walk to the small beach. The trail isn't clearly visible everywhere, but I know the way."

"Well, I guess we just have to trust you and hope for the best." Julianne smiled at him.

"Let's hope I'm not a total bastard, then." Duncan glanced at her with a wicked grin on his face. "Just watch out for the evil sheep wandering around, and you'll be fine."

Julianne was left standing there, staring after him for a few seconds, after he turned around and started walking. Was he serious about the sheep? She didn't have a lot of experience with farm animals. For all she knew, there really were evil sheep out there. Scotland had a lot of sheep.

"Don't worry. It was a joke." She turned her head to see Sabrina standing beside her with a small smile on her face.

"Are you sure? I mean Scottish sheep might—" Julianne didn't get to finish her sentence before Duncan called back to them.

"Are you coming, or am I going to have the whole beach to myself?" His face was shining with amusement.

Julianne inwardly groaned in embarrassment and started walking toward him. "Yes, we're coming."

They walked through a changing landscape of forest and grassy areas, with rocks thrown in here and there. The trail was constantly rising and falling through the uneven terrain, as well as changing direction to avoid boggy areas or dense thickets.

Everything was perfect until the sudden bleating of a sheep nearby. Julianne had all but forgotten about the evil sheep, having decided soon after they started walking that the whole thing was a joke, and there would be no encounters with sheep on their way to the beach.

A large white woolen beast suddenly emerged from some bushes and aimed straight for her. Julianne couldn't help the squeak that came out of her mouth as she took a few steps backward to get away. Only, her foot got caught on something, and she fell backward into some shrubs.

The next thing she knew, a pair of strong arms was lifting her, and she stared directly into worried black eyes. "Are you okay? Did you hurt yourself?"

Julianne shook her head before snaking her arms around Duncan's neck and laying her head on his shoulder. She felt safe in his arms, and the sheep didn't seem quite as scary anymore. It had given her a fright, but a sheep didn't hurt humans, did it?

"Is it gone?" she whispered the words close to his ear.

"No, but it's not going to hurt you. Some of the sheep around here like to be petted. Not all of them. Most of them keep their distance, but this one was obviously looking for some attention." His deep voice was soothing and made her feel safe.

"I think you can put me down now." Lifting her head from his shoulder, she met his gaze.

"Are you sure?" There was still a trace of the concern that she had seen in Duncan's eyes when he picked her up.

Julianne nodded and put a smile on her face. "Yes. But please stay close, until I've said hello to the sheep, okay?"

His eyes widened in surprise. "You want to say hello to it? After it scared you half to death?"

"Yes. Face your fears. Isn't that what they recommend?"

Duncan just nodded as he lowered her carefully to the ground, making sure she had both feet firmly on the ground before letting go of her.

She looked around and saw the sheep standing a few yards away next to Sabrina. Her friend was rubbing its woolen coat, and the sheep looked very content as it leaned into Sabrina's touch.

Julianne couldn't help the laughter bubbling up and overflowing in a burst of sound. The beast that had scared her so badly looked as dangerous as a puppy.

Sabrina smiled at her, probably having guessed why she was laughing.

"I take it the animal doesn't look as terrifying anymore?" Duncan's voice was filled with amusement, and Julianne turned her head to meet his gaze.

"Not so scary, no. I think it has something to do with how its eyes almost glaze over in enjoyment at being petted. No trace of evil in those eyes that I can see." Julianne lifted an eyebrow at Duncan in mock accusation.

He chuckled. "I think you're right. I stand corrected. Please accept my sincerest apology for misleading you, milady," he said, and bowed as he kept his eyes on her.

"I'll consider it. If this beach you've been bragging about is as good as you've made us believe." She gave him a haughty look before turning toward Sabrina.

Duncan snorted with laughter. "Let's hope it is. I wouldn't want to be on your bad side."

Julianne gathered her courage and made her way over to Sabrina and the sheep. The animal stretched its neck toward her like it was imploring her to pet it. One person giving it attention was apparently not enough.

Reaching out, she put her hand on the animal's back and let it glide over the coarse wool. It wasn't as soft as Julianne had expected, but then she hadn't known what to expect. She had never touched a sheep before.

***

Duncan watched as the two women petted the content sheep. He was impressed with Julianne for the way she had faced her fear. In his experience most people never did and chose to live with their fear for the rest of their life instead of taking steps to get over it.

A few minutes later, they were on their way again. Using his ears and nose as well as his eyes, he constantly scanned their surroundings for any more sheep. It was great that Julianne had handled the ordeal so well, but he didn't want the same thing happening again. She might feel a little more comfortable around sheep after the earlier incident, but one of them might still give her a fright if it came barging out of the bushes like before. And this time she might hurt herself.

Emerging from a small grove of trees, the beach stretched out before them. It was only about a hundred yards long but so white it was glittering like pearls in the sun.

"Wow." Julianne gasped beside him. "It's breathtaking. White sand and clear blue water. I can't wait to get in."

Duncan laughed at her use of the word *wow* again. "I have to warn you, though. The water isn't very warm around here."

Shrugging, she started walking toward the water. "I don't care. I'm hot after the walk, so it'll be nice to cool down in the water."

Oh, she's hot all right. Duncan couldn't peel his eyes away from her as she dropped her backpack on the sand and started undressing right in front of him.

"Are you coming, Sabrina?" Julianne turned to look at her friend.

Duncan barely noticed the other woman as she sat down on the sand next to Julianne. "No, I think I'll just sit and enjoy the view for a bit."

"Okay." Julianne's shorts landed on the sand, and she started taking off her shirt.

The sight of her firm round ass in tiny bikini bottoms had Duncan's cock noticing. And not just noticing but full-on preparing for action. It was only a matter of seconds before the outline of his hard length would be clearly visible through his shorts.

He let his pack fall on the sand at the same time as he shucked his shoes and shirt. Within two seconds he was running toward the water. When the cold water hit his thighs, he dived in and swam a few strokes before emerging. Standing with the water covering his lower body up to his ribs, he felt safe to turn around and face Julianne without giving her an eyeful.

Julianne had reached the water's edge and was dipping her toes in the cold water. Wincing, she raised her head and stared at him, and he nodded in encouragement.

She started wading into the water, and he followed her beautiful form with his eyes as she approached. Her full breasts were gently bouncing within her swimsuit as she moved, but he forced his gaze to stay on hers without dipping to her chest for more than a couple of seconds. He was a decent guy, and he was trying to prove that fact to himself as much as to Julianne. Although the steel bar in his shorts was implying that he was, if not lecherous, at least as bad as a teenager.

Julianne was breathing in a staccato rhythm as more of her body immersed into the cold water. The water was up to her belly and continued to rise as she came closer.

All of a sudden, she lost her footing and went under. The water wasn't deep, but Duncan still reacted on instinct. He was next to her in an instant, pulling her out of the water while she coughed and sputtered.

"Are you all right?" Flattening a hand on her lower back, he pulled her close while gently smoothing her wet hair away from her face.

"I'm…" She coughed. "I'm fine." Then she raised her face to his. Her eyes widened at the same time as her mouth dropped open.

Duncan released her so fast she almost fell again, and he put a hand on her shoulder to steady her. But he hadn't released her fast enough. He shouldn't have pulled her close at all. He had fucked up. Contrary to his intentions Julianne had discovered that he was aroused, and if she found that to be inappropriate considering they had just met, she might not want anything more to do with him. Then again, the way she had been staring at his body this morning, she might not be too offended.

"I'm so sorry." He looked away, not wanting to see the reaction to his condition on her face. "That wasn't meant to happen. You weren't supposed to know that I…" Closing his eyes, he gave up. He didn't know how to fix this. Everything he said was only making it worse. "I'll understand if you don't want anything more to do with me."

A hand on his chest made him jerk his gaze to her face. And what he saw there was totally unexpected. Julianne was grinning up at him, and it took him completely by surprise. He thought she might be embarrassed or angry with him, but she wasn't.

"Do you…" She blushed and cleared her throat. "Do you find me attractive? Is that why…" When she trailed off, her face grew a shade darker.

Duncan nodded, not able to look away from her blushing face. "Yes, very. I think you've just felt the hard evidence of that. You weren't meant to know, though. Not like that. I was trying to hide in the water. Conceal the proof of my attraction to you. But I completely forgot when your head disappeared under water."

She chuckled. "So, my clumsiness is the cause of your embarrassment."

Duncan's heart sank. His embarrassment. She thought he should be embarrassed at his own behavior, and she was right. He dropped his gaze to the water. "Yes, you're right. I'm sorry, Julianne. That was completely inappropriate."

"That's not what I meant."

He slowly lifted his eyes to her green ones. She was frowning, and he wasn't sure what to believe. Was she angry with him? Disappointed?

Julianne's expression transformed into a smile, and she placed her hand on his cheek. Putting her other hand on his shoulder, she took a step toward him as she pulled him down to her. He was completely unprepared for her lips on his, and they were gone before he had the chance to respond.

Staring up at him, she grinned. "I take your attraction to me as a compliment, Duncan. The fact that you were trying to hide it only speaks to your good character. And for the record, I'm attracted to you too."

Her hands slid down his chest and smoothed slowly over his abs to the waistband of his shorts. Duncan's breath caught in his throat as he stared at her mischievous grin. Then she spun around and dived into the water.

"You minx," he murmured as he followed her with his eyes, where she glided below the water for several seconds before emerging. Without looking back at him, she walked toward the beach and Sabrina.

Blondie was lying on her back on the beach. Hopefully, she hadn't realized what had just happened between him and Julianne.

Turning away from the beach, he walked until the water reached his chest. Palming his stiff member, he silently swore. There was no way he could get out of the water yet. The best cure for his condition was to get himself off, but that wasn't a possibility in full view of the women.

Going for a swim seemed like the only viable

option left to him. Hopefully, that would help him focus on something besides Julianne and her fantastic body. And her soft lips. And the fact that he had been too stunned to kiss her back.

"Stop. Just stop." Duncan kept his voice low as he talked to himself. "She could've kneed you in the groin for being lecherous. You were lucky." And relieved. The possibility that Julianne might walk away from him in anger had made his heart stutter in his chest for some reason. There had been a few women over the years who had been offended that he only wanted sex. Even a couple who had said no to him. But none of that had ever bothered him. There were plenty of other available women out there. But just the thought of Julianne getting a bad impression of him, scared him more than anything else had in a long time.

Duncan shook his head at his own reaction. A couple of nights with Julianne would get her out of his system. Then he would be back to his normal carefree self.

Diving under the water, he started swimming away from the beach.

***

"Did something happen between you two?" Sabrina had a small smile on her face as she glanced over at Julianne.

Julianne chuckled and sat down in the sand next to her friend. "Well, he was very happy to see me, if you know what I mean."

Sabrina just lifted an eyebrow at her in question.

"I accidently found out. He was trying to hide the fact. But I stumbled, and when he helped me, I felt it. The hard evidence of his attraction to me." She laughed as she watched Duncan swim away. "I think he's struggling to get it under control."

"But you're not angry with him?" Sabrina's question made her turn to her friend.

Shaking her head, Julianne smiled. "No, he admitted to being attracted to me. And the way he acted, it was obvious that he was trying to hide it and expected me to be angry with him when I accidentally found out. But I can't help feeling flattered that such a gorgeous man feels so turned on by just the sight of me that he loses control of his body like that. I don't think anyone has ever paid me a greater compliment."

"Not everyone would take it that way."

"I know. But he wasn't rude or obnoxious. He wasn't trying to impress me or seduce me. He was actually a bit concerned about my reaction to the state of his body, and he expected me not to want anything more to do with him because of it. That's not the conduct of a bad person, or someone just trying to seduce me without giving a shit about my feelings."

"I agree. I think he's genuinely attracted to you and wants to make a good impression." Sabrina frowned. "There's a vulnerability in him, though. You might want to tread carefully."

Julianne stared at her friend. "What do you mean by that?"

Sabrina shook her head slowly. "I'm not sure yet. He's a bit of an enigma in some ways."

"I'm not sure what to do with that information. Do you think I should keep my distance? I mean if he's vulnerable, I probably shouldn't consider getting intimate with him. Hurting him is the last thing I want to do."

Her friend was silent for several seconds before responding. "No, I don't think you should keep your distance. Just be aware that he might get more attached to you than you would expect. It's a feeling I've got. Nothing more."

Julianne lay back in the sand. She would have to go for a swim later to wash off all the sand on her body, but that was okay. The water wasn't actually that cold once you got used to it.

The feel of Duncan's smooth skin and hard body against her almost naked body invaded her mind. Not to mention the length and thickness of his hard member against her belly. The fact that he was aroused had been a bit of a shock, but not as much as the size of him. She had never been with anyone as big as him before, and just the thought had her body heating.

Julianne quickly changed the direction of her thoughts. Sabrina's words intrigued her. She had called him vulnerable. It was hard to imagine Duncan vulnerable. Big, muscular man that he was. Then again, his shoulders had sagged in defeat when she discovered his hard cock. Like he thought all was lost. Did the gorgeous man actually feel something for her beyond just physical attraction? Surely it was a bit too soon for that. If it would happen at all. Sabrina's intuition could be off.

Lying there in the sun, her brain busy thinking about Duncan, she didn't notice the man approaching until he deliberately dripped cold water on her body. Julianne rose with a shriek before stumbling a couple of steps away from him laughing. Then she turned on him, narrowing her eyes. "I'll get you for that. Just you wait and see."

He laughed. "I'm looking forward to it. Bring it on, whenever you're ready."

Julianne had intended to continue glaring at him, but seeing his face filled with laughter and mischief, she couldn't keep it up. Smiling, she turned away from him and walked toward the water. "I need to rinse the sand off my body. Just remember, you'll have to sleep at some stage." Glancing over her shoulder at him, she watched as his jaw slackened, as he realized the implications of her last sentence. That she would be there the next time he fell asleep.

Turning back to watch where she was going, she did a mental fist pump. That had shut him up. Hopefully, it wasn't enough for him to lose control of his body again, or he would have to take another long swim.

After rinsing off the sand, Julianne returned to the others. Duncan had spread a blanket on the sand, large enough for all of them to sit on. Sabrina was just bringing out her packed lunch.

Julianne went to her backpack and retrieved her towel. After drying off, she removed her lunch from her pack and was about to sit down on the blanket. Duncan's frown as he studied her body stopped her. His expression wasn't one of desire but of concern.

"Is there something wrong?" She frowned at him.

He lifted his gaze to hers. "You should put on some more sunscreen. After being in the water and toweling off, most of what you had on is probably gone."

Giving him a small smile, Julianne nodded. "Yeah. Good point. Thank you for reminding me."

She retrieved the sunscreen buried at the bottom of

her pack. Opening the bottle, she started applying the thick creamy liquid to her exposed skin. Sneaking a peek at Duncan while doing her arms, she noticed he seemed more preoccupied with his lunch than was strictly necessary. More like carefully avoiding looking at her while she was running her hands over her body. Julianne had considered asking him to apply sunscreen to her back, but upon seeing him keeping his eyes averted, she decided against it.

"Sabrina, would you mind doing my back, please?"

Her friend lifted her gaze to Julianne with a smile. "Not at all."

When Julianne was covered in fresh sunscreen from head to toe, she sat down on the blanket and picked up her lunch. Glancing over at the gorgeous man sitting less than a yard away from her revealed he was still reluctant to look at her. It was obviously time to find a safe topic of conversation, and perhaps get to know Duncan a bit better at the same time.

"So, what does taking care of an estate entail?"

The smile he gave her as he lifted his gaze to meet hers held a hint of relief. "All kinds of things, really. Trevor has quite a lot of sheep and cattle, so making sure they're all okay is a big part of it."

Julianne nodded, lifting an eyebrow at him. "And the sheep around here?"

Giving her an amused smile, he shook his head. "No, they're not Trevor's."

"Okay. What else?"

CHAPTER 5

Duncan explained about the continuous maintenance necessary to keep the main house and the other buildings on the estate in good condition. And then there was the fencing. Quite a few miles crisscrossing the property to check regularly.

"And you do all this by yourself? Sounds like quite a lot of work for just one man." Julianne's eyes had widened as he spoke about everything he took care of at the estate.

Duncan didn't consider his work at the estate so much a job as a place to stay and take care of. Trevor was the wealthy one of the two of them, but Duncan had more than he could spend. He owned a couple of businesses with Trevor that were doing exceptionally well. In addition, he had shares in several companies that were giving him a healthy dividend. If he wanted to, Duncan could retire and never have to work another day in his exceedingly long life. But he enjoyed taking care of the estate, so that was what he spent his time doing. Most of his time, anyway.

"Most of the time, I do the work alone, and I can manage just fine. But if something out of the ordinary happens, I can get help from some of the locals. They're happy to help out. At the moment Trevor is in Scotland, so he does some of the work himself. When he's not spending time with Jennie, his mate. Their attached at the hip, those two."

Julianne cocked her head at him. "Mate. Isn't that just another word for friend? Sounds like Jennie is more than Trevor's friend."

Duncan mentally kicked himself. He should know better than to talk about mates around Julianne. Smiling, he tried to cover up his mistake. "Jennie is definitely more than Trevor's friend. I wouldn't be surprised if they suddenly decided to get married. Well, if they want to. Not everyone does these days."

Amusement lit up Julianne's face. "It sounds like you think they should get married. And soon. Not a fan of people living in sin, are you?"

Laughing, he shook his head. "That's not what I meant. People should do whatever suits them." Like he had the right to judge anyone, anyway. He had no idea how many women he had fucked over the years. Most of them just once. He had always made sure they had a good time with him, but at the same time he had made certain that the women understood that they couldn't expect anything more than sex from him. Until Julianne. Taking a woman on a daytrip like this wasn't something he did, even if she brought her friend with her. But he wanted Julianne in his bed, and this was just his chosen method of getting her there. So not that different after all.

"Hm. I'm still not convinced that you're not secretly against people living together outside of wedlock. A bit older than you look, aren't you?" Julianne's eyes were shining as she kept teasing him.

At least she didn't ask more questions about his use of the word *mate*. Perhaps he should just give her the truth about his age and see how she reacted. She wouldn't believe him of course, but that was okay.

"Well, at sixty-one I guess I'm a bit old-fashioned compared to you. The youth of today have no sense of propriety and tradition." Duncan gave her a grin like he was kidding, even though he had just given her his real age.

Julianne laughed like he knew she would. Sabrina, however, didn't. She was studying him with a thoughtful expression on her face, like she was considering his words carefully to try to establish if he was speaking the truth. Not surprising really, considering Sabrina knew he was a werewolf.

Duncan was a wolf in his prime, even though he was old enough to be someone's grandfather, maybe even great-grandfather, in human years. A wolf didn't usually mate and have pups at the same age that humans did. They spent more time getting their footing in the world before settling down to start a family. It was also one of the reasons that werewolves tended to be wealthier than humans.

There were some drawbacks to being a werewolf, though, or any other kind of supernatural with a longer than human lifespan. Becoming famous wasn't really an option. No matter if it was as an actor or a surgeon. It would soon become apparent that they didn't age like they should, and they would have to fake their death or mysteriously disappear. Tedious as hell to have to hide for a long time, and the risk of recognition was high. Some supernaturals had succeeded with living on as their own child or relative, but it required some exceptionally good lawyers and connections in the correct government offices to pull that off. It was much easier to settle for a normal life and an average job. To be nobody special.

"Well, grandpa. Do you want to go for a swim? Maybe you need help getting up. Shall I find a stick that you can use as a cane?" Green eyes sparkled with glee as Julianne rose from the blanket.

Duncan played along, enjoying the sight of her happy face. "I think you might have to help me up. My knees are aching today."

"Oh, what a pity. You should probably stay here. The cold water will only make it worse, I'm afraid."

He laughed before turning to Sabrina. "Are you coming with us this time? The water is a bit cold, but it's clean and refreshing." And Duncan had a feeling she wouldn't join them unless they specifically asked her to. He enjoyed spending time with Julianne. Their easy banter and the attraction between them. Perhaps he even enjoyed it a bit too much. But he didn't want Sabrina to feel left out. She seemed to be naturally silent and pensive, but that didn't mean she wanted to be alone.

Sabrina gave him a small smile. "I think I will. Thank you for asking."

After a short swim, they packed up and started on the hike back to the car. It was an uneventful trek this time. The only sheep they spotted didn't approach them. Duncan made sure to stay close to Julianne just in case, keeping an eye out for any of the woolen animals that could be hiding in the patches of thick vegetation along the trail.

***

"Do you want to go to Mallaig? We have time to go there and have a look around if you want." Duncan opened the back of the car to put in their backpacks.

Julianne let her eyes rest on the gorgeous man who had given them a fantastic day so far. "That would be great, but are you sure you have time?"

He turned to her with a smile on his face. "Yes, this day is yours. I've got nothing else I need to do today. And I'd be happy to show you around Mallaig."

"In that case I think we'll say yes." She turned to Sabrina, who gave her a small nod in agreement.

"Good. Then get in." Duncan moved around the car to the driver's side.

The drive was fantastic, and Julianne studied the landscape and the ocean that glided past. There were several white-sand beaches close to the road as they neared Mallaig, but none of them were as beautiful and tranquil as the one Duncan had taken them to.

There were plenty of tourists milling around in the narrow streets of Mallaig. A steam train was standing at the train station puffing out clouds of vapor into the air. Their personal tour guide managed to find a parking spot, and they got out to join all the other people who were there to experience the small fishing port.

They walked around, checking out the small shops for a while, before heading down to the wharf. There were fishing boats being unloaded, and the day's catch had been good. At least from Julianne's meager understanding of these things. Which of course might have been completely wrong.

A head suddenly emerged from the water just a few yards from the wharf, and Julianne stared at it for a couple of seconds, before she was able to comprehend what it was. "A seal. There's a seal down there." She pointed as she studied it in amazement. This was the first time she had seen a seal in the wild.

"Yes, there are quite a few of them hanging around here." Duncan's deep voice came from right next to her. "They're actually quite a tourist attraction."

Julianne smiled. "I can see why. They're cute."

"Are you ladies getting hungry? I think the train will be leaving soon, so it might be possible to find a free table at one of the restaurants around here."

Julianne nodded as she turned to look at Duncan. "I could eat." She moved her gaze to her friend.

Sabrina gave a small nod. "A meal would be most welcome."

They were wandering back toward the main street, when Julianne spotted a small shop that she hadn't noticed earlier. "Please give me a couple of minutes to have a look inside."

"Go for it." Duncan smiled at her before turning to Sabrina. "Shall we check the menu at the restaurant around the corner?"

Her friend turned to her as if seeking approval, but Julianne waved them away. "Please. Go ahead. I'll be there in two minutes."

The shop had all kinds of handcrafted goods on display. So many beautiful things. She wasn't going to buy anything, but she loved the visual impressions all these beautiful pieces of art gave her, and the sense of the amount of work that had gone into making each piece. Julianne was smiling when she left the shop a couple of minutes later. She could have spent a lot more time in there.

Julianne hadn't taken more than a couple of steps away from the shop entrance when she froze. A man was standing directly in her path, blocking her progress, and not just any man. This one she knew and had come to resent, due to his progressively possessive behavior.

"Julianne." His smooth voice belied the hint of anger visible in his eyes. "Fancy seeing you here."

Fear was creeping up her spine, but she steeled herself. Steven, her ex, had never physically hurt her, but she wouldn't put it past him to do so. The way he had behaved the last couple of weeks before she told him it was over, had given her a feeling that it was only a matter of time.

"I have nothing more to say to you, Steven." Staring at him defiantly, she stood her ground. There wasn't enough room to get past him easily. Retreating back into the shop was a possibility, but she didn't want to give him the impression of having the upper hand.

"Oh, I think we have plenty to discuss. It's time you realize that I'm exactly the man you need. If you had answered any of my texts or phone calls, I wouldn't have had to chase you all the way to this godforsaken place." Anger laced his voice, and he had this strange shine in his eyes that he usually got when he was angry.

But Julianne was getting angry as well. "You have no right to follow me. This is stalker behavior, and it just makes me happy that I left you. There is no way in hell that I'm getting back together with you."

Fury flashed in Steven's gaze for a second, before he seemed to check himself. He took a deep breath and gave her a forced smile that didn't reach his eyes. "We just need to talk. I'm sure you'll remember how good we were together, once we sit down and talk this through."

"I don't think any amount of talking will change her mind. Don't you see the disgust in her eyes? You had your shot, asshole, and you obviously blew it." Hearing Duncan's deep voice was such a relief that Julianne could have cried, but she made an effort to keep her expression unchanged.

Steven narrowed his eyes before slowly turning to face Duncan, who was standing a couple of yards away from him. "This is none of your concern. What happens between me and my girlfriend is between us."

Julianne snorted. "I haven't been your girlfriend for three months. And I never will be again. Please get out of my way." She took a step toward Steven, aiming to push past him, but he put out an arm to stop her.

"I suggest you let her go." Duncan's voice had more of a growl in it than earlier, and he took a step toward Steven.

Julianne shuddered. A sensation like electricity flowed along her spine, but not in an uncomfortable way. It was a warm and exciting feeling, making her channel clench. Utterly bewildered, she took a step back toward the shop entrance.

"I just want to talk to her, wolf." The anger was gone from Steven's voice, but he didn't move. "That's a reasonable request after all the time we spent together."

Duncan looked at her over Steven's shoulder, and she shook her head at him.

"I don't think she sees it that way. Now, let her go before I have to make a point."

Steven didn't move for a few seconds until he slowly took a step to the side to let her pass.

Julianne moved past her ex without looking at him. As soon as she reached Duncan, he put a hand on the small of her back and led her away. They rounded the corner and entered the restaurant, where Sabrina was waiting at a table in the corner. The restaurant was filled with other guests.

After taking one look at her, Sabrina narrowed her eyes in concern. "What happened? You look pale."

"Steven. He followed me here. He wanted to talk." Julianne took a deep breath to try to calm down. The fact that he had managed to find her in Mallaig of all places was starting to sink in. How on earth had he done that? She had been open with friends about going to Fort William, so if he had shown up there, it would have been understandable. But him showing up in Mallaig like this was just creepy.

"What?! That asshole." Sabrina's invariably calm and collected manner was slipping, and Julianne could only stare as fury turned her friend's eyes a darker shade of blue.

Julianne's bladder suddenly contracted, and she squeezed her thighs together. Her body's delayed reaction to her fear was manifesting itself. "Is there a restroom around here?" She looked around desperately, spotting it in the corner of the room.

"Go. I'll keep an eye on the entrance." Duncan's

words alleviated an anxiety she hadn't wanted to admit to herself. That Steven would come after her and somehow manage to abduct her.

***

Duncan followed Julianne with his gaze as she quickly made her way to the restroom.

"What happened?" Sabrina's voice was clipped and angry.

He sat down at the square table to the left of Sabrina, where he could keep an eye on the entrance to the restaurant as well as the restroom. "The asshole, I take it he's Julianne's ex, had her cornered outside the small shop. He just wanted to talk to her. Or so he claimed. I'm not buying it."

"And so, you shouldn't. He's a nasty piece of work, that one." Sabrina sighed. "I thought he had given up by now. Stupid of me. He's the possessive type. They don't give up that easily."

"Don't beat yourself up. The only one responsible for this is him."

"I take it you scared him off?"

Duncan gave her a quick glance before reverting to keeping an eye out for Steven. "For now, but I'm not sure for how long. Like you said, he won't give up that easily. It's only a matter of time before he approaches her again, and I might not be there the next time." Duncan felt himself frowning at that realization. "Then there's the fact that he's a panther shifter." He let his gaze rest on Sabrina for a couple of seconds to judge her reaction to his statement.

A brief look of shock crossed her face before her expression tightened into one of anger. "I didn't know that, but it explains the sense of otherness I've had around him. Similar to the feeling I get around you, only less."

Duncan noticed Sabrina was more open around him than she had been when they met the day before. She was letting her emotions show on her face, whereas last night she had concealed her thoughts and feelings from him. He had a feeling she didn't trust easily, and the fact that she expressed herself this openly with him he took as a sign of approval.

Taking a deep breath, Duncan swung his gaze to Sabrina. He wanted her honest reaction to what he was about to propose. "I'm considering telling Julianne about shifters. She needs to know what she's dealing with in order to protect herself, and at the moment she has no idea. There's a risk that she won't take it well, and if so, she probably won't want anything more to do with me. But at least she'll have you and whatever you can do to help her. And she'll have all the facts to base her decisions on."

Sabrina was studying him for several seconds with an unreadable expression on her face. So much for seeing her reaction to his suggestion. She nodded slowly. "I think that is the best course of action. But are you willing to risk her not wanting anything more to do with you?"

Duncan swallowed, not able to answer right away. She was addressing the one reservation he had against telling Julianne about shifters, and specifically that he himself was one. Just the thought of her turning away from him in fear and disgust made his chest feel tight. "Yes. It will give her better odds against Steven. The only way for Julianne to be completely safe from him, would be for her to mate another shifter. But that's not an option. Mating is not like marriage. It's permanent. Forever. In other words, not something to be done on a whim, not even in a situation like this."

Sabrina gave him a short nod and a small smile. "I believe you're right. Let's hope it turns out better than you and me both fear. Julianne is a levelheaded individual."

Duncan sincerely hoped she was right about that, because the thought of never seeing Julianne again was giving him a feeling of dread on a level he didn't think he had ever experienced before.

The door to the restroom opened and Julianne emerged. She was still a bit pale, but she gave them a small smile as she approached their table.

The waiter chose that moment to come to their table to ask if they were ready to order, and Duncan politely asked him to give them a few more minutes. The waiter left, and Duncan turned to Julianne just as Sabrina spoke.

"How are you feeling?"

Sitting down, Julianne took a deep breath and shook her head slowly. "Still a bit shaken up. It was a shock to see Steven here. The last couple of weeks, he's been texting me and calling me every day, but I haven't answered a single text or phone call. I guess I was hoping that he would get the point if I didn't respond. That was clearly a mistake. Perhaps if I'd answered and told him to stop bothering me, he would've gotten the message."

"I'm sorry to have to say this, but I don't think there's anything you could've done to prevent him from coming after you. This is on him, not on you." Duncan didn't like giving her the hard truth, but he wasn't going to lie to her. "Are you still hungry, or do you want to leave?"

Julianne visibly swallowed. "I'd like to leave, but if you're hungry—"

He cut her off before she could continue. "No, let's get out of here."

They left the restaurant and headed to the car. Duncan scanned the people still milling around as they made their way through the narrow streets of Mallaig. But he didn't see Steven or anyone else who seemed to pay them any particular attention.

After getting into the car, Duncan turned to Julianne. "Do you have any idea how he was able to track you here?"

She shook her head as she met his eyes. "No. The only thing I can think of, is that he has done something to my phone. I still have the same phone that I had when we were together." Julianne shuddered as she said the last few words. "I can't believe that I was with him for almost six months. That I fell for him in the first place. Or fell for him isn't accurate. I let myself get charmed, but I never fell for him. That's why it wasn't difficult to leave him."

Duncan just nodded. He didn't want to comment on her romance, or whatever she'd had, with Steven. It wasn't his business. Even though the thought of Julianne with that asshole had his hackles rising. "I think you're right about your phone. You should turn it off right now and keep it off. We can get it checked later. I know someone who's an expert at that sort of thing."

Julianne gave him a weak smile. She took her phone out of her pocket and turned it off.

After starting the car, Duncan maneuvered through the narrow streets and onto the main road. "Let's stop at the estate, and I can make us some dinner. It's on the way to Fort William, anyway, and I think it would be a good place to talk and come up with a plan for how to deal with Steven." He met Sabrina's gaze in the rearview mirror, and she nodded her agreement. They needed a suitable place to tell Julianne about the supernatural world she was living in, and the estate was perfect for that.

"Thank you, Duncan. That sounds great." Julianne looked at him with relief written all over her face. "I was actually a bit worried about going back to Fort William right away. Steven probably knows where we're staying. We need a plan."

A bit worried was an understatement. Sitting this close to her in the front of the car, Duncan could smell the fear wafting off her. Julianne was terrified of being approached by Steven again. The knowledge only increased Duncan's loathing of the panther.

Parking outside the main house, they all got out of the car. Julianne was staring around her with a look of awe on her face, and there was a smile playing on her lips. It made Duncan grin seeing her like this, particularly after experiencing her fear earlier. It eased a tightness in his chest that he hadn't realized was still there after they left Mallaig.

The house was silent as they walked inside. If Michael and Stephanie were in the house, they weren't making any sounds that Duncan could hear. And Trevor and Jennie would have left for Leith's already.

Leading the way into the kitchen, Duncan went to the oven and turned it on. "I think we've got some frozen lasagna in the freezer. Does that sound okay? I can heat some baguettes and chop some tomatoes and greens for a mixed salad."

"A man who knows his way around a kitchen. I like it." Julianne grinned.

Duncan lifted an eyebrow at her. "It or him?"

She chuckled. "Both. And lasagna sounds delicious. Yes, please."

Sabrina nodded.

"Good." Duncan started gathering what he needed from the fridge.

"Anything we can do to help, please tell us." Julianne's voice came from somewhere around the kitchen table.

"Not much to it really. Just sit down and relax." Duncan was happy to prepare dinner for the two ladies. "Or come to think of it, you can set the table and find whatever you would like to drink. There are sodas and beers of various kinds in the fridge, and I think we've got some red wine in the pantry."

Duncan popped the frozen lasagna into the oven. After finishing the salad, he joined the women at the kitchen table. The lasagna would take a while to heat, so they had some time to talk. He had been debating whether to postpone their talk about supernaturals until after dinner, but they might as well get on with it. Either way it was going to be a shock for Julianne to find out the world she thought she knew was actually completely different.

"Julianne, there are a few things about Steven that you should know." Duncan held her gaze and saw her open expression change into a frown. "And it will probably be a shock to hear this."

CHAPTER 6

Julianne kept her eyes on Duncan as he spoke. His expression was serious, perhaps even a bit weary. Like he didn't want to tell her whatever it was he was going to tell her about Steven. What bothered her the most, was how he would know something about her ex that she didn't. As far as she knew, they had never met before this afternoon.

"Go on."

Duncan took a deep breath and let it out slowly. "Steven is a shifter. More precisely a panther shifter. Do you know what that is?"

Julianne could only stare at him. His black eyes were intense as he stared right back at her, and no hint of a smile was on his face to indicate that he was joking. But he couldn't be serious. It was crazy talk. The stuff of books and movies. She turned her head to Sabrina, who was sitting beside her at the table. Her friend was staring at her with the same serious expression on her face. But then Sabrina was a master of concealing her emotions. Her friend could be deliriously happy or raging mad, and you wouldn't know it to look at her. Although, she wasn't sure Sabrina was capable of such powerful emotions. Julianne had known her for almost three years and had never seen any evidence of feelings that strong.

Julianne burst out laughing. "You almost had me there, you know. So serious. I know Steven is an asshole, and it's kind of nice to picture him as such a monster, but..." The words died in her throat as Duncan visibly flinched.

He quickly turned his face away from her and rose from the table, but not before she saw his jaw tense with what looked like pain. Almost like she had dealt him a blow to the solar plexus or something.

Julianne had no idea what was going on. She felt like she had been thrown into one of those dreams where anything could happen, and everything was constantly changing.

"I'm... I'm sorry. For whatever I said that hurt you. I'm not sure I understand what just happened. Please explain to me what's going on." She was staring at Duncan's back, where he was standing a couple of yards away, facing the other way.

Julianne swung her gaze to her friend. "Sabrina?"

Her friend gave her a small smile and put a hand on her arm. "I think it would be better if Duncan explained this to you. Please listen to him carefully. He's not joking. There's more to this world than you know. Please be open-minded and remember that Duncan is not one of the bad guys."

"Of course, he isn't, but..." Julianne already knew that Duncan was a great guy. She had no problem believing that. But as for what he had said about shifters being real... No, she must have misunderstood him.

After getting up from the table, she walked around Duncan to stand directly in front of him. Looking up into his face, she was taken aback at the sadness she saw there. She reached up to put her hand on his cheek but froze when he flinched away from her touch. Julianne hadn't expected the pain that stabbed through her chest at his reaction to her, and she stumbled back a couple of steps as if he had physically pushed her. As she gasped at the pain, tears filled her eyes and overflowed down her face before she could stop them. She had no idea what was happening to her, only that it hurt. Like his rejection had physically torn open her chest.

Strong arms enveloped her, and her face was pressed into a hard chest. She made a feeble attempt to push away from him, but he didn't budge and kept her pressed tightly against his body.

"You don't have to touch me if you don't want to." Her voice broke, and she mumbled the words into his chest.

"I want to. It's all I want." Duncan's voice was scratchy, like he hadn't used it in a while, even though he had. "I'm sorry. I'm the one who should be sorry. You've done nothing wrong. But you don't know who I really am. You shouldn't touch me until you know who I am. Then you can choose whether you want to touch me or not. Make an informed decision."

The pain in her chest was subsiding, and Julianne took a deep breath to try to get her bearings. "We're kind of touching right now." A smile crept over her face and into her voice. For some reason the feel of his strong arms around her made her happy. "So, the not touching you part is impossible at the moment. Not that I'm complaining."

Duncan chuckled, and the rumbling sound coming from his chest made her smile widen. Then he kissed the top of her head. "I can't seem to let go of you just yet. Just give me a minute, okay?"

It was her turn to chuckle. "Take all the time you need. I'm comfortable right here." And she was. The pain in her chest was gone, and in its place was a warm fuzzy feeling. Julianne took a deep breath through her nose, drinking in his unique scent. It was difficult to describe, but it included a touch of woodsmoke and spices. Taking another breath, she tried to understand what her nose was telling her.

His arms loosened, and she tipped her head back to look up at him. Duncan was studying her with an amused expression on his face. "Are you scenting me?"

Smiling up at him, she nodded. "Yeah, I think I am. You smell good." And he looked so much better with an amused smile on his face, than the pain she had seen in his face at the table before he turned away from her.

Duncan all out laughed. Then he sighed and let go of her completely. Or almost completely. He took her right hand in his left one. It was large and warm and rough. Like someone working with his hands would have. He led her back to the table.

Julianne sat down next to him, holding onto his hand. She had a feeling she would need something to hold onto during this conversation, and his hand felt solid and safe, clasping hers. "I'm ready. Or as ready as I'll ever be." She turned her head to Sabrina for support, and her friend gave her a small smile and a nod.

Duncan's voice drew Julianne's gaze back to him. "I meant what I said before, when I told you that Steven is a shifter. Common for all shifters is that they can change into their animal form at will. In their human form they're stronger and faster than a typical human and have somewhat better senses. Just like humans, most shifters are decent people, but there are those who aren't." He paused, probably to let her digest what he had just told her.

"I believe Steven is one of the not-so-decent shifters." Julianne's mind was swirling around, trying to make sense of what Duncan had just told her, and that was the first conclusion she landed on. Then there was the first question she needed to ask. "How did you find out that my ex is a shifter?"

Duncan's jaw tensed, and he hesitated for a second before answering her. "I smelled it."

Julianne let that sink in. The implications of his words. There was only one explanation she could think of, and it should scare her. Or should it? Duncan was good. Shifter or not. There was no doubt in her mind he was one of the decent ones. "So, what kind of shifter are you?" Just as the words left her mouth realization hit her, as she remembered what Steven had called him. "No, wait. You're a wolf."

Breath burst from him, and she realized that Duncan had been holding his breath while waiting for her reaction.

"Yes. I'm a wolf shifter."

"And one of the decent shifters."

His jaw slackened at her words, and he stared at her for several seconds. Slowly the corners of his mouth curved upward in a smile. "You think so? I mean…I try to be. Aren't you scared of me?"

Julianne grinned as she took in his smile and the way his body relaxed in obvious relief. "No. I've got no reason not to trust you, Duncan. If you wanted to hurt me, you could've done so many times by now. Instead, you have gone out of your way to do the opposite."

"Thank you." The grin on his face was radiant, and he squeezed her hand.

The timer on the oven started beeping and Duncan rose. "The lasagna is done, but I forgot about the baguettes. I'll pop those in the oven now. They'll only take a few minutes to heat. We can start with lasagna and salad. I'm sure you're just as hungry as I am."

"Yes, ravenous actually." Julianne smiled up at the gorgeous man, who was even more exotic than she had first thought. Finding out that he was a shifter hadn't diminished her fascination with him. If anything, it had increased it.

Duncan went to the oven, and Julianne turned to Sabrina. Her friend met her gaze with a steady one of her own. A few seconds went by before she sighed and responded to Julianne's silent question. "I just found out about shifters yesterday, so I haven't been keeping this from you for long. Duncan's energy felt different, more powerful than normal, so I questioned him about it while you were in the restroom. He told me what he was."

The lasagna was placed on the table, and Julianne

tipped her head back to look at Duncan. "Why didn't you tell me as well?"

He gave her a wry smile. "Sabrina sensed that I wasn't completely human, and I decided to tell her the truth about me. I didn't feel like I had a choice if I wanted to spend time with you. She would've told me to leave if she thought that I was less than honest about who or, as she put it, what I am. You, on the other hand…" He paused as if trying to find the correct words.

"We're not supposed to tell humans about shifters. It's one of our unwritten rules. As I told you before, we're faster and stronger than humans. What I didn't mention is that we also have longer lifespans. That fact alone would create problems in our dealings with humans. I'm sure you can imagine the type of jealousy that would ensue, and the conflicts that would arise from that."

Julianne's heart sank. She had no trouble understanding what he was telling her. The arguments against telling humans like her about shifters were solid. There was no doubt in her mind that the knowledge of a superior race living among them would cause all kinds of problems. Harassment, violence, and perhaps even all-out war, which wouldn't turn out well for the humans. Well, depending on how many shifters there were in the world. If the shifters were seriously outnumbered, the humans might stand a chance. But the shifters could always increase their numbers by converting humans. Or could they?

"Julianne." Duncan's deep voice broke through her whirlwind of thoughts and reflections.

"Yes. Sorry. Just a lot to take in."

He chuckled. "I think you're taking this remarkably well."

The timer went off again, signaling that the baguettes were ready to be taken out of the oven.

Sabrina rose. "I'll get them."

Julianne had a lot of questions, but she wasn't sure where to start. And the thought that she never would have known about shifters at all if it weren't for Steven was unsettling and sad. She never would have known about Duncan being a shifter. Even if they had ended up in bed together, he probably wouldn't have told her what he was. It felt a bit like deceit, and it made her sad, even though it hadn't happened. But the fact that she knew it had been a real possibility was enough.

"Please, help yourselves." Duncan's voice pulled her out of her thoughts again.

Julianne looked at Sabrina, who indicated that she should start.

After filling her plate with the delicious food Duncan had prepared, she dug in while her mind whirled and twisted with all the implications of what she had been told, and all the emotions those implications created in her. This was her chance to ask questions and get a deeper understanding of this new world she was living in, but she had trouble focusing with all the noise in her head.

The sight of her empty plate made her frown. Julianne had eaten all the food on her plate, but she had no idea how it had tasted. She slowly lifted her head and took in the expression on the face of each of the two people sitting at the table with her. Sabrina gave her a small smile and continued eating. But Duncan…

Duncan's expression made Julianne pause. He was staring at his plate but not eating. In fact, it didn't look like he had made a dent in the pile of food on his plate at all. "Duncan?"

He snapped his gaze to hers and immediately put a smile on his face. But not before she saw the sadness in his eyes, and the smile he was giving her seemed forced. "Yes. Something you need? I'll be happy to…"

She waved his words away, and he let the sentence die on his lips, his smile faltering.

***

Duncan swallowed, not knowing what to do. Julianne had seemed to take the revelation that shifters existed, and the fact that he was a shifter, surprisingly well. And he had been so relieved. But then she had turned solemn and silent, and the longer she stayed that way, the more agitated he became. He kept it in check by focusing on how unsettling this must be for her, and that she needed time to digest what he had told her. But perhaps there was more to it than that. Maybe as Julianne spent more time thinking about shifters and what this meant, she realized that she didn't want anything to do with them, with him.

He heard a crack, and a sharp pain stabbed into his hand. Looking down, Duncan realized he had inadvertently broken the wooden handle on the knife in his hand. Gathering the pieces of the broken handle, he rose from the table and threw them into the trash. Without looking at the women at the table, he quickly strode out of the kitchen and headed for his room. He needed a few minutes alone. Just a few minutes to get a handle on his emotions. Then he would be right as rain. Or so he told himself. For some reason this whole situation was screwing with his head and his feelings in a big way.

Duncan was at the bottom of the stairs when a hand on his arm made him stop, and he realized Julianne had been calling his name. He steeled himself before looking into her eyes, but what he saw there wasn't what he had expected.

"Are you all right?" Julianne stared at him with concern in her gaze. She gripped his hand and opened it to look at his palm. The wound had already stopped bleeding. It wouldn't take long before it closed and disappeared.

"It'll be gone soon. I heal quickly." He carefully extricated his hand from her grip and looked away. "I just need a few minutes."

But before Duncan could take one step away, Julianne's arms locked around his neck, and she hugged him tightly. Her unexpected move left him stunned for a couple of seconds. He had thought she wanted to get away from him, that she was done with him. Not that anything had happened between them yet. But he had been hoping it would.

Wrapping his arms around her, he put his nose in the crook of her neck and breathed her in. Chocolate and cloves, his new favorite scents. The tension that had built since she grew silent started to leave his body, and he breathed out as his body relaxed.

Julianne gasped and squirmed against him. "That tickles."

Lifting his head, he smiled down at her. Her beauty was out of this world as she grinned up at him with green eyes sparkling. He didn't think he had ever met a more beautiful woman is his life.

Her eyes dipped to his lips, and there was a hint of desire in her gaze that made his cock take notice. She rose up on her toes and put her mouth on his. The moment their lips met, a shock like electricity sparked through him. Julianne must have felt something, too, because she moaned against his mouth. He moved his lips against her soft ones and felt his rod start hardening. There was nothing he could do about that. His cock seemed to have a mind of its own these days.

Letting his hands play along her spine, he licked the seam of her mouth to ask her permission to enter. As soon as Julianne parted her lips for him, he thrust his tongue into her mouth. He was soon losing himself in the taste of her. The feel of her. Duncan plundered her mouth with his tongue, rubbing and twisting around hers. His body was on fire with need for her, but it was too soon for that. Kissing, however, was perfect.

Julianne broke the kiss slowly, but before she pulled away, she took his bottom lip between her teeth and bit into it gently. His whole body jerked as the sensation sparked through him, causing his cock to start throbbing and his balls to pull up tightly with insistent need.

"Julianne." He'd gasped her name. Grabbing her waist, he moved her body a couple of inches away from his own. The friction between their bodies had been fantastic, but he couldn't take any more of it without running the risk of going off in his pants.

She grinned up at him with heat in her eyes before her smile turned a bit wicked. "Is that a banana in your pocket, or…" She let the sentence hang.

Duncan grinned back at her. He would like nothing better than to hoist her up into his arms and carry her to his bed. They would be good together. There was no doubt in his mind. "Oh, I'm happy to see you. Very happy to see you."

"Hm, I thought as much." Julianne palmed his cock, tracing the outline of it through his shorts.

He groaned and put his hand on hers to stop her. The feel of her hand on him, even through the fabric of his shorts, had him close to coming. "Stop. I'll embarrass myself."

Her eyes widened in shock as she stared up at him. "You're that turned on?"

"Yes." Duncan swallowed. "I want you. But not like this. Our first time is going to be in my bed, where I can worship your body properly."

Julianne gaped at him for several seconds before closing her mouth with a clack. "Oh. Okay."

He put a hand on her cheek to make sure she was listening. "But we'll leave that for another day. I think today has been eventful enough, and I want you to be sure that you want to have sex with me before I'll take you to my bed."

She nodded slowly as she kept her eyes on his. "You're right. I know you're right. But I don't have to like it." Sticking her bottom lip out, she pretended to be hurt.

Laughing, Duncan kissed her forehead before taking her hand in his and turning them toward the kitchen.

Raising an eyebrow at him, she dipped her eyes to his still hard cock. "Are you sure you want to go back to the kitchen looking like that?"

He sighed and glanced down his body to where his stiff member was tenting his shorts. "No. I forgot that we're not alone for a minute. I'll go change. Then I can hide what you've done to me."

"Oh, so now it's my fault." Julianne crossed her arms and looked at him with an expression of mock outrage on her face.

"Of course." He turned and threw her a grin over his shoulder as he moved up the stairs.

As soon as he closed the bedroom door behind him, he raced into his bathroom. There was only one way to hide his hard cock beneath his clothes, and that was to get rid of it. And it wouldn't take long with the state he was already in.

Duncan ripped his clothes off and kicked them into a corner. He wrapped his hand around his throbbing member and pumped it fast up and down. Remembering the taste and feel of Julianne as he kissed her had his balls pull up so tightly he was surprised he didn't choke on them. The thought of Julianne's hand touching him through the fabric of his shorts tipped him over the edge. The orgasm ripped through him, and he groaned as his seed shot in hard jets into the hand he had clamped over the head of his cock.

He barely allowed himself time to come down before he started cleaning up. Racing back into his bedroom, Duncan found some baggy clothes and quickly put them on as he exited his room. Running down the stairs, he estimated that he had been gone about four minutes. It shouldn't be enough for the ladies to suspect what he had been up to. At least he hoped not. It was embarrassing enough how he had no control of his body around Julianne.

Entering the kitchen, he strode to the counter and

opened a drawer to fetch himself a new knife. Turning around, he smiled at the two women at the table while showing them the knife in his hand. "I guess that gave you a demonstration of one of the challenges of being a shifter. We tend to break things, since almost everything is made to suit humans and is based on their average strength."

"And you're stronger than us. Poor you." Julianne had one eyebrow raised in challenge, but he could see the amusement in her eyes.

Duncan laughed as he sat down to eat the food he had trouble focusing on earlier. "Yes, I guess I've told you that already." He turned serious as he swung his gaze between the two women. "Please feel free to ask me questions. There must be things you want to know after everything that's happened today. I'll do my best to answer them."

Julianne's brows pushed together. "You mean you'll answer the questions you're allowed to answer." It was more a statement than a question, and Duncan saw a hint of sadness in her eyes.

It dawned on him suddenly why she had been so silent earlier. It wasn't that she was scared or disgusted by him being a shifter. He had hurt her. Not deliberately, but still. By telling her that shifters were keeping their nature a secret from humans, Duncan had inadvertently said that he would never have revealed who he was to her, if not for what had happened with Steven.

"I'm sorry, Julianne. It wasn't my intention to hurt you, but I realize that I have."

She narrowed her eyes at him while studying his face, but she didn't respond to his apology.

"You're the first human I've ever told about shifters." Then he remembered Sabrina and shot her a glance before he corrected himself. "Or that's not true. I told Sabrina. But she had already guessed that I wasn't completely human, so it's not exactly the same." He sighed. "This is how I've lived my entire life, hiding my true self from humans. I guess I'm used to it. But I understand it if you feel that I've been less than honest with you. I have. And the fact that it is how we have to live as shifters probably doesn't make you feel any better about it."

Julianne sighed and looked away from him, and he wanted to go to her. Cradle her in his arms and apologize again and again, until she gave him one of her amazing smiles. But that was not how this worked. She had to come to terms with this on her own. He couldn't force her to overlook the fact that he had kept secrets from her.

Duncan made himself eat while he waited for Julianne to say something. Or do something. Anything at all really. If she slapped him or yelled at him, or told him he was an asshole for lying to her, it would be better than this silence. At least he would know how she felt, and he could take it from there. At the moment, he had nothing to work with.

A full five minutes went by before Sabrina leaned forward in her seat while keeping her gaze on her friend. "Julianne, you know he's right. He's not supposed to tell anyone, and we're actually quite unique since we're the only humans he has ever told."

Julianne turned her gaze to him and sighed. It had felt like an eternity waiting for her to respond. "You don't owe me an apology, Duncan, but thank you. I understand why you weren't going to tell me. I mean why would you?"

He started to protest her words, but she held up a hand to stop him, and he held his tongue.

"We just met the other day. We're not exactly friends or lovers, or anything. And to be realistic, I'm not sure I would've reacted well to you telling me right off the bat. Most likely I would've thought you were off your rocker and kept my distance." Giving him a small smile, she continued. "Insanity isn't really a big turn-on, not even when covered in such gorgeous wrapping."

Duncan chuckled. "At least you don't consider me insane. I guess that's something." He turned serious. "But for the record I already consider you a friend, and you know that I have hopes of engaging you in activities a little more intimate than typically enjoyed with friends."

A chair scraping against the floor pulled their attention to Sabrina. "I think that's my cue to go for a walk in the garden or something." She didn't meet his gaze, or Julianne's for that matter.

Julianne reached out and put a hand on Sabrina's arm before she could move away. "Please stay. There won't be any intimacy. Not tonight anyway. But I have questions about shifters, and it would be nice to have you to lean on if I need it. This is still overwhelming, and I'm sure I don't know the half of it yet."

Sabrina gave her friend a short nod and sat back down on her chair. "I'll stay." Then she swung her gaze to Duncan and gave him a stern expression. "If Mr. Randy over there will focus on the topic and not get all lovey-dovey."

Duncan burst out laughing. Sabrina was objectively speaking an attractive woman, and looking at her you would think she had some experience with men. But with the mixed messages she was sending out, it was impossible to tell. One minute she seemed uncomfortable with any hint of intimacy between him and Julianne, and the next she called him Mr. Randy. He would have liked to see Sabrina finding a good lover. Someone who swept her off her feet. Duncan had a feeling it would be good for her.

"I promise I'll stay on topic from now on, Sabrina. And I'm sorry if I made you uncomfortable, but you already know I find your friend…" He deliberately let the sentence hang and winked at Julianne, before turning back to Sabrina.

Blondie narrowed her eyes at him. "Yes, but I don't need to know anything more about that." Sabrina turned to Julianne. "Ask your questions. If he acts up again, I'll kick him."

Duncan laughed, and Julianne joined in. Sabrina gave them both a small smile.

CHAPTER 7

"Okay." Julianne spoke through her laughter. "Just give me a second to try and stop my mind spinning. I think I'm still in some kind of shock, and I'm having trouble wrapping my mind around the whole concept of shifters being real." Not to mention that the world was suddenly a completely different place, full of people who could turn into animals. Or maybe not full.

"Take all the time you need." Duncan studied her face as her laughter faded away, and she took a deep breath to try to get her bearings.

"So, how many shifters are there in this world?" Julianne kept her gaze on Duncan's face, trying to judge his reaction to her question.

He scrunched up his face in thought. "That's a difficult one. I couldn't tell you."

She wasn't surprised. Julianne had expected that answer. "Is that because you don't know or because you're not allowed to tell me?"

Her question seemed to take him aback, and he shook his head while frowning at her. "There's not much I'm not supposed to tell you now that you know about shifters. Hardly anything in fact. But the number of shifters in the world... I honestly have no idea how many there are. My best guess would be about one percent of the world's population."

"Okay. How many kinds of shifters are there?" Julianne kept her gaze on his face.

Duncan chuckled. "Also a difficult question. I recently met a new kind of shifter, so my answer would have to be, more than I'm currently aware of. In addition to wolf and panther shifters, I've met or heard of lions, tigers, servals, hyenas and various kinds of bear shifters. But there might be others."

Sabrina cocked her head. "All the shifters you have mentioned are predators. Are there no shifter herbivores?"

Duncan shook his head slowly. "Not that I'm aware of, no."

Julianne stared at the beautiful man before her, wondering what he would look like as a wolf. Would he be indistinguishable from a normal wolf, or would he be different, like some kind of monster wolf?

"I'm not sure I like whatever you're thinking about right now. You are studying me like I've just grown two heads or something." There was a smile on Duncan's face as he said the words, but his eyes held a hint of uncertainty.

Julianne gathered her courage as she held his gaze. "I hope this is not too forward of me. I don't know the shifter etiquette. Would it be okay for you to show us your wolf form, your wolf, or whatever you call that side of you? Or is it rude of me to ask?"

The smile on his face widened. "I'd be happy to show you my wolf form, but only if you promise not to get scared. I can't talk in that form, so I won't be able to reassure you that it's still me you're looking at. But it is. I'll still be me, even though I'll look like a wolf."

"Okay." Julianne hesitated for a second and turned to look at Sabrina.

Her friend nodded at Julianne before shifting her gaze to Duncan. "It would be interesting to see you change. And what you look like in your wolf form."

Duncan rose from the table. "Okay. But I'll have to undress, or I'll get stuck in my clothes as I change."

Julianne felt her face heat up at the thought of Duncan taking his clothes off in front of her. Then, she frowned as she realized that Sabrina would see him naked as well. "You should turn around. That way we won't see…" Julianne stopped as she realized what she was about to say.

"I can turn around." Duncan's voice was filled with suppressed laughter as he slowly rotated away from them. He pulled his shirt over his head, revealing his wide, thick shoulders and muscular, tapered back. His shorts landed on the floor, and Julianne sucked in a breath at the sight of his firm ass and powerful thighs. The sight was enough to arouse any woman's attention, and she fisted her hands in her lap to prevent herself from using them to cover Sabrina's eyes.

Julianne soon forgot about that, though, as the man standing before her changed shape right in front of her eyes. One second he was a man, and the next he was a large brown wolf, or perhaps brownish gray. He turned to face them, and she couldn't help staring at the magnificent creature standing less than ten feet away from her. The golden eyes staring back at her were animal eyes, but she had no trouble recognizing Duncan in them. He was in there, just like he had said he would be.

Sabrina's voice startled her. "I had expected some kind of hybrid, a mix between human and wolf." There was awe in her voice. "But he looks like a wolf."

Julianne couldn't take her eyes off Duncan. "Yes, he does."

She slowly rose from the table. "Can I touch you?" It felt strange asking an animal a question and hoping for a sign that he understood her.

The big wolf nodded, and it looked so funny she burst out laughing. He sat down and opened his mouth, letting his tongue loll out to one side. Just like any other canine.

Julianne slowly closed the distance between them and reached out a hand to touch the fur on his neck. It was so soft, softer than she had expected. She dug both her hands into his fur, massaging and scratching through his coat, and he leaned into her touch, letting her understand that he liked what she was doing.

She didn't have a lot of knowledge about normal wolves, but Julianne was quite sure this animal, Duncan's wolf, was bigger than regular ones. Both in stature and in bulk. And he seemed powerful, like potential energy was stored inside him until he needed it. Apart from that he could have been an ordinary wolf, at least as far as she could tell.

He raised his snout in the air, twisting his head a

little to look at her as she continued scratching his back. When he suddenly moved, she reared back at the feel of a warm wet tongue swiping across her face. Falling on her ass on the floor with a gasp, she used her hands to wipe away the slobber all over her face.

Opening her eyes, she saw Duncan standing on his normal human legs pulling up his shorts. He had his back to Sabrina, which meant that Julianne had a full view of his front where she was sitting on the floor. He managed to pull his shorts up to cover himself, but not before she had seen what he had to offer. She had already touched his fully erect member through his shorts earlier, and the size of him had been impressive. But it was something else entirely being face-to-face, so to speak, with the thing. Even sporting a semi like he was at the moment, made her womanly parts perk up at the sight. And she was itching to reach out and touch him, stroke him, and lick him to see him fill out to his full size.

"Julianne, are you okay?"

She was jerked out of her fantasy by the sound of the deep voice of the object of her desire. Feeling her face and neck burning with what had to be a dark blush, she didn't meet his gaze. Nodding, she got to her feet and busied herself by removing imaginary dust from her clothes.

A hand on her elbow stopped her. Duncan placed a finger gently under her chin and tipped her head back to face him. She held her breath as her gaze met his, not sure what she expected to find there.

Duncan's black orbs were shining with amusement as he held her gaze. He moved his head to whisper in her ear. "You weren't meant to see that. Yet."

The word *yet* made a wave of desire roll through her body, and she shuddered as an image of him between her legs, slowly pushing his thick cock into her, took hold of her brain. "Duncan." His name coming out of her mouth was little more than a sigh, and she squeezed her thighs together as her clit started pulsing with heat.

His warm lips closed over hers, and it was like a dam broke inside her, releasing pent-up desire. Their kissing turned frantic with passion in an instant. Tongues swirling and probing, dancing and rubbing. Julianne was clinging to Duncan's big body, hands on his back pressing him as close to her as she could. Her hands found his ass, and she used her hold on him to grind her hips against his. His groan spurred her on.

Suddenly, she was spun around, and she found herself facing the kitchen counter, as Duncan's arms wrapped around her and pressed her tightly against his front.

"Can I touch you?" His voice was a low growl against her ear.

There was no doubt in her mind as to what he meant, and there was nothing in the world she wanted more. "Yes. Please."

His left hand dipped to her stomach, before sliding up beneath her shirt. Cupping her breast, he started massaging it and teasing her nipple through her bra. The amazing sensations made her moan and squirm as her channel clenched, wanting to be filled. She could feel his hard cock against her back standing proud and erect, and he groaned as she moved her body against his.

His right hand suddenly found its way down the

front of her shorts and down into her panties. She gasped as his fingers slid down between her folds and started exploring. One long digit entered her channel and rubbed against the sensitive walls. Her pelvis moved wantonly against his finger, seeking to increase the pleasure building in her lower belly. A second digit joined the first and started thrusting in and out of her, causing her whole body to move against his in desperation to satisfy the raging desire building inside her. Julianne could feel Duncan grinding his thick member against her back, groaning like he was just as desperate for release as she was.

"I need more," she whispered the words, hoping he would understand her need to have him inside her. Her brain wasn't capable of forming more words at the moment.

His left hand released her breast and dived into her panties. She was about to protest, when he found her clit and started manipulating her nub with a skill that almost blew her mind. Rubbing, pinching, and sliding over her pleasure button while thrusting his fingers inside her, had her quickly spiraling toward release.

Her knees were shaking with the effort to stand, as Duncan's hands played her body like she was a violin, and he was a virtuoso who knew exactly how to manipulate her strings to bring out the most exquisite melody. She reached behind her and grabbed Duncan's ass with her hands, both to feel his muscular ass in her hands and to have something to hold onto to stop herself from crashing to the floor if her knees gave out.

He changed his position a little to grind his cock against her ass instead of her back. She moaned at the feeling of his thick rod not far from where she wanted him. The feeling of her ass against him obviously had an effect on him. He growled, and his movements became more frantic, like he was about to lose control. His two fingers thrusting into her were joined by a third, putting more pressure on the sensitive spots inside her. Her hips were working furiously to meet the thrusts of his fingers, which seemed to increase the friction against Duncan's cock, judging by his erratic breathing.

Julianne was so close, her body reaching for the release she was craving. Duncan's fingers playing with her clit pressed down on her swollen nub, and she gasped as pleasure erupted at her center and swirled through her body. Wave after wave of pure bliss rolled through her as Duncan continued thrusting his fingers into her and rubbing hard on her clit. He suddenly jerked and gave a shout as he started coming against her ass. The feeling of his cock pulsing with his pleasure made her smile as her orgasm slowly subsided.

By the time they came down, they were both breathing heavily. Duncan carefully removed his hands from her panties, but he didn't let go of her right away. "Thank you. That was... Well, I don't think I've ever come that hard with my clothes on before."

Julianne laughed and felt her ego get a little boost from his confession. "That makes two of us. And thank you as well. But you know, I wouldn't have objected to you coming inside me. In fact, I would've liked to have you inside me when I came."

He turned her around and stared into her eyes. "Does that mean you're disappointed?"

She gave him a warm smile and shook her head. "No, not at all. What we just did was different and amazing. I enjoyed it immensely."

A huge grin spread across his face. "Good. I'm glad you liked it. I did as well." His face turned apologetic. "I'm afraid you're a bit sticky though. I am too, but—"

Julianne rose on her toes and gave him a quick kiss on his lips. "It's okay, but it would be nice to be able to take a shower."

"That can be arranged. Come." Grabbing her hand, he pulled her along with him out into the hall. "We've got several guest rooms. You can use the shower in one of them."

"So, you don't want company in your shower?" Julianne didn't expect him to, since he seemed to want them to spend a little more time together before taking the next step. That plan had sort of crashed and burned already, at least partially with what had just happened between them in the kitchen, but perhaps he still wanted to postpone being naked together.

Duncan stopped and turned to her. "I'd love to, but if we did that, I'm afraid I wouldn't be able to let you go until morning."

Julianne felt her jaw drop. That wasn't the response she had been expecting. She had thought he would give her some excuse about waiting a little to get that intimate, giving her more time to adjust to him being a shifter. Or something like that.

He chuckled. "I think we should have a shower. Separately. And then go look for Sabrina."

"Shit." Julianne had completely forgotten about Sabrina being in the kitchen when they started.

Duncan interrupted her thoughts. "She disappeared

as soon as we started kissing."

Julianne breathed out a sigh of relief. "Oh, thank goodness. I have no idea how I could completely forget." She stopped herself. "Or I do, but I should've remembered. What kind of friend am I?"

He chuckled again. "Don't worry. Sabrina already knew that we're attracted to each other. And she hasn't seemed opposed to you and me getting intimate."

"No, not as long as she didn't have to witness it. Which she almost did."

Duncan put his lips on hers, effectively stopping her. It only lasted a couple of seconds, but Julianne savored the feel of his warm mouth against hers.

"I think you have to borrow some of my clothes for now." He had his hands on her waist, some of his fingers beneath her shirt, caressing her bare skin. "They won't fit you very well, but they'll be clean."

"Um." Julianne had trouble focusing with his hands against her bare skin. "That feels nice. Your hands are so warm. Is that a shifter thing?"

His hands stopped moving, and he let her go. "Yes. Well, shit. I didn't even realize I was touching you. My body seems to have a mind of its own around you."

She couldn't help laughing. It was intoxicating having such an amazing man being so captivated by her, like he found her as irresistible as she found him. Julianne had never experienced anything like it before with anyone else, and she couldn't help thinking that what was between them was something special. It was entirely too early for that, though.

"Come. There's a room upstairs you can use. It's only a few days since I cleaned it, and no one has stayed there since." Duncan led her up the stairs to the first floor.

"Wow. A man who both cooks and cleans. Is there anything you don't do?" The more she got to know this man, the more she liked him. But what amazed her was that he wasn't already taken. He had to have piles of women throwing themselves at him. Beautiful women, far more beautiful than she. Of course, beauty wasn't everything, but there were plenty of women who were both beautiful and nice. That none of them had been able to sink their claws into Duncan yet was a miracle.

"No, not really. I do what needs to be done."

His answer made her smile. So practical.

Opening a door to her left, Duncan led the way into a large, beautiful room. "The bathroom is in there." He indicated a door to the right. "You just go ahead and have a shower. I'll find some clothes and put them on the bed for you."

Julianne smiled and turned to him. "Thank you."

CHAPTER 8

Duncan left Julianne's room and hurried to his own to find some clothes for her. He had nothing that would fit her, but she needed something to wear after he had come against her ass. Her soft round ass. It had soaked through his own shorts as well as hers, leaving them both sticky. Just the thought of what they had done made his blood flow increase to a certain appendage, and he groaned in frustration. This was crazy. The effect Julianne had on him was crazy. He couldn't remember experiencing anything like this before with anyone else. It was like he was a teenager again, with how little control he had over his body.

Rummaging through his drawers, he picked out shorts, sweatpants, a tee, and a long-sleeved shirt. That would give her a choice of what to wear. Hopefully, she would be able to make some of it work for her.

Entering her room, he heard the shower going in the bathroom. Duncan froze. She was naked in there, just a few yards away, and he could be with her in less than two seconds. Julianne had even suggested they should shower together. His dick went from half-mast to full-action mode instantly, and he shuddered at the compulsion he felt to go to her. It was only sheer force of will that made him get out of her room and close the door behind him.

His walk was stilted as he moved back to his room and into his bathroom. Staring at himself in the mirror, he shook his head. "What's wrong with you? Get a grip, Duncan, or you'll end up scaring her away." He frowned as he heard his own words. This was the first time in his life he was actively trying to keep a woman close. Well, apart from Sarah, but that wasn't the same. Duncan wanted to spend more time with Julianne. Desperately. And that wasn't how he usually felt with women. His body had needs, and he had no trouble finding women to have sex with, but he had never wanted to spend time with a woman before or after the sexual act itself.

Standing there, he let his confusion and frustration come to the surface. But for some reason he didn't feel the pain that usually followed. It was like his body's craving for Julianne was suppressing his pain, and it was a great feeling. He hadn't felt this free and happy for a long time. But would it continue for as long as Julianne was with him, or would it revert back after a while, even if she was there? He had no idea.

Taking a deep breath, he changed his focus to Julianne's safety. His mind had been poking at him for a while to make sure Steven couldn't find her. Duncan was quite sure Steven had tampered with her phone, and that was how he had been able to keep tabs on her. Turning her phone off should be enough to prevent that. But Duncan wanted to put more safety measures in place just to be sure.

He extracted his phone from his shirt pocket and found Callum's number in his contact list. Callum was a young local wolf with a knack for electronics, and he was currently setting up his own security firm. If there was someone who knew how to keep tabs on a person, or just keep that person away from the estate, it was Callum.

The young wolf picked up on the second ring. "Duncan. What are you up to?"

"Callum. I need a favor."

"Sure. Anything you need."

As always, the young wolf was eager to help out. With his brains he would have already had a high standing among the wolves, if not for his handicap. But a weakness, even something you had no control over, was frowned upon among shifters.

"I need to keep someone away from the estate. A panther. I'll text you his full name later."

"All right. That shouldn't be a problem."

"Great. I knew I could count on you to help me out."

"Of course. But are you sure the panther is the only one you don't want to come knocking? He might have friends."

Duncan sighed. He hadn't considered that. Steven had appeared to be alone in Mallaig, but that might not have been the case. And Duncan hadn't asked Julianne about it. "Good point. I'll check and get back to you on that."

"Okay. I'll be ready to roll when you give me some names."

"Thank you, Callum." Duncan ended the call.

"Fuck." He should have considered the possibility that Steven had accomplices, but instead Duncan had been too busy letting his dick rule his mind. At least there had been no signs of anyone following them from Mallaig to the estate, and there had been no cars in sight when they turned off the main road to follow the dirt road up to the main house. Unless Steven had more sophisticated means of locating them, the panther shouldn't be able to find them. The SUV was registered to one of Trevor's companies, and Trevor always made sure to hide any link between his companies and his personal name due to his long lifespan. To be able to connect the SUV to the estate would be damn near impossible unless you followed it there.

He quickly shed his clothes and turned on the shower. At least one good thing had come of Duncan worrying about Julianne's safety. His cock was no longer standing at attention.

Less than a minute later, he turned off the shower and quickly dried off. He threw on some fresh clothes and hurried out of his room to find Julianne.

Knocking on her door, he heard a mumbled reply to come in. He wasn't prepared for the sight that greeted him when he entered, and before he could stop himself, he roared with laughter. The scowl on Julianne's face only made him laugh harder, and he had to grab the door frame for support to be able to keep standing.

"This is your fault you know, so you'll be the one to explain to Sabrina why I'm wearing your clothes." Folding her arms under her breasts, she raised her chin and stared at him with one eyebrow raised in challenge.

Duncan managed to stop laughing, but only just. Not even the impending embarrassment of telling Sabrina what had happened, could take away his amusement at seeing the way Julianne was dressed. She had opted for the shorts and T-shirt. The tee was more like a dress on her, reaching almost down to her knees, and the shorts were currently lying on the floor, circling her ankles like a pair of reading glasses.

"It might be better if I find you a belt or something to tie around your waist. You can use my T-shirt as a dress, and you won't need the shorts."

Julianne chuckled as her eyes twinkled with amusement. "Well, it will certainly give you easy access, since I don't have any panties to wear."

Duncan felt his jaw drop, and his eyes dipped to the location he estimated her pussy would be hidden underneath the T-shirt. If his eyes could radiate heat, he would have singed a hole in the material right at the junction of her thighs. Swallowing, he forced his gaze back up to meet hers.

She was grinning as she stared into his eyes. Her gaze slowly lowered down his body until it stopped at his crotch, her eyes widening at the sight of his hard cock tenting his shorts. Julianne's gaze snapped back up to his. "We just... It's only been about fifteen minutes since you... How?"

He couldn't help chuckling at her surprise. "I'm a shifter. We don't need much time to reload, if you understand what I mean."

Nodding, she let her eyes drop back down to his groin. "Oh, I understand." Then, she suddenly turned away from him, almost stumbling as her feet tangled in the shorts that were still wrapped around her ankles.

Duncan stayed by the door, not sure whether to approach her or not. Several seconds went by, and he was debating what to say to Julianne when she spoke.

"If you don't want to go any further with me tonight, I think it would be best if you left me alone for a little while. At least until your… It's kind of distracting."

He breathed a sigh of relief. She didn't seem to be angry with him. Or find him creepy. She found him…distracting. To him that sounded like a good thing. But as she pointed out, they needed to focus on something else.

"There's something we need to talk about. I've got a few questions concerning your safety. With regard to Steven. When you're ready, come downstairs. I'll be down in the kitchen in a couple of minutes. Thinking about your safety has a, shall we say, deflating effect on me."

Julianne snorted and turned to him. "I'll be down in a bit."

Nodding, he closed the door behind him and went to his room to pick up his phone. The thought of Julianne's ex stalking her had his anger rising and his cock sinking. By the time he walked into the kitchen, his desire had cooled.

The leftover food was still on the table, and Duncan busied himself clearing everything away. He had just started the dishwasher when Julianne walked into the room. She had somehow managed to get his shorts to stay up around her hips.

He turned to her and smiled. "Shall we try to find

Sabrina? I think she should be here when we discuss what to do about Steven."

Julianne nodded. "Yeah. Any idea where she might be? You know this place better than I do."

"Let's try the garden first." After leading the way to the back door, he opened it and stepped outside.

Sabrina turned to them when they walked out the door. She was standing a few yards from the back door and had been facing the mountains until she heard them. Narrowing her eyes at them in accusation, she shook her head slowly. "So much for no intimacy in my presence." One of her eyebrows lifted as she took in Julianne's clothes.

Duncan started to say something, but before he could utter one word, Sabrina stopped him.

"No! I don't want to know. Just no."

"Okay, but I guess you're entitled to kick me." Smiling, he kept his eyes on Blondie to see if she still remembered what she had threatened him with.

One corner of Sabrina's mouth twitched in response to his reference to her earlier statement. "I'll keep that in mind." She started walking toward him.

Duncan prepared to protect himself, but Sabrina didn't even glance at him as she walked past them and into the house. Julianne followed her friend, and Duncan closed and locked the door behind them all. A locked door wouldn't stop a shifter from entering the house, but the sound of it breaking would warn them. On the way to the kitchen, he swung by the front door to make sure it was locked as well.

Walking into the kitchen, he observed the women opening and closing drawers and cupboards. "What are you looking for?"

Julianne smiled at him over her shoulder as she continued searching. "Do you have any tea?"

"Of course." He moved over to the kitchen counter and pulled out a drawer they obviously hadn't checked yet. "Right here. What would you like?"

Julianne and Sabrina came over to him and started rummaging through his tea collection. Taking a step back, he studied them as they read the boxes and evaluated the various options.

Pulling out a box of green apple tea, Julianne smiled at him. "Perfect. Now what would you like? We'll be preparing the tea. You can just sit down and look pretty."

"Pretty? Men aren't pretty." Duncan slowly backed toward the kitchen table, keeping his eyes on Julianne.

Smiling at him, she tilted her head a bit to the side. "Yes, some men are pretty. But you aren't one of them. You're—"

Sabrina cut her off with a sigh. Throwing her hands into the air like she was giving up, she let her gaze travel back and forth between Julianne and Duncan. "Okay, whatever you two ended up doing earlier, it clearly wasn't enough. Go find a room and fuck each other's brains out or something. In the meantime, I can have a nice cup of tea in blessed quiet solitude."

For two seconds after Sabrina's outburst, the room was deathly silent. Then, Duncan and Julianne both burst out laughing.

Sabrina was resting her hands on her waist and glaring at them, like she was debating which one of them she was going to murder first.

Duncan couldn't agree more. What he and Julianne had done earlier wasn't enough, and they most definitely would fuck. But not yet. They had more important things to attend to. The thought tamped down his amusement, and he sat down at the table.

Without preamble he changed the topic. "We have something important to discuss. Steven."

Julianne's laughter stopped abruptly, and Duncan almost regretted bringing up her ex. But this was important, and he had already waited too long. Safety measures should have already been in place, and they would have been if not for him letting his cock rule his actions.

"Yes, you're right." Julianne's serious green eyes met his. "What kind of tea would you like? I need tea for this conversation."

"Black. Any kind of black tea will be great."

Duncan stayed silent while the women prepared the tea. It was nice to see Julianne finding her way around his kitchen. Although, it wasn't his, but that was the way he thought of it. He had renovated it himself. Trevor had given him free reign as long as he kept the color scheme fairly muted. In other words no loud colors like hot-pink, toxic-green, or similar. And Duncan could live with that. He had chosen blue and dark wood as the main colors for the kitchen, and it had turned out to be a good combination. At least Duncan was happy with it.

Julianne put a steaming cup of black tea in front of him, and a cup of green apple tea in front of herself, as she sat down. Sabrina sat down as well, putting her own tea and a small pitcher of milk on the table.

Duncan added some milk to his tea and sipped the hot liquid. Putting the cup down, he looked at Julianne. "I would like you both to stay here at the estate tonight. Going back to the B and B isn't a good idea. I'm sure Steven knows where you're staying in Fort William. He has already approached you once, and he doesn't seem the type to take no for an answer. The fact that you rejected him is more likely to increase his determination to get you back, than not."

Julianne shuddered in response to his words, and Sabrina put a hand on her arm. Duncan would like nothing better than to hold her and tell her that he would protect her, but touching her wasn't a good idea at the moment if he wanted to stay on topic.

"I talked to a friend of mine on the phone earlier. Callum is a security expert, and I asked him to find a way to keep Steven away from the estate. And any close friends of Steven, if you can think of anyone who might be helping him. Callum only needs their full names to set it up."

"Thank you, Duncan." Giving him a small smile, Julianne turned to Sabrina. "I would feel much safer staying here than going back to Fort William."

Sabrina nodded to Julianne before turning to Duncan. "I fully agree. However, our things are still at the B and B. We'll need to get them at some point."

Duncan had thought about that as well. "Yes, but I think it would be best if you didn't go there to get them yourself. I can have someone pick them up for you. Would that be all right?"

"I suppose." Sabrina considered his plan for a few seconds before she continued. "But Steven can follow whoever you send to pick up our things back here."

"Not if he doesn't know which person or vehicle to follow. I've got a couple of friends running a transport business in Fort William. There are vans and trucks driving in and out of that place all day. I'm sure my friends would be happy to take your things to their warehouse. There they can load it into another vehicle and get one of their drivers to bring your stuff here. What do you think?"

Julianne chuckled. "Sounds like a good plan." Then her eyes narrowed in anger. "Asshole. I can't believe he's stalking me. I mean, whatever for? Why would you want someone who doesn't want you back? I just don't get it."

Duncan had no trouble understanding her anger. He felt it as well, along with a nagging worry for her safety. Julianne might be all right for the time being, but she would be going home soon. What then? The thought had his wolf wanting to come out, and he quickly shoved his concerns to the back of his mind. He would think about that later.

"Can you tell me Steven's full name, and that of any friends who you think might be helping him?" Duncan took out his phone and started a text to Callum. "I'll send them to Callum."

Julianne nodded and gave him the names of three men including Steven. "I can't think of anyone else who would want to help him with something like this. Unless it's someone I haven't met."

Duncan finished the text and sent it to Callum. A few seconds later, he received a confirmation from the man, that he was on it and not to worry.

"Let's not worry about Steven anymore tonight." Duncan gave Julianne a smile he hoped was encouraging. "There's no reason to believe that he knows where you're staying at the moment. You turned off your phone in Mallaig, and nobody was following us here. Callum is good at what he does. He'll put extra security in place around the estate. The best thing we can do is to get a good night's sleep. We can talk about what to do next in the morning."

As if on cue Julianne yawned. Then she smiled and nodded. "Yeah, I guess some sleep would be nice."

Getting up, Duncan gathered their teacups and the small pitcher and put them in the sink. "Okay, ladies, please follow me."

He headed upstairs to the first floor. Walking down the corridor, he opened the first door on the right, before stepping inside and turning on the light. "You can have this room, Sabrina. There's a bathroom in there." He indicated the door to the right. "There's fresh towels and various toiletries in the cabinet in there, including a new toothbrush."

A small smile formed on her face. "Thank you. You seem to be well prepared for guests."

Returning her smile, he nodded. "Yeah, you never know when someone turns up. It's happened several times recently, so I've learned to be ready."

Returning to the corridor, he pointed at the door to the room that Julianne had used earlier. "Julianne is staying there, and my room is down at the end. If there's anything you need, just knock on my door."

After saying goodnight to Sabrina, he followed Julianne to her room. "I hope you'll be all right staying here." Studying her face for any signs of fear or trepidation, he was relieved when he didn't find any. "Please come to me if you get scared. You might not feel it right now, but a lot has happened today."

Her smile was warm but also a bit melancholy. "I'm sure I'll be fine. Don't worry about me. Thank you, though."

Duncan should turn away and go to his room, but instead his eyes dipped to her lips. Forcing his gaze back up to hers, he smiled at her. "I'd like to kiss you goodnight, but if I did, I'm not sure I'd be able to stop there, so I think it might be better if I didn't. You need sleep, and time to process everything that's happened today."

Julianne grinned up at him. "I'd like to kiss you, too, but I think you're right." Her grin acquired a little wickedness. "Must be your animal magnetism."

Chuckling, he leaned down and gave her a quick peck on her cheek before turning away and starting for his room. "Goodnight, Julianne."

"Goodnight, Duncan."

He didn't turn to acknowledge her reply, just continued down the corridor toward his room. The sound of her door closing reached him just as he arrived at the door to his room.

CHAPTER 9

Julianne closed the door to the corridor and stared at it. She wanted to go to Duncan. The thought of him undressing and getting into bed had her fisting her hands at her sides to stop herself from opening the door and running after him. The man was mouthwateringly gorgeous, but that was just one reason why she wanted him. He was also kind, caring, and attentive. The perfect gentleman. Well, in some respects. Thankfully, he wasn't too much of a gentleman.

Remembering the way his cock had pulsed against her ass as he was coming had her channel clenching with need. And the way he had played her body and made her orgasm so easily. In her experience men weren't good at making women come. Most of them were too focused on their own pleasure to care, and the rest just didn't have the skills necessary. But Duncan had everything it took, and that knowledge made her horny as hell and wanting to spend the night with him.

Julianne was supposed to digest all that had happened since this morning, but at the moment she couldn't care less. The desire running rampant through her body was distracting her from any fear she might have otherwise felt. How she was supposed to rest, let alone sleep, was beyond her.

Walking into the bathroom, she stared at herself in the mirror. Her cheeks had a rosy color, like she had been outside on a cold winter day, but the cold had nothing to do with it. If anything, it was the heat. The heat pulsing through her, at the thought of Duncan's hands on her and his cock inside her.

Walking back into the bedroom, Julianne started pacing in frustration, debating whether to go to him or not. He wanted them to wait on sex, and she should respect his wishes, but the waiting seemed to be all for her benefit. Duncan wanted her to be sure she wanted him before they spent the night together, and based on everything she had learned in the last few hours, not the least about him, his reasoning was sound. But it would be great if someone could inform her body of that fact because it clearly hadn't gotten the message.

Groaning, she walked back into the bathroom. She had to do something to alleviate her body's need, or she would go crazy. Or at least not get any sleep.

Julianne removed her clothes and put them on a shelf. She turned on the shower and stepped in before the water had a chance to heat up. Shivering as the cold spray hit her, she hoped that it would cool her desire. But no such luck. Her womanly parts were throbbing and clenching, wanting to be touched and filled.

Giving in to her need, she put a finger on her clit and started playing with the little nub. She moaned as pleasure started building inside her. Inserting a finger inside herself, she started thrusting it in and out as she massaged her clit. Slowly, she was bringing herself closer to release. Not nearly as fast as Duncan had, and her body obviously remembered and missed his touch. But at least she was going to give her body some relief.

Julianne conjured an image of Duncan at the beach. His thick shoulders and sculpted pecs and abs. His beautiful black eyes and amused smile. The feeling of his hard cock against her belly as he pulled her close. And later the way he had felt against her hand as she palmed his rock-hard member through his shorts. The size and shape of him was firmly etched into her mind. To have him push inside her.

Her sudden climax interrupted her thoughts. Pleasure pulsed through her system, and she moaned as it spread throughout her body before fading away.

She rinsed off her body and stepped out of the shower. Not exactly sated, but at least her body had calmed down. Julianne had a feeling it was going to take Duncan's touch to satisfy her body completely, but that would have to come later. *Pun intended.*

After toweling off, she exited the bathroom. It was dark outside, a fact that she hadn't noticed until this moment. Come to think of it, it had been getting dark as they left the kitchen to go upstairs. Since she didn't wear a wristwatch, she had no idea what time it was. And she couldn't exactly turn on her cell phone and tip Steven off as to where she was. But it was clearly time for bed. She had no idea whether she would be able to get any sleep, but even resting her eyes for a while was better than nothing.

Remembering Duncan telling Sabrina about the toiletries available in her bathroom cabinet, Julianne went to check on hers. And sure enough, she found an unopened package with a toothbrush in one of the cabinets. As she was cleaning her teeth, her eyes landed on her discarded clothes on the floor. She would have to borrow some more of Duncan's clothes in the morning until their things from the B&B arrived, but it would have been nice to be able to dress in her own clothes in the morning. For starters they fit, and then there was the small matter of a bra and panties.

Using bodywash from the shower, she cleaned her clothes as best she could. Hopefully, they would dry by morning. For some reason it had felt good to wear Duncan's clothes. Comforting in a way. But she would have preferred to have her underthings underneath.

Getting into bed, she sighed at the feeling of the soft, cool sheets against her body. Just like everything else in this house, the sheets were high quality. Duncan's friend Trevor was obviously loaded, owning a place like this. Just the upkeep of such a place had to cost a fortune. Then again, a Maserati wasn't cheap, either, so Duncan had to be fairly well off as well. Not that she cared all that much if he had money or not.

Julianne's mind started running through all she had learned that day. Her whole world had changed in just a few hours, and she hadn't had the opportunity to process everything yet.

Shifters. There were actual shifters in the world. They weren't just fictional characters anymore, but real. The whole notion was staggering, but for some reason, she had no trouble accepting the fact. Duncan was a shifter, and she had seen him change into a wolf, a magnificent creature. And it was okay. The fact that Duncan was a wolf didn't bother her at all. It was exciting and fantastic, and it suited him perfectly. Man and beast in one. *Amazing.* She still wanted him just as much as she had before she knew what he was. Perhaps even more. That might depict her as crazy, but so be it.

At least he wasn't a vampire. The whole bloodsucking thing wasn't for her. The thought had Julianne sitting up abruptly. Vampires. If there were shifters, who was to say that vampires didn't exist as well? And witches and leprechauns and trolls. *Fuck.* Why hadn't this dawned on her earlier? She wouldn't be able to ask Duncan about it until the morning, and she was dying to know. Lying back down and staring up at the ceiling, or at least where the ceiling would be visible if the room wasn't dark, she lay there with her mind spinning.

Taking a deep breath, she tried to calm her mind. Julianne would get the answers she needed in the morning. Until then the best thing she could do was to sleep. Concentrating on her breathing, she tried to let each part of her body rest: her legs, arms, torso, and head. Focusing on the softness of the sheets and the heaviness of her body, she let herself drift.

∞∞∞

Duncan was in trouble. The fact that Julianne was in a bed just down the hall had his whole body raring to go. He wanted her again, and he had a feeling he wouldn't get it out of his system until he'd had her. Multiple times. Once wouldn't be enough with her, his wild-haired beauty. With her chocolate-colored freckles and smooth, soft skin. Green eyes sparkling with amusement as she teased him.

The feel of her tight pussy took over his mind. He had no doubt it would feel like heaven burying his cock inside her. Her sheath squeezing his cock as he thrust into her and trying to prevent him from pulling out, just like she had with his fingers.

Sitting up in bed, he wondered, not for the first time, if he was going to get any sleep at all. His rod was like granite, throbbing with the need for release, again. His balls were pulled up tight, begging to be emptied, again. But he didn't want to give in this time. His body would just have to adjust. And he needed sleep.

Lying back down, Duncan fisted his hands in the sheets to stop himself from doing something about his condition. He actively searched his brain for a safe topic to think about. Something not related to Julianne.

His mind landed on what had happened to Stephanie and Michael. Duncan found he was still wondering what would have happened if they hadn't been able to locate the two of them. Would Stephanie have been able to rescue Michael and get them both out of there? Or would the evil witch Ambrosia have prevented it? Stephanie had flayed Jack alive without knowing that someone was there to rescue her and Michael, so it was entirely possible she would have been able to save them both. That woman had some crazy-strong powers, that she herself hadn't even known about until Jack hurt Michael, and Stephanie's fury and protective instinct led her to retaliate against the panther.

Panther. Another panther was after Julianne. Just a coincidence? Or did Steven have an agreement with Ambrosia as well? It didn't quite add up, though. Ambrosia had made a deal with Jack because he was an unmated alpha, whereas Steven wasn't nearly as powerful. At least not that Duncan had been able to tell from their brief encounter in Mallaig. Perhaps it was worth keeping in mind just in case, even though he doubted that Steven was the new Jack.

At some point during his reflections, he must have fallen asleep because he woke up growling as pleasure ripped through him. The sensation of pounding into Julianne's tight, wet pussy was still there as he sprayed his seed all over his sheets, the dream so close that he found his eyes searching for her. Then reality took over, and he groaned with the realization that it was all part of a wet dream. He couldn't remember having one of those in decades.

Swearing softly, he got up and ripped the sheets from his bed. After stomping into the bathroom, he cleaned himself up before returning to stand by his bed. Well, it was official. He was going insane. Or he had turned into a sex addict and needed help. This wasn't normal. Not by a long shot.

After putting new sheets on his bed, he got in. He needed more sleep. It was light outside but still early. A couple of more hours would be good.

The next time Duncan woke up, it was due to his phone ringing. Grabbing it off his nightstand, he answered the call without checking to see who was calling him. "Yes." His voice was husky with sleep, and his irritation at being woken up was evident in his tone.

A deep chuckling sounded through the phone, and Duncan groaned. "Trevor. What do you want? It's early."

"It's eight o'clock in the morning. You're usually up by seven. What happened to you? Did a woman take you for a ride last night?"

Duncan wanted to hang up on the cheery bastard, but he didn't. "Something like that. What? You're calling for a reason, I hope. Not just to check up on my sexual encounters."

Trevor chuckled again. "Trust me. I want absolutely nothing to do with your sexual encounters."

"Good. Then what?"

"How would you like to come up to Loch Ness for a couple of days? We need some help." Trevor's tone had turned serious.

Duncan inwardly groaned. "This is not a good time. I…" He stopped, not sure how to explain about Julianne without giving away his attraction to her.

"Is this about your sexual encounters?" Trevor's voice was dripping with amusement.

"I thought you didn't want to know anything about that. But to be straight with you, both yes and no."

"And what does that mean exactly? Sounds complicated. I thought you were all about the simple things."

Sighing, Duncan sat up in bed. "I am. Usually. I didn't plan for complicated. It just happened."

Trevor's laugh rumbled through the phone. "Welcome to the real world, my friend. I hate to break it to you, but that's usually how complicated happens."

"Yeah, yeah, whatever." It was time to change the subject. Duncan didn't want to end up having to explain about Julianne. Although, it would be nice to get Trevor's opinion on this whole business with Steven. And then there was Sabrina. She was a witch, and she might have some witchy friends. Perhaps she would be able to help in their search for Ambrosia.

"Are you still there?" Trevor's voice pulled him back from his thoughts.

"Yes, sorry. Just thinking. Um, I think I might need some help as well. And there's someone here who might be able to help us with our witch problem."

"Here, as in at the estate?" There was surprise in Trevor's voice. "Is she there in the room with you listening?"

"Yes. No. I mean…" Duncan groaned. Teenager. He was acting more like one at the moment than he had been back when he actually was one. Taking a deep breath, he started again. "Yes, she's here at the estate. Well, they both are. But, no, neither of them are in the room with me. I'm not sleeping with either of them yet."

"Yet?" Trevor was laughing again. "So, you're planning to sleep with them. Is that why you can't come, because you have yet to convince them to join you in your bed?"

Duncan could have kicked himself. Why had he added the word yet? "No. It's not like that. I…" Groaning, he flung himself back down onto the bed. "Fuck! I sound like an idiot."

Trevor roared with laughter, and the sound was so loud that Duncan yanked the phone away from his ear.

After a few seconds, the sound of laughter quieted, and he brought the phone back to his ear.

"Thank you for that. I'm now deaf in one ear." Duncan tried to sound irritated, but he couldn't hide his amusement. He had no trouble understanding why Trevor was laughing at him.

"What a shame. Duncan, I think you'd better explain." Trevor was fighting to get the words out through his laughter. "I didn't realize the extent of complicated you were talking about."

Duncan chuckled. "Yes, well. I met a woman."

"That's usually how it starts." Trevor obviously couldn't help himself.

Duncan groaned. "Do you want me to explain, or not?"

"Go on. I'm listening. But I can't promise that I won't give you shit about this." It sounded like Trevor was trying to smother his laughter, his voice being a bit strained.

Closing his eyes, Duncan started again. "I met a woman in Fort William. Her name is Julianne, and she's very attractive. She's here on holiday with her friend Sabrina, who, as it turns out, is a witch. Yesterday, I spent the day with the women, showing them around the west coast. We ended up in Mallaig in the afternoon, where Julianne ran into her ex. A piece of shit panther, who's obviously been keeping tabs on her. Only she doesn't know about shifters. Well, she didn't. I told her last night. Even showed her my wolf. She took it better than I expected."

"Wait, you told her about shifters? What about her witch friend, did she know from before?"

"Well, not exactly. Sabrina has the ability to feel and

recognize power, and she confronted me about what I am the night before last. I told her, but I didn't intend to tell Julianne. Not until what happened with Steven, her panther ex. Then I decided to tell her. She needed to know to be able to protect herself."

"Yes, but as a human she won't be able to protect herself against a panther, even knowing what he is." Trevor sounded concerned.

"I know. And that's one of the reasons they ended up staying here at the estate last night. Going back to the B and B, where they were staying in Fort William, wasn't an option."

"No. Good call. Do you think they would enjoy going to Loch Ness? We could use the help of another witch. Steph is still a bit worried about using her full powers. She doesn't feel in control yet, and she's afraid of accidentally hurting someone."

Duncan was a bit taken aback at Trevor's suggestion. The thought of introducing Julianne to his friends was both scary and annoying. For some reason he wanted his friends to like her, approve of her, which was a bit strange since she wasn't his woman or anything. And he had no intention of asking her to become his woman, either. Or did he? The thought made him smile. If Julianne was his, she could stay with him. They could travel together. She would stay in his bed for more than just a couple of nights. He sucked in a breath in shock at his own thoughts. *His woman.* He had never wanted one before. He had wanted a mate, but that wasn't the same thing.

"Duncan, are you all right?" Trevor had raised his voice and sounded concerned.

"Sorry, yes. I'll talk to the ladies about going to

Loch Ness. I'll get back to you soon." Ending the call, Duncan let his phone fall onto the bed. His heart was slamming against his breastbone, as he let the whole idea of Julianne becoming his woman unfold in his mind. A tendril of fear licked up his spine at the idea, but there was another emotion that was far stronger. Excitement. He wanted this. He wanted her.

Jumping out of bed, he sprinted into the bathroom and dived into the shower. Grinning, he quickly washed his hair and skin as his body jittered with excitement. Duncan couldn't wait to tell her. To see the smile on her face, when he asked her to be his. To kiss her and... He froze. What if she said no? What if she only wanted a holiday fling? Duncan stared at the wall without seeing it, feeling his heart stutter in his chest.

Closing his eyes, he took a deep breath to calm down. He was acting like a teenager again. He needed to slow down and get a grip. Julianne had seemed eager to be with him. That was enough for the time being. They would spend some more time together, and if he still wanted her to be his woman, he would ask her. Nice and slow, or at least slower than if he was to ask her this morning.

CHAPTER 10

Julianne opened her eyes and stared at the ceiling. The room was filled with light, so it had to be morning. Moving her head to look around the room, she nodded to herself. Yes, it was all real. Duncan, shifters, Steven following her. All of it was real.

She got out of bed and went to check on the state of her clothes. Everything was dry except for her shorts. They were still a bit damp. After putting on her bra, panties, and shirt, she went to the bathroom and grabbed Duncan's shorts off the shelf. They would have to do this morning until her own shorts were dry.

She exited her room and took a couple of steps toward the stairs before stopping. Having no idea what time it was, she debated whether or not to knock on Sabrina's door. Her friend was an early riser and probably wouldn't mind even if it turned out to be quite early.

Julianne knocked and waited for a few seconds, but there was no answer. Which probably meant that either Sabrina was in the shower, or she was already downstairs.

She heard their voices as she approached the kitchen. Apparently, both Sabrina and Duncan were up and about already. It would have been nice if they had woken her up as well. But knowing them, they had probably wanted to let her sleep for as long as she needed after everything that had happened the day before.

When she entered the kitchen, Duncan spun around and gave her a bright smile filled with... She would have said love if she didn't know better.

"Good morning. How are you feeling?"

She grinned back at him. It was impossible not to. "Great. What are you making?"

Duncan turned back to focus on what he was cooking. "Pancakes. Sabrina assured me you like pancakes."

Julianne chuckled and turned to her friend, who was sitting at the kitchen table. "Yeah, she knows me. Good morning, Sabrina."

"Good morning." A small smile creased her friend's lips for a second before changing into a frown. "He didn't want any help. Insisted on making your pancakes himself."

A deep chuckle sounded from the stove. "If I'm going to impress Julianne with my cooking skills, I have to actually do the cooking myself."

Julianne felt her jaw slacken with surprise. Was Duncan serious when he said he wanted to impress her, or was he just joking? They had only known each other a few days.

"Oh, he's serious." Sabrina had somehow guessed

what she was thinking again. Although, it might have been clearly written on her face.

Not sure how to respond, Julianne just nodded.

"I'll be back in a few minutes." Her friend got up from the table and walked out of the kitchen.

Julianne was left standing in the middle of the room, not sure what to say or do. Duncan was focused on the pancakes, juggling two frying pans in his effort to impress her. There was one thing she wanted more than pancakes, though.

She walked up to him and stopped no more than a foot behind him. He shot her a quick smile over his shoulder before turning his attention back to the pancakes. Which left her free access to his magnificent back.

Starting with her hands on his shoulders, she moved them slowly down his back, using her fingers to explore every hard muscle on her way toward his ass. He was wearing a fitted tee, robbing her of the feeling of his skin against her palms, but she was still enjoying the feel of his muscles moving beneath her hands.

"Julianne." Duncan's voice had a slight growl to it.

It didn't stop her. When she reached his waist, she let her hands drop to his ass. Grabbing one ass cheek in each hand, she squeezed.

He moved so fast she didn't realize what had happened, until she found herself pressed up tightly against his chest with his mouth closing over hers. It took her a second to respond, but then she opened her mouth and welcomed his kiss. His tongue pushed into her mouth to play with hers, and she moaned as desire raced through her body.

Duncan let go of her just as fast as he had grabbed her, leaving her staggering as he was suddenly back to focusing on the pancakes he was making.

"Whoa. Ditched for food. Not exactly a confidence booster." Julianne had meant to put more snark into her voice, but she wasn't able to hide her amusement.

"Distracting a man who's trying to impress you with his cooking is unfair." Duncan didn't sound irritated, though. There was barely concealed laughter in his voice.

"Okay, I guess we're even then."

"Not by a long shot. I'll get you back tonight when I've got you all to myself. Maybe I'll restrain your arms while I—"

"Sabrina has entered the kitchen!" Her friend's loud voice rang out, effectively preventing Duncan from telling her what he was going to do to her. Which was probably a good thing, since it was still far too many hours to wait until they would have time alone together.

"So she is." Duncan was chuckling. "This was innocent, though. You didn't exactly walk in on something intimate."

"No. I realize that you could've been fucking on the kitchen table. That would've been considerably more awkward." Sabrina's voice was even and without emotions.

A sharp crack sounded through the room in the silence that followed Sabrina's statement. Duncan had dropped the bowl containing the pancake batter onto the floor, spilling the batter as the bowl broke into pieces.

Julianne almost fell over laughing. Sabrina had a

way of surprising people. She came across all proper and subdued, so nobody expected her to say anything outrageous or snarky. So, when she did, it tended to shock people.

Duncan shook his head as he chuckled. "Yes, I agree. That would've been awkward. So, there will be no fucking on the kitchen table today."

Julianne's gaze snapped to his when she caught his last word. He winked at her as he gave her a wicked grin. Then he turned to the stove and pulled the pans off the heat.

"I guess breakfast is ready. If you set the table, I'll clean the floor." Duncan's voice was neutral, like he hadn't just given her an image of them fucking on the table. Which she found she wouldn't mind at all. Just not in front of Sabrina.

A few minutes later, they were all three seated at the table, enjoying Duncan's fantastic pancakes. The man knew how to cook. But at sixty-one he would have had time for a lot of practice. Julianne inwardly chuckled as the thought popped into her head. Then, she froze as she remembered what he had said about shifters having longer lifespans than humans. Did that mean that he really was sixty-one years old? Studying his face, she dismissed the notion. He looked to be in his late twenties, thirty at the most.

"Do I have something on my face?" Duncan was grinning at her, having caught her staring at him.

Laughing, Julianne shook her head. "No. My mind is just trying to make sense of everything. I just remembered yesterday when you told me you were sixty-one, and I had a moment just now evaluating whether it was true. Don't worry, though, it's just my mind trying to come to terms with all of this."

"Is sixty-one too old for you?" A small smile was playing on his lips, but his eyes held a hint of concern.

Julianne's certainty faltered, and she stared at him. She had no idea what to believe. For all she knew shifters were immortal and ate human flesh to look young.

"Duncan, please just tell me the truth. All I know is what you told me yesterday, and I still have a lot of questions. This is one of them."

He kept his eyes on her while his expression turned serious. "It's not unusual for a wolf shifter to become close to three hundred years old. And my real age is sixty-one. I told you the truth yesterday, but with a smile so you would think I was joking."

Julianne was stunned. Duncan was older than her parents, but he didn't look like it. Or act like it. Based on his behavior, he seemed to be her age, late twenties. Did that make him young for his age or creepy? And could she apply human perceptions about age to him at all? Probably not. Considering his lifespan of three hundred years, he was at about twenty percent. In human terms that would put him at about twenty. Did that mean he was younger than her?

"Julianne, please. Say something. Sixty-one is not a lot for a shifter. I'm like a human at around thirty, just with more life experience." His voice was almost pleading, and there was worry in his black eyes.

She liked him, a lot. And the fact that he was a shifter didn't matter to her. So why should his age? It was a shifter thing, after all. Smiling, she stretched out her arm and put her hand on his. "I guess I can date a sixty-one-year-old. Unless he turns out to be hung up on the seventies or something, of course." Julianne let her amusement show on her face while inwardly cursing herself for mentioning dating. Duncan wanted her in his bed, but they had never talked about dating or this thing between them being anything other than a holiday fling.

"Good." Gripping her hand, he squeezed it and gave her a warm smile. "I'm happy that our age difference doesn't scare you."

Julianne just smiled and let go of his hand. At least it didn't seem like her mention of them dating scared him off. And that was a relief, because she found that she liked the idea of dating this man. This shifter.

∞∞∞

Duncan inwardly sighed with relief. For a minute there, he had thought Julianne was going to reject him because he was so much older than her. But she didn't. And she even mentioned dating. He didn't know if that was a slip-up or if she actually meant it, but he was going to believe the latter. And it infused him with excitement. It was exactly what he wanted. To date her, to spend time with her. Not just sex but something more. He didn't have any experience with that kind of relationship, but it was what most people wanted and searched for. And why should he be any worse at it than anybody else? He wanted to be a good date. No, a great date. And that was what he was going to be. If Julianne wanted him for more than sex. He sincerely hoped so, and so far, it seemed promising.

There was something he needed to discuss with these ladies, though, and he wasn't sure how they would respond. Hopefully, it wouldn't affect what he had in mind for Julianne.

"My friend Trevor called me this morning and wanted my help. I need to go to Loch Ness. Would you like to come with me?" Duncan swung his gaze between Julianne and Sabrina, trying to gauge their reactions.

Julianne smiled as her gaze found his. "Loch Ness? I've never been there." he looked at Sabrina. "We were talking about going to see the loch but didn't find any guided tours that weren't already fully booked."

Blondie nodded and smiled. "I had hoped to visit Loch Ness while we were here. There's something about that loch that is…interesting."

Duncan got the feeling that Sabrina had been about to say something else, but he didn't want to ask her about it. He didn't think she would tell him.

He grinned at them. "Sounds like that's a yes."

Both women nodded.

"Good. And your things from the B and B will be here within about half an hour. My friends promised me that they would check your room thoroughly, so hopefully nothing will be missing."

"Perfect." Julianne grinned. "You can have your shorts back."

Laughing, he let his eyes take in her beautiful features. "About time. I've really missed them."

"Oh, in that case." She rose from the table and started undoing the string she had tied around her waist to keep the shorts from falling off.

Duncan felt his jaw slacken as he stared at her hands fiddling with the string. The thought of seeing Julianne in her panties had his heart rate increasing, and it wasn't in order to increase the blood flow to his brain. Did she even wear panties? His cock was hardening fast, and the shorts and fitted tee he was wearing wouldn't hide the fact.

"Julianne, I'm still eating." Sabrina's stern voice startled him.

Yanking his gaze away from Julianne, he pulled his chair closer to the table to hide the way his erect member was straining against the fabric of his shorts. He searched his mind for something to say but came up empty.

Julianne's laughter brought his eyes back to her, and he inwardly groaned when he saw the wicked grin on her face. He had a feeling she knew precisely what she had done to him and was enjoying it immensely. But two could play at that game. He would get her back when she least expected it.

"Thank you, Duncan." Sabrina's voice interrupted his thoughts of retaliation against his wild-haired beauty. "Seeing as you made us a delicious breakfast, we'll take care of the cleaning up."

"Thank you, Sabrina. That's great. In that case I think I'll go pack a few things." Without knowing it, Blondie had come to his rescue. Or at least he hoped she didn't know he had lost control of his body. Again. It was one thing for Julianne to know how much she affected him, but he didn't really want anyone else to know.

∞∞∞∞

An hour later they were packed and ready to leave. Their things had arrived from the B&B, and Julianne had enjoyed changing into fresh clothes not too big or smelling of bodywash. Like the day before, she had gotten into the passenger seat to sit beside Duncan, and Sabrina was sitting in the backseat. The big man himself was checking the house to make sure everything was locked up.

"I think you should go easy on him." Sabrina's voice was a bit reprimanding. "What you did to him at breakfast? The way he clenched his teeth I thought he was going to crack a molar."

Julianne burst out laughing. Duncan's expression when she had been pretending to take off the shorts she was wearing had been priceless. The heat in his eyes had been amazing, and she was almost surprised it didn't burn her. Perhaps she had overdone it, though. There was no doubt in her mind that he had lost control of his body again, evidenced by the way he had scooted his chair closer to the table to hide his lower body from view. And the way he had shot out of the kitchen as soon as Sabrina had said that they would be cleaning up. "Yeah, maybe that was a bit much. I didn't expect his reaction to be quite so tense. I thought he was going to laugh."

"Remember when I said that I sense a vulnerability in him? I think he needs someone to care about him. Someone to love him. He needs more than just sex. Are you prepared for that?"

Turning to Sabrina, Julianne stared at her friend in shock. "Are you sure?"

Sabrina gave a short nod. "Quite sure. And he wants you more than he himself realizes yet. I think he'll suffer greatly if you reject him."

Julianne's heartrate sped up, and she could feel her

own pulse pounding in her throat. She wanted Duncan, but did she want him that much? The way Sabrina was talking it sounded like Duncan might be proposing marriage at some stage, and Julianne found that thought to be a bit overwhelming. At least so soon. But she did want him for more than sex. She wanted to date him and see where that would take them.

The driver's side door opened, and Duncan smiled at her, but Julianne wasn't able to produce a smile back. She was still too stunned by Sabrina's words.

His happy expression died and turned into a concerned one. "What's wrong? You look shocked. Has something happened?"

Julianne's mind raced to come up with a plausible explanation for her shock, and suddenly she found one. "Do vampires exist too? And trolls and witches?"

Duncan's concern faded and was replaced by an easy smile. "There are a number of other supernatural beings around. Vampires are one of them."

"Shit." Dread crept up Julianne's spine like icy tentacles, and she felt herself go pale. For some reason the thought of shifters hadn't scared her. It had been a shock to learn that they existed, but they didn't make her afraid. That might have something to do with Duncan being a shifter, and a kind, caring, gorgeous one at that.

"Just like with shifters and humans there are good and bad individuals of all supernatural kinds. No kind is all bad or all good." Duncan's voice was calm, and it was having a soothing effect on her.

Taking a deep breath to try to force her body to relax, she turned to look at him. His lips were curved in a gentle smile as he focused on the road ahead, and she realized that the car was moving. They had already left the estate behind, and she hadn't even noticed.

Julianne turned in her seat to look at her friend in the backseat. Sabrina had an unreadable expression on her face. "Did you know about this?"

Her friend swallowed. "Not entirely. But I..." Taking a deep breath, Sabrina started again. "There's something I need to tell you, that I've concealed from you. I should've told you long ago, and in a manner, I've let you know some of it."

Julianne stared at Sabrina, not sure exactly what to expect. Her friend actually seemed a bit flustered and uncertain, and that was a first. Sabrina had secrets, but Julianne had known that all along. She hadn't wanted to push her friend to share more about herself, figuring she would when she felt comfortable enough to do so. And Sabrina had shared more as they got to know each other, giving her the feeling that few other people actually knew her friend better than Julianne herself did.

"You know that I can sense things, about people and about situations. You've taken it to be some kind of intuition, and I've let you think that. But it's more than that. I've got other abilities as well that I haven't shown you. That nobody knows about except for a few people in my family. And even they don't know all that I can do."

Studying her friend's face as she spoke, Julianne saw the wariness there, and she realized that Sabrina was scared. Scared of being rejected for being whom she was. Was that the reason why Sabrina was so guarded around people? Was her friend scared of slipping up and causing people to reject her for being different? That explained a lot. But there was one person Sabrina seemed to be less guarded around.

"But Duncan knows. Did you tell him, or did he guess?"

Her friend seemed a bit stunned. Sabrina obviously hadn't realized that Julianne had noticed how she was more relaxed around Duncan than she usually was around new people. "He knows. When I asked what he was, he understood that I was different as well. Duncan asked me what I was, and I told him. I felt safe telling him since I could sense that he's a good man, and he's a supernatural himself."

"So, what are you exactly?" Julianne kept her gaze on Sabrina, trying hard not to feel betrayed by her friend.

"I'm a witch. It runs in the female line of my family. Not everyone gets the abilities, but both my mom and my grandmother are witches. We keep it concealed from everyone, making sure not to show our abilities around other people. I've let it slip a little around you, and in time I hoped to be able to show you everything. You're not judgmental like most people, and I consider you my best friend."

Julianne didn't know what to say. Her best friend was a witch. And from what she could understand, it involved more than what Julianne had taken to be a highly developed form of intuition.

"Don't be too hard on her." Duncan's voice made Julianne turn to him. He glanced at her before swinging his gaze back to the road. "It's not easy having abilities that are outside of what is considered normal. You constantly have to be in control, make sure you don't do anything that raises suspicion that you're anything other than human. If I were to compete against humans in the Olympics, I'd easily win at every sport with my speed and strength. I have to be careful what I do at all times around humans. That's why quite a few supernaturals stay with their own kind and keep away from humans as much as possible. It's just easier that way. Everyone likes to be themselves and supernaturals are no exceptions."

Julianne knew he was right, but it was still a lot to take in. She hadn't had time to think about the implications of being someone who shouldn't exist. Someone who was considered a fictional character or a figure from folklore. There had been times in her life when she had been reluctant to show people her true self, thinking she was different or not good enough, but that had only been a case of insecurity. To truly be different and always have to behave within certain boundaries that weren't natural for you, that was a whole other ballgame.

"I'm sorry. I... This is a lot to take in. Please don't mistake my silence for disapproval. It's just..." Julianne struggled to find the correct words to describe what she was thinking. Probably because her mind was a swirling mass of feelings and questions. She really just needed a hug. And if she did, perhaps Sabrina did as well. "Can we stop? Just for a couple of minutes."

"Of course. I'll find somewhere to pull over." Duncan sounded a bit concerned, but he didn't say anything to confirm it.

Julianne stared straight ahead. She was having some kind of reaction to everything she had learned in the last twenty-four hours, and she knew she would tear up if she met Duncan or Sabrina's eyes.

The car slowed down, and Duncan turned off onto a narrow dirt road before stopping the car. Julianne got out of the car and took a few deep breaths to try to prevent her tears from falling. The sound of a car door opening alerted her to someone getting out of the car behind her. She steeled herself and focused on her breathing to try to stay in control.

"Julianne." Sabrina's voice sounded from a little behind her.

Julianne fisted her hands at her sides. There was only one way to handle this. Facing it head on. Before she could talk herself out of it, she turned to Sabrina and closed the distance between them. She threw her arms around her friend and pulled her into a tight hug. "I'm so sorry, Sabrina, that you've had to hide your true self from me. I can't imagine what that's been like. But at least from now on you don't have to do that anymore. I don't care what you are or what you can do. You're my best friend. I accept you just the way you are."

Tears streamed unchecked down Julianne's cheeks. Neither she nor Sabrina were prone to hugging, but at some point during Julianne's speech, Sabrina's arms wrapped around her to hug her back.

"Thank you."

The sound of Sabrina's wobbly voice had Julianne pull back and look at her friend, and she was shocked to see the tears filling Sabrina's eyes. Never before had Julianne seen her friend cry. Sabrina didn't typically show any strong emotions.

Julianne shook her head and smiled through her tears. "You don't have to thank me. I'm your friend.

Acceptance is an important part of friendship."

Sabrina laughed, but it was filled with bitterness. "You'd be surprised how often that's not true." Her friend carefully extricated herself from their hug and took a step back. "I mean it when I say thank you, Julianne. And I don't want you to be sorry. You've got nothing to be sorry for. All you've done is to be a good friend to me, as far as I've let you. It's been my choice not to share more of myself with you than I have."

"Okay, but from now on you have to be yourself around me. No holding back." Julianne grinned. "Even if I can't promise not to be shocked if it turns out that you can fly or turn into a frog, I'll get over it and accept it."

Sabrina smiled. "I can't fly or turn into a frog. Not that I've ever tried to turn into a frog."

"Good to know."

"Now I think it's time we got back in the car." Sabrina's gaze swung to something behind Julianne.

She felt a hand on her shoulder. Turning around, Julianne had to tip her head back to meet Duncan's black eyes. The warmth there unleashed a corresponding warm sensation in her chest, and she felt a pull toward him. There was suddenly only an inch separating their bodies, and she couldn't remember noticing either of them moving. Duncan leaned down toward her, and she rose up on her toes to meet his lips with her own.

His arms came around her and pulled her tightly against his body while plundering her mouth with his tongue. Julianne's whole body heated, and she retaliated by sinking her hands into his hair and gripping it with her fists as she forced her tongue into his mouth and started exploring. Groaning, he tightened his arms even more around her, and she could feel something hard forming against her belly.

Julianne abruptly ended the kiss and grinned up at him. "I think we'd better continue this tonight when we're alone."

The heat in his eyes virtually seared her, and she almost expected him to start kissing her again. Instead, he nodded. But before he let her go, he leaned down and murmured in her ear. "Until tonight. It's going to be a long day."

"It is." She'd sighed the words as her body tingled with anticipation. If he had suggested to go into the forest and fuck, she probably would have agreed to it. Her body had been aching for him ever since their stunt in the kitchen the night before, and knowing what they had planned for later only made it worse.

Duncan adjusted his shirt to cover his erection before moving around the car to the driver's side. Before leaving the estate, he had put on a loose shirt over his tee. Which was a good thing since it effectively hid his hard length.

They all got back into the vehicle, and after turning around, Duncan pulled back onto the main road. They drove in silence for a couple of minutes before he cleared his throat.

"I need to prepare you both for what's going to happen when we get to Loch Ness. And thanks to you, Julianne, for asking about other supernaturals, and you, Sabrina, for telling us that you're a witch. It just got a whole lot easier for me." Duncan shot Julianne a smile.

"You're about to take part in a witch hunt. I know that sounds medieval at best, but Ambrosia is an evil witch who will stop at nothing to gain more power. We need to find a way to stop her."

"Ambrosia." Sabrina sounded pensive. "I've never heard of her. But I don't know a lot of witches outside my own family. We've kept our powers mostly to ourselves. How do you know about her and what she wants?"

"I'm getting to that. Just let me tell you a little about the people you will meet first. We're going to Leith's house on the shore of Loch Ness. He's an old friend of mine. Then there's Trevor and his mate, Jennie."

Julianne turned to look at Duncan. "Trevor, who's your friend and owns the estate. And Jennie, his mate." Keeping her eyes on Duncan's face, she continued. "What does mate really mean, Duncan?"

He chuckled. "For a shifter a mate is your partner for life. Once mated there's no going back. A mating bond can't be broken. And you wouldn't want to."

Julianne frowned. Mating sounded serious, far more serious than marriage. "How do you know who to mate?"

Pain seemed to flash across Duncan's face for a moment, but it was gone so fast Julianne was left wondering what she had actually seen.

"Well, you usually sense it when you're near the person. Some shifters can tell right away when they meet their mate, but others need a little more time to figure it out."

Julianne debated whether to ask her next question but decided it was better to know as much as possible.

"Are all mates shifters?"

"Actually, no. Jennie is human. That's one of the reasons Trevor didn't realize at first that she was his mate. And to complicate things, she's terrified of dogs, so meeting his wolf was difficult. Thankfully, she managed to get over her fear of Trevor's wolf and accept him. Within a week of meeting each other for the first time, they were mated."

"A week?!" Julianne's voice was filled with disbelief. Sabrina's words about Duncan came back to her with a bang, and she felt her whole body stiffen in shock. There was no real bang, of course, but that was how it felt in her mind. Was she Duncan's mate? Was that what Sabrina had been trying to tell her? And if she was, did he know? Based on what Sabrina had said, it sounded like he didn't. Perhaps he hadn't figured it out yet. And it certainly would explain the strong attraction between them. The way he lost control of his body, and how her body constantly ached for him. But a week? That was too soon. She wouldn't be ready to agree to be with him for the rest of her life in only a few days. That was crazy. They didn't know each other well enough for that yet. Not even close. Duncan was an amazing man, and given more time she could see herself agreeing to marry him...or mate him. But not in a few days.

"Julianne!"

Duncan's deep voice flowed through her and made her channel clench. It was almost like the response she'd had when Duncan had spoken to Steven. Not as powerful but close. She hadn't understood what was happening to her in Mallaig, but with her current knowledge she thought she did.

"Yes, sorry. Still a lot of new information to process." Julianne tried to smile, but she wasn't sure if she managed to pull it off convincingly. Probably a good thing that Duncan kept his eyes on the road.

"No need to be sorry. I said your name several times, and when you didn't respond, I started to get worried. But I understand your need to digest all of this. For what it's worth I'm proud of you for handling this so well. I'm not sure I would've handled it half as well myself."

Julianne mentally shook herself to get rid of the tension in her body. "You were telling us about your friends. Please go on."

"Okay. I've mentioned Leith, Trevor, and Jennie. Then there are Michael and Stephanie. I talked to Trevor as I was locking up the house, to confirm that we're coming, and he told me that Michael and Stephanie are staying at Leith's house as well. Which is both admirable and surprising after what they suffered at the hands of Ambrosia and her ally. They're the reason Ambrosia was stopped in her first attempt at increasing her power. Or at least we assume that it was her first attempt. Michael is a shifter, a serval, from America, and Stephanie is a witch. She didn't know that she was a witch, however, until Michael was hurt, and she burned the alpha panther responsible to a crisp. I've never seen anything like it."

"Well, strong emotions can be a challenge for a witch. It's harder to stay in control if you get angry or distraught."

Sabrina's comment made Julianne turn around to look at her friend. "Is that why I've hardly ever seen you pissed off, even though you've had reason to be?"

Julianne looked at her friend with a new understanding and a sadness that Sabrina had to live with those kinds of restrictions, preventing her from expressing herself using the same emotional spectrum that Julianne took for granted.

Sabrina smiled. "Don't feel sorry for me. I'm used to it by now."

Julianne studied her friend's face, but as usual Sabrina's carefully controlled expression was hard to interpret. "If you say so. It sounds limiting."

"I think we should let Duncan continue." Sabrina kept smiling, and Julianne knew that she had been dismissed. Apparently, there were some things her friend still didn't want to talk about.

CHAPTER 11

Duncan glanced at the blond woman in the rearview mirror. If there was one thing he had noticed about her, it was that she was always in control. And he found himself wondering what it would take for Sabrina's control to slip. He wagered it would take a lot. The control she possessed she had perfected for many years already, and even if she was in a situation where she could let go, she would probably find it difficult to do so.

He told the ladies what had happened to Michael and Stephanie at the hands of Ambrosia and Jack, the alpha panther.

"Panther, like Steven." Julianne uttered the words like a statement, but Duncan could hear the unspoken question in her voice.

He glanced at her. The woman who had his brain almost short-circuiting from lust. It was sheer luck that he decided to put on a loose shirt before leaving. At least it made his condition less obvious. Showing off his hard cock wasn't something he relished doing when he wasn't in the act of pleasing a woman. But the knowledge that he would take Julianne to his bed later was playing havoc with his control.

"I don't believe there's any connection between Steven and Jack. From what I could tell, Steven isn't an alpha, and his accent places him in London. I don't think Ambrosia would care one whit about him. Her goal is to increase her own power, and an alpha has the most power in a pack or, in the case of panthers, a clan. I wouldn't worry too much about Steven right now. The chance of him finding you while you're in Scotland with your phone turned off is miniscule."

Julianne sighed. "I guess, but I still don't understand why he wants me back. We were never that good together and with his looks, if not for his personality, I'm sure he would have no trouble finding someone else."

A burning sensation flared in his chest, and Duncan inwardly swore. Julianne saying that Steven was good-looking made his fur itch beneath his skin, or at least that was what it felt like. He realized it was just his pride taking a hit, but he felt a strong compulsion to prove to her who was the better man. And it sure as hell wasn't the panther.

"Some men just want what they can't have." The irritation in Sabrina's voice made Duncan look at her in the mirror. It sounded like she was speaking from experience. "That might well be the case with Steven. He got more and more possessive toward the end of your relationship. Probably in response to you losing interest in him. A man like him doesn't take that kind of rejection well, and he wants to prove that he can get you back."

Julianne turned to her friend. "Yeah, I guess you're right."

Duncan broke into their conversation. "Well, ladies. The water you see straight ahead is Loch Ness. We'll be at Leith's house in just a few minutes. Are you ready to meet everyone?"

Smiling, Julianne turned to him. "They're friends of yours so they can't be that bad, right?"

Duncan chuckled. "No, they're good people. In any case I'll have your back."

"My back, huh? I had the distinct impression there were other parts of my anatomy you'd rather have."

"Children, behave." Sabrina's stern voice from the backseat made Julianne snort with laughter. "I hope there are some adults where we're going. It'll be a nice change from the teenagers I've had to put up with for the last couple of days."

"I wouldn't bet on it." Duncan couldn't hide his amusement. "Newly mated couples are very, how shall I put it, amorous. The only one sane at the moment will be Leith, the owner of the house."

"In that case it sounds like Leith is my safest bet for a normal adult conversation."

Chuckling, Duncan nodded. "Yes. He's a bit quiet. Only says something when he has something intelligent to say. I think you two will hit it off perfectly."

Sabrina's jaw tensed for a second at his words. "I'm not here to hit it off with someone."

"I know." Duncan smiled. "And I'm sorry. I couldn't help myself. Don't worry about Leith coming on to you. He's not like that. He's a truly nice, decent man. If anything, he's a bit too serious. I think you'll like him."

"Hm, I guess we'll see." Sabrina didn't sound convinced.

"Yes, we will. We're here." Duncan pulled off the road and drove down to a house situated on the shore of Loch Ness. The house was large, but it didn't give off that impression with how it was placed in the sloping landscape in a tiered fashion. Large trees surrounded the beautiful house, helping it fit into the terrain and shielding the property from prying eyes.

***

They parked next to a Ferrari in front of the house. Sabrina let her gaze wander around the magnificent house and property. It was a large house yet subdued both in color and form. She had never seen anything like it. No property had ever appealed to her the way this one did. It almost made her curious about its owner.

They all exited the car, and Duncan opened the back to take out their luggage. He handed Sabrina her bag with a smile, and she was just opening her mouth to say thank you when a deep voice spoke behind her.

"Duncan, my friend. Good to see you. It has been a while."

The man's voice seemed to flow over her like warm, soothing water, making her feel welcome and safe. Wanted even, like he had been expecting her, which was a strange feeling.

Gripping her bag like a safety blanket, she slowly turned around, curious to lay eyes on the man with the remarkable voice.

"And welcome, ladies. I am Leith. I hope you will

feel at home here during your stay."

Sabrina's gaze landed on a tall, lean man. But lean in Leith's case didn't equate with weak. His arms emerging from the T-shirt were corded with sleek muscle, and she had a feeling that was true for the rest of his body as well. The thought made her face heat with a blush that took her completely by surprise. This wasn't how she normally thought or acted around men, at least it hadn't been since her powers started manifesting when she was sixteen.

"Leith." Duncan walked forward toward the man, thankfully bringing Leith's attention away from her. "It's been too long."

The men gripped each other's forearm firmly in some sort of special greeting. Perhaps it was how shifters typically greeted each other. Although, Duncan hadn't mentioned what Leith was, so Sabrina wasn't certain the man was a shifter. He could be another kind of supernatural. The only thing she was sure about was that Leith wasn't entirely human. She could sense immense power in him, but it was well concealed, and she doubted many witches would be able to pick up on it. Her ability to sense other people's power and personality was well developed, and with her new insight into the supernatural world, a lot of her previous experiences took on new meaning.

Duncan introduced Julianne to Leith, before the owner of the house swung his gaze to Sabrina.

"And this is Julianne's friend Sabrina." Duncan's voice was laced with amusement, and she wondered if he had noticed her blushing.

"Welcome, Sabrina, to my home." Leith covered the distance between them and slowly extended his hand.

She was about to shake his hand, but he surprised her by closing his hand softly around her fingers and bringing them to his lips. While holding her gaze hostage with his dark-green eyes, he brushed his soft lips lightly over her knuckles. It was like time had stopped, and Sabrina was drowning in his warm gaze. Then he lowered her hand, and one corner of his mouth lifted in what she took to be a small smile.

"Now come with me into my house, Sabrina. I have coffee, or something stronger if that is your wish."

"Coffee." Her voice sounded strange, and she swallowed to try again. "Thank you, Leith. A cup of coffee sounds like heaven right now."

"Let me take your bag for you." Leith kept his gaze on her as he extended his hand toward the bag she was still holding. But he didn't take it until she nodded her consent.

He turned away from her to lead the way into his house, and Sabrina rolled her eyes at her own behavior. What was wrong with her? She was behaving like a teenager with a crush.

Duncan and Julianne were walking ahead of her as they followed Leith into his house. Julianne turned her auburn head to Sabrina with a wicked grin and mouthed something that looked like the word *wow*. She had obviously seen Sabrina's reaction to Leith. Which was an indication that Sabrina would have to be on her guard in the future. No more losing her head over the man of the house.

However, upon stepping into the hallway, Sabrina found something else snagging her attention. Every surface of the room was made of dark wood, but what caught her attention were the carvings in the wood. There were small scenes carved directly into the walls. Stepping closer to one of them revealed a woman standing knee-deep in water in all her naked glory. A man was standing behind her, but he was mostly hidden by the woman's form. The woman had her eyes closed and her head tipped a little back, and Sabrina found herself wondering if the man was touching her. Or if he had snuck up on her without her noticing and was about to grab her. Either scenario was possible, and the fact that the man's face was partially hidden only made it more intriguing.

"Your coffee, Sabrina."

She jerked at Leith's voice, having been so entranced by the image that she hadn't heard him come up behind her. Perhaps like the woman in the carving. Slowly she turned to him and looked up into his eyes.

"I am sorry that I startled you. It was not my intention. I can see that you have found one of my images."

Words seemed to elude her. Instead, Sabrina nodded as she felt herself drowning in his eyes. It took her a few seconds to get her bearings enough to look away.

"They're amazing and must've taken a long time to create." Her praise sounded flat to her own ears, but she had trouble finding intelligent words around this man. Was she attracted to him? The thought both scared and tantalized her.

"Thank you. Your approval means a lot to me."

His words drew her gaze back to his. It had sounded like he put extra emphasis on the word *your*, like her approval in particular was important to him. But his expression gave nothing away, and she realized that she was probably putting too much meaning into his words.

The corner of his mouth lifted in a small smile, like he could hear her internal debate. Like he could read her like she so often read other people.

"Your coffee," Leith repeated and lifted the cup in his hand a little as if to draw her attention to it. "I believe you said coffee sounds like heaven."

"Yes." Sabrina felt her eyes widen as she realized why he had come to find her in the hallway. It wasn't to spend time with her but to deliver the coffee she had asked for. Her face heated as mortification gripped her and made her body stiffen, where she stood in front of him.

She focused on the cup and lifted her hand to take it from him when she felt his hand loosely close around her upper arm.

"Please come with me into the kitchen, and we will find you a seat, my angel. Your hand seems to be shaking a little, and I cannot have you spilling hot coffee on yourself. That is unacceptable."

Moving her gaze to her hand confirmed he was right. Her hand was shaking. A new emotion replaced the mortification she had been feeling. Fear. Fear that she was going to lose control of her powers and hurt people.

"No, I have to go outside. As far away from people as I can get."

But before she could move, a sense of calm flowed through her, and it was coming from Leith's hand gripping her arm. Lifting her gaze to his, she was amazed by the light in his eyes. They were glowing like emeralds. Beautiful and completely enchanting.

"You will not lose control, Sabrina. You just need a few minutes to sit down and drink your coffee in the kitchen with us."

Staring into his eyes, she felt herself nodding. She turned away from him and walked through the door that she had seen Julianne and Duncan walk through earlier.

They were seated at the kitchen table with cups in front of them, perhaps waiting for Leith and her to join them. Sabrina sat down on a free chair, and Leith placed her coffee in front of her.

"So, did you get stuck out there?" Julianne's face was filled with amusement, probably about to say something more embarrassing about her time in the hallway with Leith.

Sabrina was about to respond when Leith effectively stopped Julianne's plans to tease her before they could be launched.

"Sabrina was studying my carvings, paying a respect to me and my home that is highly appreciated."

Julianne actually blushed at the little sting in Leith's words. "I'm sorry. I didn't mean—"

Sabrina cut her off, not wanting Julianne to feel bad. "I know. You should have a look at the carvings in the hallway. They're both beautiful and intriguing."

Julianne smiled and waved her hand around. "You should have a look around in here."

Letting her gaze glide around the kitchen, Sabrina felt her jaw slacken in utter amazement. The hallway had some amazing carvings, but this room... There were carvings on the walls a few places, but the most elaborate carvings were covering the wooden beams in the ceiling. They were all cut into unique shapes and patterns.

A huge hearth was built into one wall of the room, made of natural stones in different shapes and sizes but all somehow fitting together. On the mantel and on various shelves around the room was a selection of what looked like ancient artifacts, giving her the feeling of being in a museum. And the wall space not covered by carvings or shelves was covered with old paintings.

"My other guests have gone for a swim, but they will be back soon. I believe they are eager to meet you ladies." Leith was standing by the kitchen island, coffee cup in hand. His eyes were back to their normal dark green, a color matching well with his long copper-colored hair.

Sabrina let her gaze wander around the kitchen again, but soon found her eyes drawn back to the man of the house. She started when his dark-green gaze met hers, and she quickly averted her eyes. Leith was easily the most captivating man she had ever met in her life, but she knew very well there could never be anything between them. He deserved someone more in control of her powers, someone who could… No, not going there. She was done contemplating that which she couldn't have.

CHAPTER 12

Julianne kept an eye on her friend. Sabrina hadn't been able to hide her reaction to Leith. He had clearly made a deeper impression on Sabrina than any man Julianne had ever met before. And if Julianne wasn't mistaken, Leith was quite taken with Sabrina as well. He wasn't an easy man to read with his mostly solemn expression, but there had been clear signs that he liked her friend.

"There are two free bedrooms." Leith looked at Sabrina. "One is on the lower level. It is quite small, but I think it will suit you, Sabrina."

Her friend's head turned to Leith, and she nodded. "Thank you. That sounds perfect."

Leith gave Sabrina a small nod before swinging his gaze to Julianne and continuing. "The bedroom on this level is across the hallway. It is quite large and should suit your needs, Julianne and Duncan."

Julianne nodded as she felt heat rising in her face. As far as she knew, Duncan hadn't told Leith they would be sleeping in the same room, but somehow the man had figured it out anyway. It reminded her of Sabrina's ability to read people. Maybe Leith was a witch as well? Duncan had never mentioned what kind of supernatural the man was, but Julianne was almost certain he wasn't human.

"Both the other couples are staying on the middle level, and my bedroom is on the lower level." Leith looked at Sabrina as he said the last words, and she snapped her gaze to his.

Julianne almost laughed out loud at the shocked expression on Sabrina's face, but she managed to stop herself in time. She had a feeling Leith wouldn't approve of her laughing. He seemed unusually protective of Sabrina.

"Thank you, Leith." Duncan was sitting next to her at the table, and he leaned forward a little as he spoke to his friend. "Anything we can do while we're here just tell us. You're brave taking us all in like this."

"It is no trouble, my friend." Leith gave Duncan a slow nod. "You are always welcome here. All of you." His gaze swung from Duncan to Julianne to Sabrina, where it lingered.

Oh, the man was smitten all right. He had even placed Sabrina on the same level as himself. Of course, with the size of the bedrooms, it seemed logical, but Julianne had to wonder if the man had an ulterior motive. And looking at how Sabrina responded to the man, Julianne couldn't help wishing it would work out between them. Leith seemed like a nice man. Perhaps he would be the one to make Sabrina happy, and bring out the light she was hiding inside. Because it was there—Julianne had seen glimpses of it at times, but her friend hid it well. Too well.

"I think it is time for lunch." Leith moved to the large gas stove and turned it on to preheat the oven. "There will be warm bread rolls, cold meats, cheese, and a variety of vegetables and fruit. I would greatly appreciate some help."

Duncan was up before Leith had uttered his last words. "I'll help." Before moving away, he turned to Julianne with a smile. "Why don't you two ladies go and have a seat on the terrace. You can enjoy the view of the loch from there." Duncan indicated the terrace outside the kitchen windows.

"But don't you want some help preparing lunch?"

"No, we can handle it." Duncan grinned at her, his warm gaze heating her blood. "I'm sure there'll be work to do after lunch, so you should enjoy the view now while you can."

Nodding, Julianne got up and turned to Sabrina.

Her friend rose from the table and followed Julianne out onto the terrace. They walked all the way up to the railing, staring at the magnificent view of the water, and the mountains rising out of the water on the opposite side of the loch.

"Wow." Julianne kept coming back to that word. "With all the amazing places I've seen in Scotland and around the world so far, you would think that at some stage nothing would impress me anymore. But this is fantastic. And to have this kind of view from your own house. I just can't think of a better place to wake up in the morning, than to a place with this kind of view. It's both calming and awe-inspiring at the same time."

Sabrina laughed softly. "I couldn't agree more. And I don't think I've ever seen a house so happily situated.

It blends into the landscape like it was meant to be here, like it was all part of a greater design."

Julianne walked to the door to the kitchen and closed it firmly before returning to Sabrina.

Turning to her friend, she kept her eyes trained on Sabrina's face to gauge her reaction. "What about the owner of the house?"

Sabrina snapped her gaze to Julianne's but didn't say anything for several seconds. When she spoke, she seemed to weigh her words carefully before letting them out. "Leith is a nice man. I have nothing but respect for him, and you know that's not usually the case with me. But that's all."

"Sabrina, please. I saw you blush, and that's a first. I've never seen you so affected by a man. Ever. And he seems taken by you too."

Sabrina held up a hand to stop Julianne. "That doesn't mean anything. Nothing will happen between Leith and me. It can't."

Julianne debated whether to let the whole thing go. Let Sabrina off the hook. But watching the obvious chemistry between Sabrina and Leith had gotten Julianne's hopes up on her friend's behalf, and she didn't want to let it go so easily. "Why not, Sabrina? Why not at least give it a shot? If it doesn't work out then so be it, but don't you think you would regret it if you never gave him a chance? I don't think a man like him will come around again anytime soon."

Staring out over the water, Sabrina didn't respond. Her expression was unreadable as her gaze was fixed at a point in the distance. Yet it didn't look like she was seeing the beautiful scenery anymore. Her friend's focus seemed to be inward.

Julianne kept silent. She had pushed Sabrina far enough. Anything her friend did or let happen, had to be her own decision. Julianne could only hope that Leith got through to Sabrina because she had a feeling those two would be great together.

Someone opened the door to the terrace, and Julianne turned around. She smiled when she saw Duncan standing in the doorway.

"Ladies, please come inside and meet the rest of the houseguests."

Julianne walked up to him, and Duncan put his hand on the small of her back as they walked back into the kitchen.

There were four people in the kitchen Julianne had never met before. From Duncan's earlier description of these people, she knew they had to be Trevor, Jennie, Michael, and Stephanie, but she had no idea who was whom. Two of them stepped forward to greet her. A tall well-built man with short sandy-blond hair and brown eyes, and a beautiful woman with long blond hair and dark-blue eyes.

"Hi, I'm Trevor. Nice to meet you. I've already heard so much about you from Duncan. All good, I assure you." He gave her a grin filled with amusement, before swinging his gaze to Duncan, who let out a groan.

"And I'm Jennie, Trevor's mate. I'm so pleased to meet the woman who's made such an impression on Duncan." Jennie's smile was happy and genuine, giving Julianne the feeling she was relieved for some reason.

"I'm Julianne. It's nice to meet some of Duncan's friends. We had the opportunity to stay at your house for a night. A truly amazing place."

"Thank you." Jennie smiled and nodded before turning to Sabrina. "And you must be Sabrina. It's so nice to meet you. Another witch. I'm new to all this supernatural stuff, so forgive me if I get a bit excited."

Sabrina smiled. "In that case you have something in common with Julianne. Although, as it turns out, I didn't know that much about supernaturals either until a couple of days ago. Apart from witches, that is."

A man with short black hair and light-brown eyes came forward, his arm wrapped around the waist of a woman with long chestnut-colored hair and hazel eyes. The man wasn't as tall or broad as Duncan and Trevor, but he was still tall and muscular compared to most men.

"I'm Stephanie, but please call me Steph." The woman smiled at Julianne before turning to Sabrina. "I understand you're a witch like me, or maybe not exactly like me. I only realized I was a witch a few days ago. Any pointers you can give me would be much appreciated."

Sabrina smiled and nodded. "I'd be happy to help you. It must be overwhelming having just found out."

"Oh, it is. I think I'm still in shock. If it wasn't for Michael, I'm not sure how…" Steph stopped. "Sorry, I should let Michael introduce himself."

Michael smiled down at Steph before turning his head back to look at Julianne and Sabrina. "I'm Michael, and this beautiful woman is my mate." His gaze swung back to Steph, and the love in his eyes made Julianne avert her eyes, like she was witnessing something private.

"Okay. Listen up, people." Duncan's voice sounded from over by the large kitchen island. "Lunch is ready.

So, if someone can set the table, we can eat."

Julianne hadn't noticed that Duncan was no longer by her side. Meeting all these new people had snagged her attention away from the big, gorgeous man for a little while, which was almost a first since she had met him. But these people were important to him, his friends, and she wanted to make a good impression.

Jennie and Trevor volunteered to set the table, and a few minutes later, they were all seated. All eight of them. Duncan was sitting next to her, and on her other side was Jennie. Trevor was sitting next to Jennie at the other end of the table. Across from Duncan and herself, Leith had managed to secure a seat beside Sabrina, and her friend was looking mildly nervous at having the man so close. Or at least Julianne assumed that was the reason for Sabrina's unusual facial expression. Steph and Michael were sitting across from Jennie and Trevor, with Steph in the chair next to Sabrina.

The conversation around the table soon flowed comfortably, and Julianne was listening with a smile on her face as Jennie was telling her how Trevor and Jennie first met. Julianne had no trouble believing Jennie and Trevor cared about each other. It was all there in the way they touched and looked at each other often. But the fact that they had met less than two weeks ago was harder to believe. You could develop feelings for someone quickly, but to love someone so much that you knew you wanted to spend the rest of your life with that person…that was something else entirely. That kind of certainty didn't develop overnight. It required time to grow and mature. But Julianne didn't voice any of her thoughts on the subject. It wasn't her place.

Jennie finished her tale and was soon busy talking to Steph about something. Julianne found it hard to follow the conversation, her mind having reverted to what Sabrina had said about Duncan before they left the estate. Vulnerable, needing someone to love him. Was Julianne prepared for that?

"Julianne, are you with us?" Duncan's low voice in her ear brought her back from her thoughts. "Are you worried about tonight? I'd promise that I'd go easy on you, but since I'm not sure I'd be able to keep that promise, I'd better not."

At his words she snapped her head around to look at him, only to freeze when she ended up with her face barely an inch from his. There was a trace of heat in his eyes, and she watched as his mouth curved into a wicked grin.

"Duncan!"

Julianne had whisper-shouted his name, and the room fell completely silent. Then laughter erupted around the table, and she tipped her head forward to hide her face as it started burning with embarrassment. She had just met these people, and this wasn't how she wanted to make an impression.

Trevor's voice broke through the sounds of laughter. "This is the Duncan we all know and love. If you want him, you'd better get used to his antics. Just pay him back using the same coin. He can take it."

A large, warm hand grasped hers, and she glanced at their joined hands without raising her head. Conversations started up around the table again, and she slowly relaxed.

"Where's your bite, Julianne? I know you have no

trouble retaliating. You've done it before." Duncan's voice was close to a whisper, and she could detect a note of concern in it.

Lifting her head, she met his gaze. "I've just met these people, and they're your friends. I want to make a good impression, or at least not a bad one."

The smile that spread across Duncan's face was warm and understanding. "Just be yourself. You're wonderful just the way you are. They will love you just the way I…" He stopped. Eyes widening as if in shock, he turned away abruptly. "You know what I mean."

And she did. His words didn't bother her, since it was just a phrase. A way to say his friends would accept her for whom she was.

So maybe it was time for Julianne to retaliate, just a little. She leaned in and whispered in his ear as she squeezed his hand. "I've got no intention of going easy on you tonight. I want to squeeze your cock while you fuck me hard and fast." She put her other hand on his thigh and slowly slid it up toward his groin. Julianne had no intention of actually going that far while sitting at the table, but she counted on Duncan not realizing that.

Duncan yanked his hand out of her grip and rose from the table in one motion. It all happened so fast Julianne was left still leaning toward where his ear had been a fraction of a second before.

"I'm… I just…" There was a low growl in his voice as he struggled to say something. Giving up, he rushed out of the room.

Julianne had just started wondering if she should go after him when the whole table erupted with laughter.

She turned in amazement to see what was so funny and found all eyes on her.

"I believe the smartass got what was coming to him." Trevor barely managed to get the words out through his laughter. "Very good, Julianne."

CHAPTER 13

Duncan stormed out of the house, silently berating himself for being so stupid as to bait Julianne. His body had been giving him hell all day, but he had been able to keep it under control. At least most of the time. Knowing what he and Julianne would be doing later was almost driving him insane with lust, and they were barely finished having lunch. Their time alone together was hours away.

He had only wanted to push her a little, wondering if she was struggling the way he was, but instead he had provoked her to retaliate. And what a retaliation it was. Duncan would have been proud of her if not for the fact that his cock was so hard, he could have used it as a sledgehammer. And he had no idea how to persuade his member to relax. Images of Julianne on her hands and knees as he pounded into her tight pussy were running on repeat in his mind, inspired by her vivid dirty talk.

"Duncan?" Julianne's voice behind him startled

him. Completely lost in his desire for her, he hadn't even heard her approaching.

He looked at her over his shoulder. "I'll be there in...a little while." Who knew how long it would take him to get some semblance of control?

"Did I make things hard on you?" Her voice sounded like she was about to burst out laughing.

Groaning, Duncan closed his eyes and let his head tip forward. He was so fucked, and she knew it.

He could hear her approaching, but he didn't move. Julianne knew exactly what his problem was. Whether she saw the outline of his hard dick through the fabric of his shorts didn't make any difference at this stage.

Her hand gripping his had him opening his eyes and turning to her. She met his gaze with a small smile on her face.

"Come." Julianne started to go back to the house, but he resisted.

"I can't go in there like this."

"I know." She cocked her head at him. "We're not going back to the kitchen. Trust me, we're not going to see the others."

Duncan wondered what she was up to, but he let her lead him into the house. They continued down the hallway until she opened a door on the left and pulled him inside before closing the door behind them.

A bedroom. Their bedroom while they were staying with Leith. He turned to her. "Julianne, this isn't a good idea. I want you so much, just the sight of the bed is enough to make me consider forgetting about the others for the rest of the day. But we can't. I—"

"Duncan." Julianne stepped up to him and shook her head. "I'm just going to help you with the steel rod in your pants. It won't take more than a few minutes with the state you're in. And I promise you that I won't taunt you for the rest of the day. I don't want you walking around with a hard dick all the time. It can't be healthy. And someone might notice."

The feel of her hand on his hard cock had him sucking in a breath. Even through the material of his shorts, it felt fantastic having her hand on him. She gripped the waistband of his shorts and started sliding them down his hips.

"Wait." Putting his hands on hers, he stopped her from taking his shorts off. "You're just going to jerk me off to help me out?"

"Well." Julianne grinned up at him. "I do get to finally see you naked. At least for more than half a second. And I get to touch you. So, you won't find me complaining."

Duncan swallowed as her words washed over him. A warm feeling spread throughout his chest, making him wonder what was happening to him. Julianne wanted to make him come, and she wasn't asking for anything in return. All this was for him. And it wasn't because she didn't want him like he wanted her, because being this close to her he could scent her arousal.

"I want to make you come first." He stared into her eyes intently. "I can't make love to you, because then we won't be getting out of this room today, but I can use my mouth and fingers to give you pleasure."

Her jaw dropped as she stared back at him, desire making her eyes a bit unfocused. "I..." Clearing her throat, she tried again. "That sounds good. I would like that. But after I bring you—"

"No." He cut her off. "I know this might be selfish, but if I make you come after you have gotten me off, I'll be just as hard by the end of it. Trust me on that."

Julianne nodded. "Okay, but that doesn't really sound selfish to me."

Duncan just smiled down at the beautiful woman standing before him. Leaning down, he put his mouth on hers.

She eagerly responded to his kiss. Opening her mouth and tangling her tongue with his in a wicked dance. It spurred him on, and while continuing to kiss her passionately, he used his hands to snap open the button of her shorts and unzip them. Letting go of her mouth, he slid her shorts down her legs along with her panties until she was standing before him with her lower body bared to him.

"Duncan." His name was a sigh on her lips as a shiver ran through her body, and she squeezed her thighs together. The sight made him realize just how turned on she was, and his cock started throbbing insistently, trying to convince him to push inside her channel.

He smiled up at her as he kneeled before her. "Open your legs for me, Julianne."

She moved her legs farther apart to give him access, and he placed his hands on her thighs, gently sliding them up toward her center. She gasped as he slid a finger between her folds, and he almost gasped as well when he felt how wet she was. Her juices coated his finger and slowly trickled down his hand; he had to clench his teeth to prevent himself from throwing her on the bed and filling her with his cock.

Taking a deep breath, he leaned forward and licked

up her slit all the way to her clit. The small nub was swollen, and he used his mouth to lick and suck on it, until Julianne's legs started shaking, and she was making small mewling sounds.

Pulling back, he looked up to see her eyes hazy with her need to come. But her legs were going to give out soon, so they would have to change this around a bit.

"Take a step back and lie back on the bed. I can't have you falling for me. Not like this anyway." He grinned at her as she backed up and lay down.

"Duncan." There was desperation in her voice.

He moved in between her legs. "Don't worry, sweet pea. I won't leave you hanging."

Putting his mouth back on her clit, he circled it with his tongue as he slowly breached her entrance with two fingers. Her hips bucked, trying to make him penetrate her deeper, and he obliged by thrusting his fingers deep inside her.

Julianne moaned and thrashed her head from side to side as he used his fingers and mouth on her. When he felt her sheath start to flutter against his fingers, he vibrated his tongue against her clit.

Her whole body tensed as she came. Her thighs tried to close around his head, but he used his shoulders to keep them open while he continued the vibration against her clit and the thrusting of his fingers inside her to draw out her pleasure.

When she started coming down, Duncan raised his head and stared into her hooded eyes. *So beautiful.* Julianne was so beautiful like this. He wanted to see her exactly like this again and again.

"Wow." Her voice was weak and shaky. "That was… Actually, I don't have words to describe how that was. You're amazing. I think you have to give me a couple of minutes before I can move."

Chuckling, he rose from between her legs and lay down beside her on the bed. "Good. If you were able to get up immediately after I made you come, it would've been embarrassing."

"Oh, you've got no reason to be embarrassed. Trust me." She gave him a weak smile.

Rolling onto his side and supporting his head with his hand, he let his eyes skim over her body from the top of her head to her toes. Everything about her was beautiful. Her smooth skin, her freckles, her hair, her eyes. The swell of her breasts visible through her shirt, and the glistening dark curls between her legs, hiding her pink pussy from him at this angle. *Hips and thighs perfectly made for a man to hold onto, as he…*

Her hand palming his cock had his thoughts stutter to a halt. He landed on his back as she rose up above him and pushed him down.

"I'm getting a bit impatient to see you and touch you." Julianne crawled over him to position herself above him on her hands and knees. "You've already touched me twice, but I've yet to touch you. It's time to rectify that."

Duncan felt his throat go dry as he stared up into her grinning face. Whatever she wanted to do to him, he would let her. Even if she decided that she wanted him inside her immediately, he wouldn't be able to say no. His friends would just have to wait because he was powerless against this woman.

She moved backward until she kneeled by his lower legs. "You have to help me get your shorts off." Gripping the waistband, she started inching his shorts down his hips and thighs as he lifted his lower body off the bed. His cock sprang free from its confinement, and Julianne gasped at the sight of him.

"I knew you were big but..." Her eyes were wide as she stared at his straining rod. Then, she yanked his shorts down his legs and left them around his ankles.

He wasn't prepared when she leaned in and licked him, using one solid stroke from root to tip. The feel of her warm, wet tongue was heaven, and he moaned as the throbbing in his cock intensified.

"So hard yet so soft." She straddled his legs and leaned forward.

His mind was getting muddled with his need, but he picked up on one word that didn't make sense to him. "Soft?"

"Your skin. It's like the most luxurious velvet."

She leaned forward and wrapped her mouth around the head of his rod, and he lost the ability to think. All he could do was feel as she took as much as she could of him into her silky, wet mouth. Her hand gripped the base of his member and slid up and down as her mouth worked his tip and as far down his shaft as she could reach without choking. The feel of her tongue stroking and swirling around the head of his cock had him fisting the bed sheets in order to hold on. He didn't want to grab her head and accidentally choke her.

Duncan could feel himself getting close already. His body had been eager for her touch since he first met her, and when she was finally touching him, he was going to come in less than two minutes. But he couldn't help it. That was the effect Julianne had on him.

Her hand closing gently around his balls broke him. Pleasure shot through him like a dam had suddenly failed, and he roared as his seed pumped into her mouth and the ecstasy of coming threatened to blow his mind. The pleasure pulsed through him before slowly fading away, leaving him more sated than he had been in a long time.

Duncan didn't know how much time had passed when he slowly opened his eyes. Turning his head to the side, he took in the beautiful woman beside him.

Julianne grinned and raised her head. "I thought you might've fallen asleep, so I wanted to give you a few minutes before trying to wake you."

Chuckling, he grinned back at her. "No, I'm not sleeping. I'm just very relaxed. Thank you. I haven't been this relaxed since I met you. My body has been amped up with wanting you all the time, and even getting myself off hasn't helped."

Julianne leaned in and gave him a gentle kiss on his lips. "Anytime, Duncan." She raised an eyebrow at him. "But I hope this doesn't mean that tonight's off. I'm kind of—"

He sat up abruptly. "No. Absolutely not. Tonight's on. I hope you're not expecting to get much sleep, because we'll be busy doing far more enjoyable things than that."

***

Julianne's jaw dropped at Duncan's words and enthusiasm about the night they were going to spend together. And having seen how fast he recovered after coming last night, she had no trouble believing they would spend most of the night having sex. But if she was going to be honest with herself, she would have liked to start early, like right this second. The sight of his huge cock, and the feel of his hardness and velvety skin against her tongue, had reignited her womanly parts. And only his words, that he couldn't make love to her until this evening, had stopped her from straddling him and taking him inside her.

At least Duncan was relaxed. And since that had been her goal when bringing him into this room, she was happy with how it had turned out. She could wait until later. He had already made her come so hard she had probably killed a few braincells, so a break until later was good for her. Or so she was going to tell herself.

"Have I shocked you?" Duncan's eyes were filled with concern as he looked at her. "Please don't worry about tonight. We'll take it as fast or as slow as you want to. If you need sleep, I'll let you sleep."

Julianne chuckled at his concern. The caring side of Duncan was one of the main reasons she liked him so much. His perfect body was a definite turn-on, but his personality played a big part in her attraction to him. "I'm not worried, Duncan. I just wish we could start right now. But I can handle the wait, and I'm looking forward to having sex with you all night. If you can handle it." Julianne uttered the last few words as she got off the bed and moved toward the door to what she assumed was a bathroom.

Rustling behind her alerted her to his movements a second before he stood in front of her, effectively blocking her path to the bathroom.

"You don't think I can handle it?" His eyes were narrow like he was irritated with her for doubting his stamina, but the twitching of his lips gave him away.

She cocked a hip and folded her arms across her chest. "Well, I don't know. It took me no more than a minute to make you shoot."

Duncan flinched like she had hit him, and she inwardly cursed herself for saying something so stupid.

Flinging her arms around his neck, Julianne held him close as she spoke to him. "Sorry. I'm so sorry. I know you have stamina, and I know you recover fast. Please don't be angry or hurt. I didn't mean it like that. Please forgive me. I'm so stupid. I can't believe I said that. I—" She stopped when Duncan broke into her frantic speech.

"Julianne, relax. Look at me."

Reluctantly, she loosened her hold on him and looked up into his face. The smile there made her breathe out a sigh of relief and smile back at him.

"So, you're not angry with me, then?"

"No, I don't think I could ever be angry with you. You're not afraid to tease me and give me shit, just like I'm known to do to others. It's one of the things I like about you." Duncan grinned and put his hands on her hips. "And I look forward to proving to you that I can go all night. But I think you should put some clothes on, or I'm not going to be able to wait."

Laughing, Julianne stepped back. "Then move out of my way, so I can get into the bathroom and clean up."

∞∞∞∞∞

Sabrina was alone in the kitchen with Leith. They had finished cleaning up after lunch and were sitting at the kitchen table having another cup of coffee. After

Julianne had left to find Duncan, it hadn't taken more than a few minutes before the other couples had excused themselves and disappeared as well. Leaving her alone with the remarkable man of the house. The one thing she had decided not to do while she was a guest in his house.

"Are you sure there is nothing you would like with your coffee, my angel?" Leith's dark green gaze was on her.

Against her better judgement, she met his gaze. She really should find a good reason to excuse herself from his presence. "Thank you, Leith, but no." And why did he call her *my angel*? They barely knew each other.

He gave her a small nod.

Sabrina suddenly realized there was something she could ask him that would keep their conversation neutral. The last thing she wanted was for him to start asking questions about her.

"I understand that you are trying to find a witch, Ambrosia. Duncan told us what happened to Steph and Michael. Have you found any clues as to her whereabouts?"

Leith took a sip of his coffee while studying her face. Putting his cup down, he cleared his throat. "We have contacted several shifter groups in these parts and further north. So far, we have had no luck in finding her. She is most likely searching for an unmated alpha to use for her purposes, but most of the clan leaders and pack masters we have spoken to are already mated. We have only encountered two alphas not yet mated. Both of them are people of high integrity, and I do not believe any of them would fall for Ambrosia's promise of power."

"Why do you distinguish between clan and pack? What's the difference between the two?"

"Thank you, Sabrina, for your questions. I apologize for my assumption that you are already acquainted with the shifter terminology and structure. Pack is used for a group of wolf shifters led by an alpha wolf, whereas clan is used for a group of panther shifters. A clan is led by an alpha panther. Wolves and panthers are the predominant kinds of shifters in Scotland. Other kinds of shifters do exist here but are limited to one or two groups per kind, and they are not nearly as powerful as the wolves and panthers. Hence, we are concentrating on the packs and clans in our search for Ambrosia."

Sabrina nodded. She couldn't help noticing the way Leith was speaking. It was a strange blend of modern and old-fashioned, like he was trying to fit into the modern world but sometimes reverted to old habits. Which put his age far beyond what she had assumed based on his looks. If he had been human, she would have put him somewhere in his early thirties, but he was more likely around Duncan's age or perhaps older. If he was a shifter. If he was some other kind of supernatural, there was no way for her to guess his age.

Telling herself to stay on the subject she had started on, she asked him another question. "Do panther clans have something to do with Scottish clans?"

One corner of Leith's mouth curved up slightly in what Sabrina had decided was his way of smiling. She had yet to see a full-on smile on his face or hear him laugh. Even when everyone had laughed at Duncan and Julianne's antics at lunch, Leith had only shown his version of a smile. It seemed to be his way, but she found herself wanting to hear him laugh.

"A good question, my angel. Scottish clans are a human structure, with each clan constructed of extended family, or kin if you will. A panther clan is a group of panthers often having no family ties. It is enough to pledge yourself to the clan. Usually the clan members live within a relatively small area, but you can be part of a clan far away from where you live. The same applies to the wolves."

It was nice being alone with him, when she could maintain a distance between them, and there was no immediate danger of any personal questions. And if she was going to be honest with herself, she liked the sound of his voice. Leith was obviously happy to answer her questions, so she continued.

"So how does the clan or pack select its alpha?"

Leith took another sip of his coffee before answering her. "A shifter comes into his or her power in puberty, and each individual's power level determines where they end up in the shifter hierarchy. An alpha shifter has more power than other shifters, and they are quite rare. That is why most shifter clans or packs are large, and every alpha is expected to become a leader. Sometimes alpha power runs in families, but not always."

"Are all alphas equally powerful?"

"No, some are more powerful than others. And that has been the reason for many feuds between shifter groups throughout history."

Sabrina frowned as she considered what Leith was telling her. Specifically, the fact that all alphas were expected to become leaders.

"So, how does an alpha become a leader?"

"Good question. That is not always straight forward. Some clans and packs practice a form of succession. A young alpha will take over for the old one if certain criteria are met. The criteria may vary but can be related to age, power level, family ties, etcetera. Other groups use a more brutal method for choosing a leader. Or it is not really a choice as such. The alphas fight to determine who is the most powerful, and whoever wins assumes leadership."

"What happens to the alpha who loses?"

"Well, if he is not killed, he can try to win another group. Or he can try to gather shifters who are not currently part of a group. There are a number of shifters who have not actively chosen to be part of a group, or who do not want to be part of a clan or a pack. They live by themselves or among shifters with a similar mindset."

Sabrina stared at Leith. "It sounds like there might be a few alphas out there who're not currently leaders. Have you contacted them about Ambrosia?"

Leith's brows pulled together as he stared at her. "No. We have not. You make an excellent point, Sabrina. I believe you have just found a flaw in our plan."

CHAPTER 14

Julianne felt a bit awkward as she approached the kitchen with Duncan. She had no doubt that the others had figured out why they were gone so long. It was only a little over half an hour since they left the kitchen, but still.

She was surprised when they entered the kitchen to see only Sabrina and Leith sitting at the kitchen table. None of the couples were there.

"You set off quite a stampede you know." Leith turned to them, and Julianne saw the corner of his mouth curve up a little in a weak imitation of a smile.

"Where did they go?" Duncan sounded just as confused at Leith's words as she was.

"Newly mated couples. Where do you think? The lust in the air is somewhat potent around here these days."

Julianne felt heat rising in her face, not sure what to say in response to Leith's blunt words.

She started when Duncan burst out laughing. "Yes,

and I guess it didn't lessen with our arrival. At least you seem to have found a fellow sufferer."

Sabrina lifted an eyebrow at Duncan. "I've been putting up with you two for a couple of days now. I wasn't aware that the other couples are just as amorous."

Julianne chuckled. "I'm sorry, Sabrina, but in my defense, you told me it would be good for me to find someone to bump pelvises with."

"Oh, so that's all I am, someone to bump pelvises with?" Duncan folded his arms across his chest and stared down his nose at her with an offended expression on his face. Then his face broke into a wide grin. "But I guess that's not so bad. I can think of worse activities."

Julianne laughed.

"Yes, well. I believe we've got more important things to discuss." Sabrina's expression was neutral, but her skin tone was a little rosier than usual.

"Would you like some coffee or tea?" Leith rose from the table and moved over to the coffee machine.

Duncan smiled. "Coffee would be great, Leith." He nodded toward the table indicating to Julianne that they should sit down.

"Yes, please. I think I need a coffee." Julianne took a seat beside Duncan.

"Sabrina?" Leith turned his head and looked at her friend over his shoulder.

Sabrina glanced at Leith and gave a small shake of her head. "No thank you, Leith. I think I've had enough coffee for a while."

"Would you like some tea?" Leith kept his gaze trained on her friend.

Smiling, Sabrina shook her head again. "No thank you. I'm fine."

Julianne watched the exchange with interest. Leith was extremely attentive to Sabrina's needs and welfare. For a man not prone to dishing out big smiles, he was perceptive and warm. Leith clearly appreciated his friends and wanted everyone to feel welcome, but there was something unique about the way he treated Sabrina.

Sounds from the kitchen doorway brought Julianne back from her thoughts. Trevor and Jennie walked into the kitchen. The happy smiles on their faces brought a smile to Julianne's face as well. Those two were like the perfect couple. So happy and secure in each other's love. It was like they radiated love and warmth, giving everyone a boost of energy and joy.

"At least we're not the last to show up." Jennie chuckled and let her gaze linger on Julianne and Duncan. "I thought that would be you two."

Julianne couldn't help the blush that crept over her face, even though they hadn't been the only ones engaged in bedroom activities after lunch.

"We've come all the way up here to help out. And you can't even be bothered to be present for the important discussions." Duncan was trying to look offended, but his eyes were twinkling with barely restrained laughter.

"Careful, Duncan." Trevor grinned. "I seem to recall someone too hot for a woman to even finish his lunch, let alone speak. How old are you again? Seventeen?"

"Boys, stop." Laughing, Jennie pulled Trevor toward the kitchen table. "Or, we'll never get anything done today."

"Would you like some coffee?" Leith was still by the coffee machine.

Jennie nodded enthusiastically. "Yes, please. Thanks, Leith."

Trevor nodded with a smile on his face.

Duncan's expression had sobered, and he was suddenly all business. "I've told Julianne and Sabrina about Ambrosia, and what happened to Steph and Michael at the hands of Jack and his panthers. Have you managed to locate the evil witch yet?"

"No." Trevor sighed and gave a brief description of what they had done so far. By the time he was finished, they were all enjoying the coffee Leith had made for them.

Frowning, Duncan stared at Trevor. "So, she hasn't been in contact with any packs or clans around here or up north. I know of at least three shifter groups out east, but none of the alphas are unmated. There's a panther clan not far from Glasgow and a pack just to the north of Perth. The pack alpha is mated, but I don't know about the clan alpha."

"He's mated." Trevor narrowed his eyes in consideration. "We might have to start contacting some of the groups further south."

"Sabrina." Everyone's eyes swung to Leith as he spoke. "Please tell everybody about the flaw you discovered in our strategy."

Sabrina's eyes widened a little as her gaze snapped to Leith's. "I… It wasn't like that."

"Oh, it was, my angel. You made an excellent point."

The warmth in Leith's gaze as he kept his eyes on

Sabrina made Julianne smile. And he had just called her friend his angel. This was just getting better and better. Not the least of which was Sabrina's reaction to this man. The ice queen was melting into a puddle at Leith's feet.

Sabrina turned to look at Julianne before she spoke. "I just asked about the alphas not currently leading a pack or a clan. If one of them holds a grudge, that alpha might be easy to convince."

"Fuck!" Trevor rose from his seat at the table and started pacing. "That's an excellent point and something I should've thought of. I'm one of those alphas for fuck's sake, only now I'm mated and therefore not a target. There are others like me out there who don't want to lead, but there are also those who have been beaten or surpassed by another alpha."

"Well, then we need to contact them." Jennie followed her agitated mate with her eyes.

Trevor swore again. "If only it were that easy. I only know of one such alpha, and I have no idea where he is. I can get someone to find him, but there are bound to be others out there."

Leith nodded slowly. "We need to talk to all the packs and clans again and gather information about solitary alphas. Although I am an alpha, I am somewhat of a special case. Besides, I have not been contacted by Ambrosia, and I don't consider myself at risk of her machinations even if she was to contact me."

Julianne nodded to herself. Leith had just confirmed that he was a shifter. She had no idea what he meant when he said he was a special case, but as long as he treated her friend well, Julianne didn't care.

This whole discussion about shifters and alphas had made Julianne think of another question she had about supernaturals. "What about other types of supernaturals? Don't they mate or form some kind of similar bond?"

Duncan smiled at her. "No, most supernaturals either marry or perform some other kind of ritual to celebrate the union of two people. But it's no more than an agreement. It's not an unbreakable bond like the one shifters have as mates."

"So, Ambrosia has no reason to target any other supernaturals than shifters in order to gain power?" Julianne threw the thought out there to provoke these people who knew a lot more about supernaturals than she did.

Silence reigned in the room for a full minute before Leith spoke. "There may be other ways for a single witch to gain power, but I have little knowledge of this. A vampire will gain power with age and so will a few other kinds of supernaturals. A vampire can also increase his or her power by drinking from a more powerful individual. However, old vampires do not typically want to share their power and will seldom offer blood to younger vampires." He paused before getting to his feet. "I think I will go for a swim. My mind works better surrounded by water."

Julianne felt herself frown as she watched Leith walk out the door. "Um, why—"

Duncan cut her off, having obviously understood what she was about to ask. "He has to tell you that himself. It's his story to share." Smiling at her, he took her hand in his before turning toward Trevor. "Have you made a list of the packs and clans you have contacted?"

Nodding, Trevor went to a small side table and picked up a laptop. He brought it back to the kitchen table and turned it on. "We have a list with location and the alpha's name and phone number. We need to add the details for the shifter groups to the east and south."

"Okay." Duncan leaned in as Trevor logged in and opened a spreadsheet. "We can split it between us and get started."

"Jennie can cover a few. As my mate she's accepted as part of the shifter community. She's already talked to some of them. Between the three of us, we can get through most of them in a couple of hours. When Michael and Steph show up, they can start logging all the info about the solitary alphas, and any other useful information we get."

"Anything you would like us to do?" Julianne indicated herself and Sabrina.

Duncan smiled at her before turning to Sabrina. "Is there anything you can do to try and locate Ambrosia? I know you have no idea who she is, but if you can think of a way to find her, that would be valuable."

Sabrina gave him a slow nod. "I'll have to think about it. I'm not aware of any way to locate a random person. If she had been someone I'd already met, perhaps I would've been able to give you a rough location."

Julianne felt her jaw slacken in awe. "You can locate someone you know no matter where they are?"

Her friend gave her a small smile. "I can, but it requires a lot of energy. It's usually much easier to just pick up the phone."

Julianne snorted. "Yeah, I guess. Modern technology trumping witchcraft. So, have you tried finding a phone number for this Ambrosia? There can't be that many people in Scotland called Ambrosia. If that's her real name, of course."

Trevor and Jennie both stared at her before Trevor answered. "No. We haven't tried that. Apparently, there are quite a few things we haven't thought of. I wonder what we would've done if you ladies hadn't joined us?"

Shaking her head, Julianne smiled. "You would've thought of it in time. And in any case, she might not even be listed. I can't check, though, since I can't turn on my phone."

"We can use mine." Sabrina rose and walked around the table to where Julianne was sitting with Duncan. "Maybe we can go somewhere else while the rest of you start making phone calls."

"Good plan." Duncan let go of Julianne's hand. "There's a living room downstairs. Just follow the stairs in the hallway down one level."

"Okay." Julianne rose from her seat next to Duncan, but before she moved away, she leaned down and gave him a quick kiss on his soft lips. It was more public display of affection than Julianne was usually comfortable with, but she might not see him for a couple of hours, and she needed something before she left. As she straightened, she was happy to see a smile on his face. Then he stood, and before she realized what he intended he was cupping her head and kissing her hard. It lasted only a few seconds, but she was still a little breathless when he let her go.

"I'll be downstairs when you're done." Sabrina was

already by the door to the hallway.

"Wait up, I'm right behind you." Julianne hurried after her friend as she chuckled. Both from the happiness spreading through her and Sabrina's curt comment.

The living room was filled with art and artifacts just like the kitchen and hallway upstairs. The difference was that the carvings in the walls of the living room were much bigger, and a whole sequence of events seemed to play out on the walls almost like a cartoon with no speech. It was amazing but not the reason why they were in this room. They had an evil witch to find.

"Okay." Julianne walked up to Sabrina, who was studying one of the wall carvings. "Shall we check the phone directory?"

"Yes." The word was drawn out as Sabrina obviously struggled to pull her eyes away from the scene that had snared her attention.

Julianne studied the carving Sabrina was staring at. "Leith is extremely talented. I've never seen such detailed and expressive carvings before. I'm not sure I understand the scenes he's portraying, but I don't know a lot about art."

Sabrina turned to her and smiled. "Perhaps we're not meant to understand them, just be intrigued by all the possibilities in the scenes."

"That's deep, and way too artsy for me." Julianne smiled. "Phone directory?"

Nodding, Sabrina turned away from the carving, and they sat down next to each other on the sofa.

Their search for Ambrosia came up with fourteen listings. They were mostly business names, and a couple of listings were men with the surname

Ambrosia. There were only two women. However, an internet search revealed that they were both old ladies. None of them were the Ambrosia they were looking for.

"Well, that was a waste of time." Julianne sighed. It would have been so nice if they had found the woman's number and address, but of course that would have been too easy.

Footsteps sounded from the stairs coming up from the bottom level of the house, and a few seconds later, Leith came to a halt at the top of the stairs, staring at them. He was wearing shorts and holding a shirt in his hand. "I am sorry, ladies. You have to excuse my state of undress. I did not think to check if this room was occupied, or I would have put on my shirt before making my entrance." As he spoke, he was staring at Sabrina.

Julianne turned to look at her friend and almost burst out laughing. Sabrina was staring at Leith with wide eyes and her mouth hanging open. Ogling would be the correct term for what her friend was doing, and Julianne silently cheered her on. It was so nice to see Sabrina reacting to a man, and particularly to a man like Leith.

Sabrina suddenly snapped her mouth shut with an audible clack and tipped her head forward to hide her face. "I'm sorry. That was impolite. I didn't mean to stare at you like that."

"I do not mind, my angel. Not in the least. Please do not be sorry. If anything, it was my fault for assuming that this room was empty."

Julianne didn't say anything and kept her eyes on Sabrina.

"I will be upstairs if there is anything you ladies need."

Julianne turned her head toward Leith and smiled. He had put on his shirt. Nodding once to Julianne, he walked up the stairs to the upper level of the house.

"That was...interesting." Julianne couldn't hide the amusement in her voice.

"No, that was embarrassing." Sabrina sighed and lifted her head to meet Julianne's eyes. "Leith is a nice man, but there can't be anything between us. I don't want there to be anything between us."

Frowning, Julianne studied her friend's face. Sabrina usually hid her feelings well, but at the moment there was sadness in her eyes. "I don't understand, Sabrina. You said yourself that Leith is a nice man, and he's clearly taken by you. Why not give him a chance? He's a respectful and caring type of man. I think the two of you would be good together."

Her friend shook her head and looked away. "It's better for both of us if I keep my distance. He'll find someone else who's more suitable for him."

Julianne had no idea what was going on with Sabrina. Her friend had been in relationships before. Not exactly loving relationships, but amicable at least. So why was a relationship with Leith out of the question? Was Sabrina scared because she could see herself actually falling for the guy? That might be an explanation.

Julianne put her hand on Sabrina's arm. "I'll support you no matter what you decide to do, Sabrina. I don't understand, but I'll support you. And if you at some point feel comfortable telling me why, I promise I'll listen and try to understand your reasons. You're a rational woman, so there must be good reasons."

A small sad smile curved Sabrina's mouth as she turned back to Julianne. "Thank you, Julianne. I think I'll need your support. But I can't tell you why. Not right now. It's too hard."

"Okay. Whenever you're ready then."

CHAPTER 15

Duncan ended the call and looked at his notes. So far, he had gotten the names of two alphas not leading a shifter group. One wolf and one panther. The panther was mated, so that left the wolf.

Trevor was sitting at the other end of the kitchen table, whereas Jennie had preferred to sit outside on the terrace.

"Any luck?" Duncan looked over at his friend, who had just ended a call.

Trevor shook his head. "Not really. I got the name of two alphas that are not part of a pack, but both are mated. Or one is no longer mated. Apparently, he killed his own mate. Really nasty piece of work, but he's already been mated so he's not a person of interest for Ambrosia. You?"

"A wolf. I just tried calling him, but there was no answer. I left him a message to call me back, without any details as to why. Just in case he's already in Ambrosia's clutches. Better chance of getting the truth from him if he's unprepared for my questions."

Trevor nodded. "Good thinking. I've got two more names on my list to call."

"Same. Let's sum up when we're done."

Trevor nodded again and picked up his phone.

Duncan talked to the last two alphas on his list, but neither of them had any relevant information. One of the alphas mentioned there had been an old alpha in his pack, but he had recently died. So, not relevant.

"I've got one." Trevor looked up from his notes. "An alpha panther. Lives somewhere secluded up north. Alone and without a phone. Not mated the last time anyone spoke to him. That was three months ago."

"Is he the type to be susceptible to Ambrosia's lure of power?"

"Well, that's the thing. He was supposed to mate a woman. It was some kind of family agreement. Apparently, he balked at the mating, but when the woman turned around and chose someone else, he was furious. That was about a year ago, and he left the clan shortly afterwards and moved up north. If Ambrosia knows about him at all, he might be the type that would be willing to agree to her plans."

"Yes." Duncan narrowed his eyes in thought. "We need to talk to him. Did you get an address or directions for how to find him?"

"Well, sort of. The alpha I spoke to just had a rough idea of where this guy was staying. Let's check what Jennie has found out." Trevor smiled as he looked at the entrance to the terrace.

Jennie walked into the kitchen, smiling. Walking over to Trevor, she gave him a quick kiss before sitting down with a sigh. "Nothing. None of the alphas I've talked to knew of any solitary alphas that are unmated. What have you found out?"

Before anyone could answer, Leith walked into the kitchen.

Duncan smiled. "You're just in time to get the results of our search."

Leith gave them a short nod and sat down.

Duncan told them about the alpha wolf he hadn't been able to get ahold of, and Trevor told them about the secluded panther up north.

Jennie scrunched up her face in thought. "Two alphas who might cooperate with Ambrosia, assuming she is still in Scotland. And assuming that we've managed to identify all the alphas. If there's another unmated alpha out there that we don't know about, we have a problem."

Trevor took Jennie's hand in his. "Yes, I think that about sums it up."

Duncan rose from the table. "I think I'm going to ask Julianne and Sabrina if they want to go for a swim."

"Do you mind if I join you?" Leith was already rising from the table.

"Of course not." Duncan struggled to keep a straight face at Leith's obvious eagerness to spend time with Sabrina. Hopefully, Blondie would give the man a chance.

The ladies were sitting on a couch in the living room when Duncan and Leith descended the stairs.

"Do you ladies want to go for a swim?" Duncan met Julianne's eyes as he walked up to the women.

"Yes, that sounds great." Julianne quickly rose from

the couch before frowning and turning to look at Sabrina. "Will you join us?"

Sabrina shook her head. "No, you go ahead. I think I'll take a little nap if you don't mind."

"I will show you to your room, my angel. Just let me get your bag from upstairs." Leith turned and hurried up the stairs.

"Okay, I need to find my bikini. I'll be back in a sec." Julianne gave Duncan a big smile as she moved past him toward the stairs.

Duncan nodded and followed her, his eyes roving over her round behind as she walked ahead of him up the stairs. His cock took notice, and he quickly looked away, trying to focus on something else.

They met Leith at the top of the stairs carrying Sabrina's bag. "Please enjoy your swim. I will make sure Sabrina is satisfied with the accommodation I have offered her."

Duncan grinned at Leith. "Caught you by surprise, didn't she?"

Leith's expression gave nothing away when he replied. "I do not think I understand what you are referring to."

"Of course, you don't." Duncan laughed as Leith hurried down the stairs with Sabrina's bag.

Duncan and Julianne changed quickly and returned down the stairs to exit the house at the bottom level. There was a small beach about two hundred yards along the shore from the house, and there was nobody else there at the moment.

Julianne dropped her towel and took off the shorts and tee she had put on over her bikini. The sight of her in her bikini had Duncan's heartrate increasing, and he quickly averted his eyes. After removing his T-shirt, he started walking slowly down toward the water. He was such an idiot inviting Julianne for a swim. What had he assumed was going to happen when he saw her in her bikini again? It wasn't going to take much to shatter his control, but if he could keep his eyes on something else until they were in the water, he might have a chance.

She came up beside him, and he smiled down into her face. Grabbing her hand, he tugged her along into the water.

Gasping, she slowed her steps. "Slow down, it's cold."

He chuckled. "Better to be quick if it's cold. You'll get used to it faster."

"Okay, if you say so." Julianne suddenly flung herself into the three-feet-deep water. Two seconds later she came up sputtering and shivering.

The sight had him grasping her and pulling her close against his body. It was almost like an instinctual reaction to seeing her cold and shivering.

Julianne held onto him for a few seconds before loosening her grip. She rose up on her toes and put her mouth on his.

Duncan groaned at the feel of her lips moving softly against his. When she opened her mouth, their tongues started dancing and his control shattered.

He tightened his arms around her as his cock rose up between them. Their kissing turned more frantic, and Julianne squirmed against him, clearly as turned on as he was.

Breaking the kiss, he stared down into her face, taking in the desire in her eyes. "Come. Let's go a little deeper."

Walking her backward into deeper water, he didn't stop until it reached her neck. He grabbed her hips and lifted her. "Wrap your legs around my waist, sweet pea."

"Okay." Her voice was breathy.

The feel of her warm center against his cock as she wrapped her legs around him had his hard member throbbing with the need for release.

He took a few more steps until the water covered them up to their shoulders. Then he stopped and held her gaze, as he started rocking his hard cock against her pussy.

Her eyes widened as he moved against her. She started moving her pelvis, and the friction between them increased. Duncan growled as his balls pulled up and his body prepared for release.

"Duncan, I want you inside me."

He almost choked with how much he wanted exactly what she was asking. "I—"

"Please, I need you inside me." Julianne's voice was strained with her need to come.

Duncan knew he should say no. Or did he? He couldn't come up with any good reasons as to why he should say no to this amazing woman.

"Okay." He moved her weight over on one arm and used the other to pull down his shorts. Then, he reached between her legs and pulled her bikini bottoms to the side to give him access to her warm, wet channel. Using one finger he breached her entrance and pushed inside, and Julianne gasped and squirmed against him.

"Duncan, please."

He pulled out his finger and used his hand to guide the head of his cock to her opening. While watching her face, he pushed slowly inside her. Julianne's jaw slackened, and her eyes became unfocused as he pushed farther in. She was so tight, just like he knew she would be. He was only about halfway inside when her internal muscles clamped down on him, and he growled as his cock was crushed so hard it bordered on pain.

"Julianne, please try to relax. I'm a bit stuck." He smiled at her, but it might have been a bit strained.

She nodded. "I'm trying. You're just so big, and the water isn't helping either. I think my body decided that you're too big for me or something."

"Am I hurting you? I'm so sorry." The thought hadn't crossed his mind before, but when it did, his desire died and his cock started softening.

"No. You're not hurting me. You don't have to pull out." She tilted her head at him as his soft cock slipped from her body.

"I'm sorry, Julianne. The thought that I might be hurting you... Perhaps it's better if we continue this tonight in a bed." He studied her face for any signs that she was in pain or angry with him.

Smiling, she nodded. "Maybe you're right." She closed the distance between their mouths and kissed him.

Duncan relaxed as they kissed, slower this time. Not the hectic frenzy from before. He liked this kind of kissing just as much as the more passionate kind. As long as he got to kiss Julianne.

She slowly pulled away, but he kept looking into her eyes. A warm feeling was spreading through his chest. A feeling that was telling him to hold her tightly and never let her go.

"Will you be my girlfriend?" The words tumbled out of his mouth, almost tripping over each other. He suddenly felt icy fear creeping up his spine. What if she said no? What if she didn't want him? What if he had scared her when he got stuck inside her?

Julianne burst out laughing, and Duncan froze. Reluctance he would have understood, but he hadn't expected ridicule. His whole body seized up, and pain erupted in his chest, making his heart stutter. At least that was how it felt.

"I'm sorry." The words fell dead from his mouth, and he looked away from Julianne's face. He took a few steps to a place where he could safely put her down with her head above water, and let her find her footing before taking a step back.

"Duncan?" There was still amusement in her voice, and the pain in his chest flared.

"I understand." He started walking toward the beach, not waiting for her to follow. His chest was tight, and every breath he took caused pain to radiate out through his body. He needed time alone.

"I'd love to be your girlfriend."

It took him a few seconds before her words registered in his frayed mind. Then he stopped. *Did she really say...*

Turning around, he was surprised to see she was right behind him. He hadn't even heard her move.

"You would?" Duncan was afraid to get his hopes up. "But you laughed at the idea."

"Yes. No. I..." She sighed before starting again. "Yes, I'd love to be your girlfriend, Duncan. I wasn't laughing at the idea of being your girlfriend. I was laughing at the term girlfriend, used by you, a sixty-one-year-old. It sounded funny to me. I'm sorry. I realize now that my laughing hurt you. That wasn't my intention."

"So, you're my girlfriend now?" His heart was hammering wildly in his chest as he stared at her.

"Yes." She grinned up at him.

He grabbed her and kissed her hard. She was his. Julianne was his. All he wanted to do was scoop her up, carry her up to their bedroom, and make love to her. Again and again until she begged for mercy. And why shouldn't he when she had agreed to be his?

Lifting her into his arms, he carried her out of the water. He intended to leave their things and come back for them later, but Julianne had other plans.

"Put me down." She grinned up at him.

Duncan reluctantly put her down on the beach, but he didn't let her go. "I want to make love to my girlfriend."

Julianne laughed. "No more waiting until tonight, huh?"

"No, I think I'll spontaneously combust before that. I want you. I've wanted you since the moment I first laid eyes on you. But I don't just want you in my bed. I want to spend time with you doing everyday things. Just be in your life."

He wasn't prepared for the tears that filled her eyes. "Julianne? Did I say something wrong?"

Shaking her head, she threw her arms around his neck and held him tightly. "Sorry. I guess I'm a bit overwhelmed. You're just so amazing, and I didn't expect you to want me. At least not for more than a holiday fling. I want you in my life, and I want to be a part of yours."

"Well, then it's settled." Chuckling, he nuzzled into her neck. "You're stuck with me now."

"Good. I want to be stuck with you." Julianne let him go and grinned up at him through her tears.

"Let's go." He grabbed her hand and turned in the direction of the house. "I'm kind of eager to get you into bed. It's important that I make up for the disaster in the water."

Julianne laughed. "Just let me grab our things." She tugged at their joined hands.

Duncan let her go and watched her run and gather their clothes and towels before coming back. Taking them from her, he balled them all up and carried them under one arm. He gripped her hand and tugged her along toward the house.

"In a hurry, are you?" Julianne half ran beside him to keep up with his long strides as they moved along the path leading to Leith's house.

"Sorry." Slowing his pace to a comfortable walking speed, he threw her a smile. "As I said, eager."

"Yes, you did say that." She smiled up at him. "But you're going to have to wait a few more minutes, I'm afraid. I have to check on Sabrina. She's...sad."

Duncan's smile faded a little. He liked Blondie. She was solemn and a bit too quiet, but she was a good person. And she cared about Julianne and had clearly supported her as she broke off her relationship with Steven. And that alone was enough for Duncan to consider Sabrina a friend and care about her well-being.

"Is there anything I can do?"

Shaking her head, Julianne gave him a small smile. "No, I'll just check how she's feeling.

"Okay. I'll be waiting in our room."

They reached the downstairs entrance to the house, and Duncan stopped. He removed the ball of clothes from under his arm and extracted Julianne's towel. "Do you want this?"

"Yes, thank you." Her eyes dropped to his shorts, and she laughed. "There's a large snake in your pants."

"I know. Is this better?" Duncan held his towel up in front of him to cover the huge bulge in his shorts.

"Much." Julianne's eyes were glittering with amusement.

Duncan opened the door to the house and indicated which room was Sabrina's. Leaving Julianne to talk to her friend, he took the stairs two steps at a time.

Getting to their room unseen by any of the other people in the house was a relief. He quickly took off his wet shorts and wrapped the towel around his waist.

His thoughts touching on Steven earlier reminded Duncan that there was something he needed to do. He found his phone and called Callum.

"Duncan. I was just about to call you."

Duncan's anger toward Steven was rising, and his voice was a bit growly when he responded. "What has happened?"

"Actually, nothing. Steven hasn't been anywhere near the estate at all. Since I started tracking his phone last night, he's been around Fort William."

"Oh, that's good."

"Yes, and you know the other names you gave me? Both of them are in London, so there's no reason to keep track of them."

"Even better. It seems Steven was acting alone, and that he was using Julianne's phone to track her." Which meant the panther was no longer a threat, as long as Julianne's phone stayed off.

"The panther is stalking your friend?" Anger was evident in Callum's voice. "Do you want me to do a background check on this guy? Might be good to know a bit more about him."

"Julianne's my girlfriend actually." Duncan could hear the pride in his own voice as he pronounced her importance to him. "Please do a background check on the panther. Julianne can't stay off the grid forever, and it would be good to know if we can expect any more trouble from the asshole."

"Will do, and congratulations." Callum laughed. "She must be some woman to have snagged your attention for more than one night."

Duncan chuckled. "She is." And he deserved the little sting in Callum's comment. It was a well-known fact among the wolves in Fearolc that Duncan was a no-strings man. "I'll pay you for your work, Callum. I don't expect you to do this for free, you know."

"No, don't even think about it. You're my friend. I'm happy to do this for you. And it's not taking me a lot of time. I'll get back to you as soon as I've got more information."

"Thank you, Callum."

"No problem."

Duncan ended the call. At least Steven wasn't an issue at the moment. And as long as the panther stayed away from Julianne, they could deal with him later. Which made Duncan realize he had forgotten to tell

Callum they had relocated to Loch Ness.

But before he could send a text to Callum, the door opened, and Julianne entered the room and closed the door behind her. "Ready for me?" She bit her bottom lip as she dropped her towel onto the floor. Taking a step toward him, she reached behind her back and unsnapped her bikini top.

The sight of her bare breasts had Duncan's jaw dropping. He hadn't had an opportunity to play with her breasts yet. This was the first time he laid eyes on them, and he felt his hands itching to touch the soft globes.

Duncan didn't even realize he had moved, until he filled his hands with her perfect mounds and squeezed them gently. He bent down and took a nipple into his mouth, suckling and biting the pink tip.

Julianne moaned, and he smiled against her breast before moving over to suck her other nipple into his mouth. Releasing one breast he let his hand skim down her side to her hip, before changing direction and plunging into her bikini bottoms.

She sucked in a breath as he found her clit and started circling the little button with his middle finger.

"Duncan." Her voice was already a little breathless. "Let me…get on…the bed."

Which was a good idea, since he doubted she would be able to stand for long if he kept going.

Letting go of her, he took a step back as he smirked. "Well, go on then. I'm waiting."

Julianne lifted one eyebrow at his cocky demeanor and closed the distance between them. Before he realized what she had planned, she tugged the towel away from his body. Her hand closed around his hard cock and slid up and down his shaft a couple of times.

"Julianne." He gripped her wrist gently and tried to make her stop, but she just shook her head and continued stroking his straining member.

"Please, Julianne. I don't want to come without you." His voice was shaky with how close he was to release already.

She let go of him and took a step back as she smirked up at him. "Still waiting?"

"Minx." His cock was throbbing with his need for release, and he fisted his hands at his side not to grab her and throw her on the bed.

Chuckling, she took off her bikini bottoms and lay down on her back on the bed. Her legs were bent at the knee and spread wide, giving him a grand view of her pink pussy.

Groaning, he climbed onto the bed between her legs. "I'm going to give you an orgasm first before I enter you."

She frowned. "No, you—"

"Julianne. I want to make sure your body is prepared this time before I enter you. The last thing I want is to hurt you."

A smile spread across her face. "Okay. But you didn't hurt me, you know."

"Good." Duncan slid his hands under her ass and angled her pussy a little upward. Keeping his eyes on her face, he leaned in and started licking and sucking on her clit.

It didn't take long before she was moaning and rocking her pelvis against his face, eager for more. He pulled one hand from under her ass and used two fingers to slide into her tight, wet sheath. She mewled as he pumped his fingers into her while continuing to work her clit. Adding a third digit, he used his fingers to massage her channel walls as he thrust them inside her. When he felt her walls start to flutter, he vibrated his tongue over her clit.

CHAPTER 16

Julianne came with a scream, thrashing her head from side to side as pleasure racked her body, leaving her breathless and shaking with the power of her orgasm.

As she came down, she felt Duncan's head resting on her belly, and she lifted her hands and ran her fingers through his hair. He sighed in response, and she smiled.

Duncan was her boyfriend. He had asked her. It was so unexpected and funny that she had almost ruined the whole thing by bursting out laughing. But thankfully he had understood, and he was really her boyfriend. The gorgeous and kind man was hers. It was unbelievable.

"What are you thinking about?" He was staring at her face with his lips bending in a small smile.

Julianne had been so wrapped up in her own thoughts she hadn't noticed him moving. "You, being my boyfriend." The warm happy feeling in her chest must have reflected on her face, because his smile widened into a warm and happy grin.

"And as your boyfriend I would like to make love to you." Duncan crawled up her body until his cock bumped gently against her entrance. Supporting himself on one elbow he used his hand to line himself up. Slowly he pushed into her, stretching her channel wide.

It felt so good, but she could feel her body wanting to resist the intrusion. Then, he pulled back out a little before sliding into her again, a little farther in this time. He repeated the procedure a few times, his jaw tensing each time, until he bottomed out inside her.

"I've never felt so full before. It feels amazing." Her voice was husky and didn't sound like hers at all.

"Good." Duncan spoke through his teeth. "You have to give me a few seconds. I can't move just yet. You're so tight."

Julianne felt herself frowning. That didn't sound good. "Am I too tight? Is it painful?"

"No, no." He chuckled. "Being inside you is too good. I don't want to embarrass myself by coming before you do."

"Oh." She grinned at him. "I've already had an orgasm, so it's your turn. I don't mind."

He shook his head slowly. "But I do. I want you to come while I'm inside you."

She felt him pulling out slowly before thrusting back in, and she gasped as pleasure tingled through her nerves and settled like a hot ball in her lower belly. He repeated the motion, and she grabbed his ass cheeks to hold on. His long wide shaft was touching places inside her she'd never even known she had. He kept thrusting inside her, gradually increasing his pace, and she angled her hips to meet his movements.

"Julianne." Duncan's voice was strained as he whispered her name. Sweat was running down his face, and his muscles were taut. He was trying to hold back his own orgasm, and it was clearly taking its toll on him.

"I'm...so...close." It was hard to speak while he moved and created the most amazing sensations in her. So powerful she might actually come from just having him inside her. If that happened, it would be a first for her. She usually needed her clit stimulated at the same time.

He changed his position slightly and pushed into her hard. It brought her right to the edge, and she heard herself mewl. Digging her fingers into the tense muscles of his ass, she hoped he understood she wanted more of what he had just done. Julianne had lost the ability to speak.

Thankfully, he understood, and it only took two hard thrusts for her to tip over the edge. Pleasure exploded through her from her center as her channel seized his cock in a tight grip. Duncan roared, and his shaft pulsed inside her as he came, the movement increasing her pleasure even further. She held onto him for dear life as wave upon wave of utter ecstasy tore through her and shook her body.

It felt like a long time before she finally came down. She was breathing hard, still holding onto Duncan with arms and legs wrapped around his powerful body. He was breathing hard as well, and his cock was still buried deep inside her. But the pressure of him inside her was lessening.

"Wow." Julianne whispered the word. "That was...

I don't know if I've got words strong enough to describe how that was. I've never felt anything like it."

"Good." He kissed her shoulder before lifting his head and looking at her. There was wonder in his eyes. "That was incredible. I've never come so hard in my life. When your muscles clamped down on me, I thought my cock was going to be crushed to hell, but instead I came so hard my balls feel empty."

"Empty, as in..." Julianne swallowed as her gut plummeted. "Protection. We didn't use any protection."

Duncan sighed as he looked into her eyes. "I'm sorry. I should've thought of that. We'll use condoms from now on, okay? I'm sure we'll be fine this once."

Julianne stared up at him. "You don't seem that worried."

His lips widened in a smile. "I'm sorry. I know we've just met and it's not the right time, but I've always wanted pups. The thought of you carrying my child is amazing to me."

Her jaw dropped at his words. That was so not what she had expected to hear. It gave her a warm feeling that he'd be there if she became pregnant with his baby, but the thought also scared her. It was way too soon. They didn't know each other nearly well enough to have kids together. "Let's wait a little while with that, okay? I just want to enjoy being your girlfriend for a while. We can discuss children later."

Chuckling, he leaned in and kissed her slowly before pulling back. "Yes, I know it's too soon. But I think you would look sexy growing my pup inside you. Just saying. I've heard your boobs will get bigger when—"

"Duncan!" Julianne cut him off, not ready to hear this right after he had just come inside her for the first time. Then, she realized what he had just said. "Are my boobs too small?"

"What? No." He growled at her. "Your body is perfect." He lifted himself off her a little and stared between them as if to underline his words.

Julianne laughed. "Okay, I believe you."

"You'd better. I'm the expert here."

"Oh, really?" She narrowed her eyes at him.

"Of course. I like women and you like men, so..." He waggled his eyebrows at her.

Laughing, she nodded. "Okay. I can accept that."

Duncan carefully rolled off her, his soft cock sliding out from inside her. He got up off the bed and went into the bathroom. She heard water running and was about to get up from the bed when he came back with a small wet towel. He put one knee on the bed and leaned over her as he gently cleaned between her legs. When he was done, he winked at her before returning to the bathroom with the wet towel.

Julianne followed him with her eyes as he came back out of the bathroom and started rummaging through his bag.

She sat up on the bed and swung her legs over the side to get out.

"Oh no, forget about that. I'm not done with you yet."

Julianne turned her head toward him, and her eyes landed on the large box of condoms in his hand. Then, her gaze lowered to his groin, and her jaw slackened at the sight of his semierect member.

"Unless you don't feel up to it." The challenge in

his voice was softened by amusement.

Her channel chose that moment to clench, like it wanted to be filled again. "I feel up to it." She mumbled the words as she kept her eyes on his growing shaft. It was rising proudly from between his legs, already close to fully erect.

"Then wipe the drool off your chin, sweet pea, because I'm coming to get you."

Duncan moved over to the bed while taking a condom out of the box and tearing off the wrapper.

"Give it to me." Julianne stretched out her open hand toward him. "I'd like to put it on."

"Okay." Smiling, he put the condom in her hand and moved to stand in front of her.

His cock was fully erect, the skin stretched and shiny around the thick head. She closed one hand loosely around the base of his shaft and caressed slowly upward. His skin was so silky, and it felt so nice against her hand. It had felt nice against something else as well a little while ago. The thought made her shudder with remembered and anticipated pleasure.

"Julianne. If you want me inside you again and not going off in your hand like a teenager, you have to put the condom on me now and stop touching me."

Tipping her head back to look up at him, she pouted. "But I like touching you."

"And I'll be happy to let you touch me to your heart's content later, but right now I want to fill you again. And I'm not above begging." The heat in Duncan's eyes was amazing, but he didn't do anything, letting her decide what she wanted.

She put the condom against the straining head of his cock. Looking up into his face, she started rolling the tight sheath down his shaft. He shuddered as she smoothed her hands down him to finish the job.

"Okay. How would you like me?" Grinning up at him, she moved around on the bed until she was on her hands and knees in front of him.

His eyes were burning with desire as he climbed onto the bed and moved in behind her. Using his legs, he spread hers wider before nudging her entrance with his tip. But instead of entering her right away, he reached around and put a finger on her clit. He slid the finger down into her folds, coating it with moisture, before moving it back to her clit. She was still sensitive from all they had done and tried to squirm away from him, but he locked her in place by putting a hand on her hip and curling his big body over her back.

"Duncan." His name was like a prayer on her lips as he continued manipulating her sensitive button. Her channel started clenching, wanting to be filled, and she pushed her ass back against him. "Please, I need you inside me."

He didn't wait for her to ask him twice. Still holding her hip, he nudged into place at her opening before surging forward a couple of inches. She gasped as the head of his cock spread her wide open. He started moving using quick strokes until he was buried inside her to the hilt. Julianne was fisting the sheets in her hands and trying to support herself while her body was about to erupt with the pleasure Duncan was creating in her.

***

"Oh, Duncan."

Duncan grinned as he heard Julianne moaning his name again and again while he pounded into her tight, wet sheath. He wouldn't last much longer, but judging by the sounds she was making, she wouldn't either.

He changed his angle a little, and Julianne made a mewling sound as he felt her vaginal muscles start fluttering. One more thrust and her muscles clamped down on his cock like a vice, only a hell of a lot more pleasant.

Julianne screamed his name as she came apart, and he roared as he went with her. His shaft was stuck inside her as it jerked with his seed spilling. Pleasure pumped through his system, filling him with an ecstasy so potent his fangs lengthened. Nuzzling into her neck, he opened his jaws and enclosed her shoulder close to her clavicle and…stopped. He quickly turned his head to the side before biting down. On air.

Julianne screamed again as her sheath tightened with an extraordinary force. Duncan roared as his shaft was crushed so hard it bordered on pain. Pleasure tore through him even more violently than before, and he lost himself in the powerful orgasm that shook his body. He could feel his cock jumping wildly inside Julianne as she kept screaming, obviously in just as much ecstasy as he was.

When the orgasm eventually let him go, he was lying halfway on top of Julianne where she was sprawled on her stomach on the bed. They were both breathing hard, and he had a hard time convincing his body to move.

He managed to lift himself up on one elbow, and he looked down at the beautiful woman sprawled beneath him with a smile. They were dynamite together; there was no doubt about that.

Julianne still had her eyes closed, and Duncan took

the time to study her neck and shoulder to make sure he hadn't broken her skin. There was no sign of any scrapes or blood, and he breathed a sigh of relief. There might come a time when he decided to take a mate, even though he wouldn't be able to have his true mate. And the idea of mating Julianne didn't feel bad to him. It didn't feel bad at all. But this wasn't the time for that. He would have to be sure before asking her to become his mate.

He kissed across her shoulder to her neck before leaning in and whispering in her ear. "So beautiful."

Julianne smiled and cracked open an eye to look at him. "Thank you. You're not so bad yourself."

"Would you like a shower?"

She lifted an eyebrow. "Will you join me?"

He nodded and smiled down at her. His girlfriend. It felt amazing knowing that she was his.

"In that case you have to get off me."

He rolled off her and put his feet on the floor. Getting up, he moved toward the bathroom. "Are you coming?" He glanced at her over his shoulder and chuckled. She was still lying in the same position.

"Yes."

"Okay."

Duncan walked into the bathroom and turned on the shower before disposing of the condom. He stepped under the spray and just stood there, letting the water pour over his head and down his body.

A lot had happened in just a few days. From being a perpetual bachelor with no hope of being anything else, he suddenly had a girlfriend and was actually considering taking a mate. He might become a dad, after all, something he had thought was lost to him.

Just a few days and a remarkable woman had changed his life. He suddenly had everything he wanted. It didn't matter that she wasn't his true mate, because they were good together. Fantastic together even. And not just in bed.

Hands on his back startled him. Julianne had snuck up on him. He turned around slowly and smiled down at her. "Took you long enough."

She laughed. "Well, I think you have to blame yourself for that. You've worn me out."

"Already?" Duncan smirked at her.

But she didn't respond with a smart remark like he had expected. "I'm afraid so. I'm quite sore."

"Ah." He smiled down at her. It wasn't surprising with how tight she was. "I guess we'll get some sleep tonight after all."

Julianne tipped her head forward, hiding her face. "You're disappointed."

Closing the distance between them, Duncan put his arms around her and pulled her close. "No. We'll have plenty of sex, just not tonight. We'll…cuddle."

She chuckled and looked up at him. "You said that word like it's foreign to you."

"You mean cuddle?"

"Yes."

He cocked his head as he stared into her green eyes. "I'm not sure I really know what it means. I don't think I've cuddled before."

Julianne looked shocked as she stared up at him. "What? You've never cuddled with any of your previous girlfriends?"

Duncan shook his head. "I've never had a girlfriend before. I've never wanted one before you."

The look of shock on her face intensified as she stared at him. "How is that possible? Why? I mean you're... Please don't take this the wrong way. But you're old compared to me." She narrowed her eyes at him. "Someone hurt you. When you were young. That's why you've avoided relationships all these years. She obviously hurt you badly. What a bitch."

Duncan felt his jaw drop open in shock and surprise at her words. Julianne had just told him his life's story. Or close enough. It had been his choice to not even try to have a relationship with a woman after Sarah left. It had taken him a year to work up his nerve and get Sarah out of his system enough to actually have sex with another woman. And even then, it had felt wrong to him in the beginning. That feeling had faded over time, but he had never had any desire to spend time with a woman beyond sex. Until Julianne.

"I..." He hesitated, not sure how much to tell her. It was probably better not to mention that Sarah was his true mate. Julianne already knew about mates, and it might hurt her to know she would never be to him what Sarah could have been. Not that he wanted Sarah anymore. She had been, as Julianne so eloquently put it, a bitch. "You're right. I was seventeen and scrawny for my age, and she was the first woman who showed any interest in me. The first woman I had sex with." Just the thought left a sour taste in his mouth. "She ignored me after that, and ridiculed me when I finally plucked up the courage to ask her out. It destroyed me for a long time."

"An extremely long time apparently. If I ever get my hands on her, I'll kill her." Julianne's eyes were lit with fury on his behalf.

Duncan chuckled. It felt good to have someone care about him. Someone who knew how he had been treated and was angry because he was hurt. He probably should have told someone a long time ago, but it wasn't the pain that had stopped him. It was the thought of telling someone that he was so undesirable as a mate, that even his true mate wouldn't have him. And that was a fact he'd probably take to the grave with him. It was better that way.

"Have you seen her since she used you and stepped on your feelings? I hope she hasn't been around to terrorize you all these years."

"No. I moved to America six months after she ditched me, and I came back just a couple of years ago. Last I heard, she was mated to a wolf down in Wales."

"Good. At least she's far away. So, she's a wolf like you?" Julianne was studying his face, most likely trying see his reaction to her question.

"Yes." He smiled down at her. "But let's forget about all that. I'm lucky to have found you, and I want to focus on us." Leaning down, he gave her a soft kiss before pulling back. "It's time to get clean, I think."

"Yes. I wouldn't mind scrubbing your back. And other things." Grinning, she reached for the bodywash. "Turn around."

Duncan obliged with a smile. "So bossy."

Her hands slid over his wet skin, spreading soap all over his back before moving down to his ass. That part of his body was apparently much dirtier than his back, judging by the time it took to clean. His traitorous cock was reacting to her soft hands gliding over his skin, and he was already at half-mast by the time she ordered him to turn around.

Julianne ignored his swelling shaft and started cleaning his chest, paying a lot of attention to each muscle from his shoulders to his abs. By the time she started washing his legs, still ignoring his groin area, his cock was rock hard.

When she was done with his legs and feet, she moved to his arms, and Duncan couldn't help the groan that escaped him. He had been hoping she would focus on another dirty part of his body first.

She looked up at him with a stern expression, but he noticed the way she was biting her trembling lower lip to keep from laughing. Julianne knew exactly what she was doing to him, and she was loving it.

With his arms finished, she poured more bodywash into her hand, but before touching his body she grinned up at him. "Or perhaps you would like me to wash your hair first?"

"Julianne, please touch me." His voice had a growl to it, and his request sounded more like a command.

Slowly, very slowly, she reached out toward his throbbing member. She closed one hand around his stem and squeezed a little, before coating his swollen shaft in bodywash.

Duncan shuddered at her touch. His cock was a bit sensitive after the amazing sex they had just been having, and he groaned with the incredible sensations building in him as she slid her hand up and down his length.

"Julianne." His knees were turning to jelly, and he put a hand on the wall to support himself. He wasn't sure he'd be able to stand through this, but he'd try.

She increased her pace, squeezing his straining shaft a little as her hand moved up and down. He was close to release, and his legs were shaking with the powerful sensations Julianne was creating in him. When he felt her other hand cup his balls and massage gently, he plummeted over the edge.

Duncan was vaguely aware that he sank to his knees as his cock started spilling his seed in hard spurts. Julianne was holding his jerking member as pleasure surged through him and swirled through his body. When his orgasm slowly faded away, he opened his eyes to find Julianne on her knees in front of him. She was looking at him with heat in her beautiful green eyes, clearly affected by what she had done to him.

"Sweet pea, thank you. That was amazing. You're amazing. Do you want me to do something for you?"

Looking away from him, she shook her head. "I'm sore. I don't think—"

He didn't let her finish. "Even your clit? I'll be gentle."

Swinging her gaze back to him, she studied his face for a few seconds, seeming to consider his offer.

Getting up on shaky legs, Duncan reached a hand down to Julianne to help her up. When she was standing in front of him, he leaned in and kissed her slowly, gently. She opened her mouth and sighed when their tongues tangled and caressed each other. Slowly, he maneuvered her around and pressed her against the wall. He reached between them and slid his hand slowly down her belly until he reached the apex of her thighs. Gently, he pressed his thumb against her clit.

Julianne didn't react like it was uncomfortable, but he didn't want to take any chances.

"Does it feel okay, or is your clit sore as well?"

"It feels good." Her voice was a bit huskier than

normal.

"Do you want my mouth on you?"

She nodded. "Yes, please."

Duncan smiled as he kneeled in front of her, and Julianne followed him with her eyes. He focused his attention on her pleasure button.

Using his hands, he spread her open before leaning in. He started sucking gently on the small nub, and Julianne gasped and squirmed.

"Hold still, sweet pea." Pressing her more firmly against the wall, he flicked his tongue against her rapidly, and she moaned and tried to squirm out of his grip.

"It's too good, Duncan. I'm close."

Well, that was fast. She was obviously extra sensitive as well. He vibrated his tongue against her clit, and she squirmed and uttered small cries, but he kept going. Then, she screamed and fisted her hands into his hair as her body shook with her orgasm. He gentled the vibration of his tongue against her but didn't stop until her body sagged against the wall.

"Don't let me go. I don't think I can stand yet," Julianne whispered.

Duncan chuckled as he looked up into her face and met her hooded eyes. A sight he was going to see often if he had any say in the matter.

He rose to his feet while keeping his hands on Julianne, holding her against the wall so she wouldn't fall. As soon as he stood before her, he took her in his arms and just held her. It was so nice having her body close to his, skin to skin, just feeling her soft body against his hard one. He had a feeling he'd like cuddling with Julianne. Just having her close and knowing that she was happy and safe.

She tipped her head back and looked up at him. "Shall we finish our shower?" A small smile was playing on her lips.

Duncan nodded. "But I think it might be best if we don't wash each other, or we'll never get out of here. We've probably used most of the hot water already, so…" He let his sentence hang.

"Agreed. Why don't you finish first, since you were almost done before we got carried away."

He smirked. "You mean you got carried away. I just let you clean my body."

"Oh really? I seem to remember someone begging me to touch his hard cock." Julianne lifted an eyebrow at him in a challenge.

"I didn't say that."

"It was implied."

"Says you."

"Well, I'll keep that in mind. Next time I'll just go ahead and wash your hair instead."

Duncan laughed. "Okay, you win. I can't risk you not wanting to touch me next time."

Julianne smiled and shook her head at him. "Too easy. Now get under the shower."

"Yes, ma'am."

Duncan quickly shampooed and rinsed his hair and washed off the remnants of their shower activities. Then, he got out to allow Julianne time to wash. He toweled off quickly and went into their bedroom. After putting on fresh clothes, he sat down on the bed to wait for Julianne to finish.

When she came out of the bathroom, her wet hair was hanging down over her shoulders. She smiled at him before bending over her bag.

Duncan's gaze traveled over her curves, taking in the vision of her like he had never done before. Whenever they had been naked together, or partially naked, they had always been so desperate for each other that he had never really taken the time to study her naked form. And what he saw was perfection. Every part of her body appealed to him, and it was nice just being able to appreciate the sight of her without instantly losing control. Duncan still wanted her, but not with the uncontrollable desire from before. He was in control, and the fact that he knew she was his might have something to do with it.

"What do you think the others are thinking?" Julianne glanced at him as she started dressing. "We disappeared again. I'm sure they know exactly what we've been up to. At least with the noise we've been making." A blush crept over her face.

Duncan chuckled. "Oh, they know exactly what we've been doing. But if you think for a minute that they disapprove, you're wrong. They're happy for us. Sure, they might give us a hard time about it, but that's just a sign that they care. And I've been giving them a hard time, so they're kind of obligated to hand it back to me now that they've got the chance. So if anything, you have to blame me."

"Well, that makes me feel better." Julianne lifted an eyebrow at him in mock irritation.

He rose from the bed and closed the distance between them before giving her a light kiss on her lips. "I'll protect you, sweet pea. You're my girlfriend now, so you're mine to care for and protect."

The warm glow in her eyes hit Duncan directly in

his chest, igniting a warmth that spread to cover his whole body. It wasn't a sexual kind of heat but something else. Something he had never felt before, and it felt good. It caused him to throw his arms around Julianne and pull her close. He should probably let her go so she could finish dressing, but he needed a few more seconds or minutes or… He didn't know. Duncan had no experience with this feeling of need that wasn't desire.

CHAPTER 17

Sabrina knew it was time to get up and face the others again. She had stayed in her room for too long already, but she just hadn't been able to pluck up the courage to see Leith again.

The sight of him shirtless circled through her mind, like it had done countless times during the last few hours she had been hiding in this room. She had been right the first time she laid eyes on him. His torso had been corded with muscles, each of them defined and well developed yet not overwhelming. More like a swimmer than a bodybuilder. Mouthwatering.

She hadn't been able to hide her reaction to the sight of him, and he had noticed her openmouthed staring. Even enjoyed it. Or at least that was the feeling she got.

After that Sabrina had needed a place to hide for a while. To get her bearings, clear her head, and try to forget the effect Leith had on her. Instead, he had offered to show her the room he had assigned to her, on the same level of the house as his own. He hadn't given her a chance to refuse his offer, and she probably wouldn't have refused it even if he had given her a chance to do so. It would have been discourteous. And she couldn't be impolite and ungrateful to Leith. He was a decent and honorable man, treating everyone around him with respect and care.

Leith had walked ahead of her down the stairs to the lower level of the house, carrying her bag like it weighed no more than a feather. He was a shifter of some kind, an alpha, but his comment about being a special case had intrigued her. Sabrina would have liked to ask him what he'd meant by that, but she wouldn't. Any interest she showed toward him might result in him asking questions about her. And that was something she wanted to avoid at all costs.

The room was small but beautiful. Unlike the other rooms she had seen in his house so far, the walls were painted. And instead of elaborate carvings, the walls were covered in paintings. Not the framed kind of paintings, but detailed paintings created directly on the walls, of fish and sea creatures and the world below the surface of the ocean. She had been taken by them instantly, almost forgetting the man in the room with her. Until he spoke.

"I built this house for my future mate, decorating it to please her. Hoping that it would help me persuade her to accept me, if I was ever lucky enough to find her." Leith's voice had been even and warm.

Sabrina hadn't known how to respond to Leith's words, so personal yet presented in such a straightforward manner. So she didn't say anything, just kept studying the paintings on the walls.

"This room is intended for any children we may be blessed with."

Spine stiffening, she'd stared at the wall, no longer seeing the paintings. *We.* He had said *we.* He couldn't have meant… And of course, he didn't. It was a statement that included his mate. It had nothing to do with her, Sabrina.

She'd let out a shaky breath, and consciously forced her body to relax before turning to him. Pasting what she hoped was a pleasant smile on her face, she spoke in a surprisingly calm and controlled voice. "Your mate will be a lucky woman. I hope she'll appreciate all this. You've put so much of yourself into this house. It's the most beautiful house I've ever seen, both inside and out."

"Thank you, Sabrina. You honor me with your words." Leith bowed his head a little while keeping his gaze locked with hers. "Now I will leave you to rest, my angel."

He'd backed slowly out of the room while watching her and closed the door softly behind him.

She had been left standing there, her mind still spinning with his words and all their possible implications. Her gut was telling her that Leith had chosen his words carefully. That there had been intention behind every word. And she had learned to trust her gut. It was seldom wrong. But she didn't want to understand the meaning of his words, and his true intention behind them.

Sabrina sighed as she pushed her thoughts to the back of her head. It was time to face the others.

A knock on her bedroom door startled her, and the

thought of Leith on the other side of the door had her nervously smoothing her hair back from her face.

"Sabrina?" Julianne's voice sounded through the door.

She breathed out, realizing she had been holding her breath. "Yes, just come in."

Julianne opened the door and smiled. Her hair was wet from swimming or a shower or both. Happiness seemed to radiate out from her pores. There was no doubt that Duncan was making Julianne happy.

∞∞∞

Duncan walked into the kitchen to find Trevor and Leith at the kitchen table. Through the windows he spotted Jennie sitting on the terrace speaking on her phone.

"What happened to Michael and Steph? Have they checked in after lunch at all?"

Trevor chuckled. "I wouldn't speak that loudly if I was you. They turned up right after you went for a swim, but swimming was just an excuse for you, wasn't it?"

Duncan laughed. "Not really, but I guess we got a bit carried away. I…" He stopped. Should he tell them that Julianne had agreed to be his girlfriend? It was very new, but Trevor and Leith were his best friends, and probably the people who knew him best. If he couldn't tell them, who could he tell? "I asked Julianne to be my girlfriend, and she accepted. We needed some time to ourselves after that."

Surprise registered on Trevor's face. "Girlfriend." It was more a statement than a question.

Leith's expression was unreadable as he studied Duncan's face.

"Yes." Duncan nodded. He was grinning like an idiot, and he knew it. But that was how Julianne made him feel. Unbelievably happy.

"I am happy for you, my friend." Leith stared at him. "Love has found you at last."

Duncan froze. He hadn't said that. He hadn't mentioned the L-word at all. What was between him and Julianne was fantastic. It might never qualify as… He couldn't even bring himself to think the word. That was something reserved for true mates. But he didn't need it. Julianne was amazing, and what they had was more than he had ever thought he'd have. It was all he wanted.

"Why are you looking shocked and uncomfortable, my friend? Is she not your true mate?" Leith kept staring at him in that uncanny way he did sometimes. Like he knew something Duncan didn't.

"No, she's not my true mate." Duncan swallowed. This wasn't something he wanted to discuss, but he didn't see any way around it.

"You seem very certain. How can you be this sure that she is not?"

"I…" Duncan looked down at the table, unable to meet Leith's eyes. "I met my true mate years ago. When I was young. She didn't want me. I wasn't good enough for her."

Trevor sucked in a breath and swore.

"But you have asked Julianne to be your girlfriend, knowing she is not your true mate?" Leith didn't let up with his questions.

Duncan nodded. "Yes, and I'll treat her right even

if she's not..." He paused, not sure how to end the sentence. After a few seconds of silence, Duncan lifted his gaze and met Leith's stare. "I care about Julianne, even though she's not my true mate. It's even crossed my mind to ask her to be my mate one day, and the thought appeals to me. I think we would be good together. I know I must be a bad person to be able to consider mating another after meeting my true mate, but so be it. That's just something I have to accept about myself. If I hadn't met my true mate, there would've been nothing unusual about it. Shifters take mates that aren't their true mates all the time. Finding your one and only isn't that common."

Trevor frowned. "When exactly did you meet your true mate?"

"About six months before I went to America."

"So you were about..." Trevor stopped.

"Seventeen. She was a couple of years older than me."

Leith put the glass he had been holding onto the table and leaned forward. "She was the woman who introduced you to the lure of a woman's body." It wasn't a question.

Duncan nodded slowly. "Yes, I... She was the first woman to show any interest in me. I fell for her instantly." The thought made him wrinkle his nose in distaste. "But when I told her that she was my true mate, she called me immature and stupid. After that she wanted nothing to do with me."

Leith stared into his eyes. "There is a simple solution to this. I will call your true mate and invite her here. She can explain why she chose not to accept you all those years ago. I am sure she must have had compelling reasons not to. I am sure Julianne will understand. I will comfort your girlfriend while you—"

Duncan was up and around the table in less than a second, his face an inch from Leith's. "Julianne's mine. You'll never touch her." Nobody was going to comfort Julianne other than himself. Ever. Leith was supposed to be his friend. What the hell was he playing at?

"Oh." Leith raised an eyebrow at him. "Julianne is yours?"

Duncan frowned. "Yes." He'd already said that. What was wrong with Leith?

"But what if your true mate would like you to share her bed? Play with her—"

"Stop." Duncan took a step back and almost gagged. The thought of… No, he couldn't even think about it.

"Julianne." Leith uttered his girlfriend's name, and Duncan felt his stomach settle. Then his friend continued. "All these years you have mistaken infatuation for love. Just because a woman shows you some interest and introduces you to the world of pleasure, does not mean that she will be important to you for the rest of your life. You even feel sick at the thought of touching her now."

Duncan stared at Leith, not sure if he understood what Leith was talking about. He had managed to suppress his need for his true mate. That didn't exactly mark him as a good shifter.

"Yet the mere mention of Julianne's name calms you. She makes you happy, and you have no trouble showing your friends that fact. And you would happily fight me, your friend, if I touched her. Before you mate her, I think it would be good for you to have sex with another woman just to—"

Bile rose in Duncan's throat. "Stop! I'll never have sex with anyone else."

Leith just stared at him. "Because Julianne is yours."

"Yes, Julianne is mine. Forever. I don't want anyone else. Please understand." Duncan was getting fed up.

Leith snorted. A sound unusual for him. "I understand perfectly, my friend. Do you?"

Duncan frowned.

Trevor laughed. "You're just as dense as I was with Jennie. She's your mate, you dimwit. Julianne's your true mate."

Duncan stared at Trevor before turning to Leith. They were both staring back at him. Trevor with a big grin on his face and Leith with one corner of his mouth curved slightly upward. His mind was spinning with Trevor's last words. Could it be correct? Was Julianne his true mate? His heart warmed at the thought, like it had known all along. The warmth spread through his chest as Julianne filled his mind. Her laughter, her snark, her screams of pleasure. His. She was his. Truly his.

"Mine. She's mine." Duncan wasn't sure he had said the words aloud.

"Yes, she is." Leith nodded.

"I have to tell her." Duncan hurried out of the kitchen as he uttered the words.

Julianne felt numb as she walked along the road. Duncan had asked her to be his girlfriend. His first ever girlfriend. It had meant something. At least she had thought that it meant that she was special to him somehow. Even after such a short time, a couple of days, she had counted on him caring about her. She had been so sure of it.

The conversation she had overheard between Duncan and Leith in the kitchen had changed that. It kept replaying over and over in her mind.

"I am happy for you, my friend. Love has found you at last." Leith's voice mentioning love had made her stop before entering the kitchen.

There had been a pause, and she had just decided to move when Leith continued. "Why are you looking shocked and uncomfortable, my friend? Is she not your true mate?"

"No, she's not my true mate." Duncan's serious voice made her heartrate speed up.

"You seem very certain. How can you be this sure that she is not?" For some reason Leith was pushing Duncan.

"I… I met my true mate years ago. When I was young. She didn't want me. I wasn't good enough for her."

Someone gasped and swore. It sounded like Trevor, but Julianne wasn't sure.

"But you have asked Julianne to be your girlfriend, knowing she is not your true mate?" Leith's words made tears prick in Julianne's eyes. Apparently, that wasn't a good thing.

"Yes, and I'll treat her right even if she's not."

Julianne hadn't been able to stay and listen any

longer. Silently, she'd walked down the hallway and out the front door, before hurrying up the drive to the road.

She had been walking for a few minutes, and Fort Augustus was visible in the distance. Hopefully, she would be able to get there before anyone noticed she was gone. She needed time to process the shock of knowing she was second rate to Duncan. There was no doubt as to who his true mate was. He had already told Julianne about the woman who broke his heart when he was seventeen. He had just failed to mention the woman was his true mate. And that changed everything.

Julianne wasn't sure why she was reacting so badly to the news that Duncan had a past love. A lot of humans had loved and lost, yet still found new love that lasted for many years, even for the rest of their lives sometimes. But that was just it. A human could find love again, but she wasn't so sure that a shifter could. From the conversation she had overheard, it sounded like love was something that was unique for a true mate, which meant that Duncan would never be able to love her. He cared about her, Julianne was quite sure about that, but he would never love her. Not like she loved him. And that was the problem. Why she had reacted too much. Julianne had already fallen in love with him, even after such a short time, and it hurt that Duncan would never feel the same way about her.

The big question she needed to answer was: Would she be able to stay with him knowing that he would never love her back? And the answer was that she didn't know. It might be best to cut all ties immediately, while the relationship was still young. Forget about him somehow, the most amazing man she had ever met.

A car slowed down beside her, and she automatically took a step to the side, out of the road. She kept her face turned away from the car. Her heartrate sped as she realized it must be Duncan or one of his friends.

"Do you need a lift?" It was a woman's voice, and not one she had ever heard before.

Julianne turned her head and took in the woman smiling at her. There was no one else in the car besides the woman, and Julianne felt herself relax. Slowly, she nodded. A lift to the village would be good. She would get there faster. Hopefully, Julianne could find a place to hide for a while, until she could think this whole thing through and decide what to do next.

Opening the passenger side door, she got in. "Thank you for giving me a lift." Julianne swiped at her cheeks to remove her tears before turning to the woman. She was beautiful, with long red-gold hair and deep-green eyes. Her clothes were elegant. The white blouse she was wearing was shimmering like it had gold threads woven into the material, and the long green skirt was made in a similar fabric. It made Julianne feel underdressed and mousy in comparison, but she hadn't exactly dressed for a party.

The woman glanced at Julianne as she drove toward the village. "I'm staying in a little cottage in Fort Augustus. Why don't you come with me to freshen up a little? You seem a little worse for wear, if I might say so. You have obviously been through an ordeal."

"I…" Julianne debated her options. She didn't

know this woman, and she wasn't sure that it was a good idea to accept the woman's offer. But what choice did she have? Julianne hadn't brought any money, so hiding out in a café or a restaurant wasn't an option. "Thank you. That's very nice of you. I won't stay long."

The woman smiled. "Long enough for a cup of tea, I hope. It would do you good."

Julianne nodded. "Yes. A cup of tea sounds nice. Thank you."

"Then it's settled."

CHAPTER 18

Duncan stared at the people gathered in the kitchen. Everyone was there. Everyone except Julianne. He had checked every room in the house. Twice. Even checked outside. She wasn't there. The last one to have seen her was Sabrina, but that was half an hour ago. Julianne had only checked in with her friend for a couple of minutes before going up to the kitchen. Or so she had claimed. But why hadn't she shown up? He had been in the kitchen with Leith and Trevor talking about… The conversation ran through his head, and he felt his body go cold.

"She must've heard us. When we talked. You asked me about love." He stared at Leith. "I said that Julianne isn't my true mate, but I'd treat her right. Fuck! She probably thinks I only want her because I can't have the one I want. Like a replacement. She probably left before she heard the end of our conversation. Julianne doesn't know that I love her. She thinks I don't care about her, that she's just a pastime for me." He stared around the room at all the concerned faces. "I fucked up. Please help me find her."

"Of course." Trevor spoke, and the other people in the room nodded in agreement. "But we need a plan."

"Yes, we—" Duncan's phone rang, and he ripped it out of his pocket. *It might be…* Callum's name was showing on the screen. He felt himself frowning as he debated whether to answer the call. Duncan didn't care about information about Steven right at the moment, but Callum might be able to help in his search for Julianne.

"Callum."

"Hi, Duncan. I thought you'd like to know—"

Duncan didn't have time for Callum to finish. "Callum. I don't care about Steven right now. Julianne is missing. I need your help finding her. Can you help me?"

"Of course. I'll do whatever I can. Do you have any idea where she might be headed?"

Duncan sighed. He was such an idiot. If only he had understood that Julianne was special a little earlier. If only he hadn't been such a blue-eyed baby when he met Sarah. If only… But this was not the time for self-reproach and regrets. "We're just outside Fort Augustus at Leith's place. She—"

Callum didn't let him finish. "You're what? That's where Steven is. He arrived a couple of hours ago. Still there as far as I know. I'll check to make sure."

Duncan felt his heart stutter as fear crept up his spine. His skin itched as his wolf wanted to come out to look for his mate. Protect his mate. "Please check and tell me exactly where Steven is." He met Sabrina's worried gaze, and her eyes narrowed in anger when she understood what he was saying.

"He's…" Callum stopped. "Fuck! He's been moving around the central area of Fort Augustus since he arrived. Not staying in one place for any amount of time. Five minutes ago he turned off his cell phone. I can't pinpoint his location. I'll try local cameras in the area and see if can find him that way. It'll take me a little while. I'm so sorry."

"No, this is not your fault, Callum. It's mine. Just tell me if you find out anything useful. I have to go."

"I'll get back to you soon. Good luck in your search."

"Thank you." Duncan ended the call and stared at Sabrina. "Steven is here. Has been for a couple of hours. If he sees Julianne, he'll take her. I have no doubt about that."

"I can find her." Sabrina stared at Duncan.

"Steven, as in her ex?" Trevor frowned.

Duncan swore. "Yes, Steven is Julianne's ex. Panther. Asshole. Wants her back. He's been following her. Now he's here in Fort Augustus. Has been for a couple of hours. I've got no idea how he's been able to track her here, since her phone is turned off. We have to find Julianne. Now. Before he does."

Sabrina turned to Leith. "You have to help me. Add your power to mine so I can pinpoint her location."

Leith nodded. "Of course, my angel. I am at your disposal."

"Thank you. Let's use the living room downstairs."

Duncan spoke as he watched Sabrina and Leith move away. "Sabrina, do you need more help?"

She shook her head and glanced at him over her shoulder. "No, Leith's help will be enough."

Duncan nodded and turned to the remaining people gathered in the kitchen. Trevor, Jennie, Michael, and Steph were all ready to help him find Julianne. "Let's go to Fort Augustus. If I were Julianne, that's where I'd go if I wanted to get away from here. And Steven is there, so if we find him first that'll help too. At least we can make sure that he doesn't have Julianne, and if he does… Well." He didn't need to elaborate on what he would do to Steven if the panther had his mate. Everyone in the room knew it wouldn't be pretty.

"Do you have a picture of Steven?" Jennie's eyes clearly showed her concern. "We don't know what he looks like."

Duncan swore. "Of course, you don't. Give me a second." He quickly texted Callum to ask if he had a picture of Steven or could find one.

It only took a few seconds before Callum sent him a photo of the asshole panther, and Duncan distributed it to everybody in the room.

"Okay. Let's go." Duncan strode out the door.

∞∞∞∞

Julianne followed the woman into the small cottage. The way she saw, it the cottage wasn't in Fort Augustus as the woman had claimed. It was remotely located in a wooded area to the north of the village. There were a couple of houses nearby, but they weren't within sight of the cottage. Julianne should have made the woman stop on the way out of the village, but it had felt a little awkward since the woman had been so nice to her. And how dangerous could one woman be, anyway?

They entered a tiny hallway before moving into the combined kitchen and living room. It was tastefully decorated but seemed to lack any personal touches. The woman bid Julianne to sit at the kitchen table, before putting the kettle on and placing two mugs on the table.

"Are you feeling better?" The woman sat down on the other side of the table, leaning forward and staring at Julianne intently like she wanted to know what had happened to her.

Julianne felt herself frowning. She had no intention of telling this woman anything about herself or what was going on. "Not really, but a cup of tea will be nice."

The woman stared at Julianne for a few seconds before sighing and sitting back. "I'm afraid I haven't been entirely honest with you, and I'll tell you why in a minute. First, I would like to introduce myself. My name is Ambrosia."

Julianne rose so fast she almost stumbled. She ran for the door. But just as she moved through the doorway, she crashed into a big form.

Stumbling back, she almost fell as someone snarled.

"You let the wolf fuck you." Steven's voice rose as he spoke, ending in a shout.

Julianne froze, staring in disbelief at Steven. What was he doing there? How did he know where to find her? She shivered as ice seemed to wrap around her spine. Julianne had turned off her phone and not turned it on even once since they left Mallaig the day before. But Steven had found her, anyway. And he was with... It all fell into place. Ambrosia was a witch. She probably knew how to locate a person. But why would she bother to help Steven? As far as Julianne knew her ex wasn't anyone special.

Julianne frowned when she noticed that Steven had stopped moving. His face was calm, and his eyes a bit unfocused like he was in a trance. Ambrosia had said something right after Steven yelled. But Julianne had been too stunned at the sight of Steven to catch the words Ambrosia had uttered.

"I believe he is rather annoyed with you for cheating on him with another shifter." Ambrosia stepped into view as she moved to stand next to Steven.

Julianne snorted. There was nothing remotely funny about this situation, but she couldn't help her exasperated laughter. Probably a sign that she was going crazy, but so be it. She deserved to go crazy after everything that had happened the last couple of days.

Then anger took over. "Steven is a possessive asshole. I left him three months ago, and I haven't looked back even once. I don't care if he's paid you to help him find me. He can go to hell and stay there."

"Well, to be honest I don't care how you feel about him." Ambrosia's eyes were cold as she stared at Julianne. "He wants you as his mate, and I'll make that happen. Whether you'll mate him willingly or not is up to you."

"What?" Julianne felt fear and anger swirl inside her, not sure which emotion would take over. She wanted it to be anger. It was better than fear.

"I'll wake him now. I suggest you go sit on the

couch." The witch stared at Julianne. "He'll probably want to hit you, and I'd like to prevent that."

Julianne's anger was winning. "Just let me go outside, and that won't be a problem."

Ambrosia just stared at her. "If you want me to let him beat you up before he mates you, that's fine."

Duncan had called this woman evil, and Julianne was just realizing how right he was. Backing up slowly, she went to sit down on the couch. She was stuck there, apparently the next victim to be used by Ambrosia to gain power. But Julianne would fight with everything she had to avoid being mated to Steven. She would just have to bide her time for a suitable opportunity to get away.

"Steven." Ambrosia spoke in a calm voice.

The man frowned like he was just waking up and realizing where he was. "Julianne." He moved his gaze a little sluggishly around the kitchen area before turning toward the living room. Anger flashed in his eyes when he spotted her on the couch. "You reek of wolf. How can you expect me to fuck you when you stink of wolf?"

Disbelief and disgust filled Julianne as she felt her jaw slacken.

It must have shown on her face, because Steven's features contorted in rage, and he yelled at her. "Why do you look at me like that? I'm much better than a wolf. And I'll prove it to you. You know you love my cock inside you."

A calm descended over Julianne as she sat there listening to Steven rant in desperation. Because that was what he looked like. A desperate man. She had no idea why, but he wanted her to say yes to him. It was important to him that she accept him. And for some strange reason, she felt sorry for her ex.

Julianne spoke to him in a calm voice. Her anger was gone, at least temporarily. "I'm sorry, Steven, but I don't love you. I never have and never will and mating you won't change that fact. I'll just resent you even more for forcing me into something I don't want. By mating me you'll make both our lives miserable. Is that really what you want?"

Steven hesitated and swung his gaze to Ambrosia. "Can't you make her love me? Admire me?"

Shaking her head once, the witch spoke. "No, but you'll gain a lot of power. You'll be king of the panthers. That's far more valuable than love." Ambrosia wrinkled her nose in disgust as she uttered the last word. "And don't let her fool you into believing that she won't care about you once you're mated. She will, she just doesn't know it yet."

∞∞∞∞

Sabrina was sitting cross-legged on the floor in Leith's living room. The man himself was sitting directly in front of her with his hands on her knees. That way they had eye contact, and he could support her with his power. She could have done this on her own, but having access to someone else's power would increase the momentum of the locating spell as well as the precision of the results.

She had explained to Leith what she was going to do. Calling it a locating spell was misleading since a spell implied the use of words. There were no words involved in this process, only power. A lot of power. It might have been more natural to ask Steph to help her with this, since Steph was a fellow witch. But being supported by another witch who had just discovered what she was and didn't know the extent of her power, was a risk Sabrina didn't want to take. Leith had control of his power. It was smooth and even and solid. And most importantly, Sabrina trusted him.

Staring into Leith's dark-green eyes, she nodded once. "I'll start now. Just give me your power evenly, not too much in the beginning."

"Okay." He kept his eyes on her. "Anything you need me to do, just tell me."

She nodded before closing her eyes and picturing Julianne in her mind. Using her power, Sabrina reached for her friend, trying to get to her. Focusing on Julianne's image, she tried to see her features and her surroundings in more detail.

Leith's power started flowing into her knees and up through her body. It was smooth, warm and strong, like it was geared toward making her feel good.

Sabrina focused more intently, drawing on Leith's power, feeling it blending with her own and sharpening the image of Julianne. It was like looking into a microscope and adjusting the knobs until the image gradually came into perfect focus.

Julianne was sitting on a couch in a living room. She looked calm and unharmed. There were two people in the room with her. A woman and a man. Sabrina recognized the man. It was Steven. Zooming out, she could see the house from above, a bit like an aerial photo. Zooming out even more, she saw the small house and the landscape surrounding it. Sabrina repeated the process a few times until she was sure she knew the exact location of the small house.

Letting her power decrease, she opened her eyes to stare directly into Leith's glowing emerald orbs. They were so beautiful she could easily have forgotten where she was and what she was doing. But she didn't have time for that. Clearing her throat, she spoke. "I know where she is."

"Good." Leith's voice was darker than before, and the sound raced through her body to settle between her legs. That was when she noticed how wet she was, and her clit felt swollen and achy like she was already halfway to an orgasm. Gasping at the feeling, she felt a pulse of power shoot from Leith's hands on her knees to her center, pushing her need even higher.

"No!" Sabrina pushed Leith's hands away from her knees and scooted back away from him.

His eyes widened in surprise and shock before he quickly looked away from her. "I am sorry. I am so sorry, my angel. I did not mean to…" His voice faded before he got up off the floor and adjusted his shirt.

Sabrina's eyes lingered on his crotch for a couple of seconds too long. He had adjusted his shirt to cover that area of his body, but not before she had seen the long thick ridge through the fabric of his shorts. He was obviously just as affected by the power they had used as she was.

This whole situation was thoroughly embarrassing, but Sabrina didn't have time to worry about that at the moment. "I know where Julianne is." She pulled out her phone and found the map with a satellite image showing the area around Fort Augustus. Zooming in, she pointed at the house where her friend was. "Here. In this house. Steven is there, along with a woman I've never seen before."

Leith nodded once. "I will call Duncan and give him directions." Leith extracted his phone from his pocket. Duncan answered immediately, and Leith told his friend exactly where to go before hanging up.

Sabrina stared up at Leith as he ended the call. "Are they far away? Do you think they'll find the house without our help?" Perhaps she should go as well, just to make sure they found the correct house? She was convinced Duncan would move heaven and earth to find Julianne, but she was worried that he might get the directions wrong.

Leith looked into her eyes and lifted his hand as if to touch her arm. Then he seemed to think better of it and let his hand drop to his side. "They will find her. It will only take a few minutes. Do not worry, my angel." He sighed and looked away for a second before bringing his gaze back to hers. "Please accept my sincere apology for using my power to…" The man seemed unsure how to complete the sentence. He took a deep breath and started again. "My actions were deplorable. Please tell me what I can do to recompense for my inappropriate behavior."

Sabrina kept her eyes on him. It seemed out of character for him not to know exactly what to say in a given situation. He was so calm and collected all the time and always in total control. She had a feeling he was just as rattled by what had just happened between them as she was, and that being flustered wasn't something Leith was used to.

Smiling up at him, she wanted to put a hand on his arm to reassure him, but she didn't. It was better not to tempt fate by touching him again. "Let's just forget that ever happened. I don't know about you, but I've never experienced that kind of…side effect before when using my power. I wasn't prepared for it, and I'm guessing you weren't either."

The corner of Leith's mouth lifted a little as he stared at her with what looked like relief in his eyes. "Thank you, my angel. You are too generous in forgiving my violation. Can I do something for you? Would you like a cup of coffee or tea, or perhaps something stronger?"

Sabrina nodded, trying to keep her concern for Julianne from taking over. There was nothing else she could do at the moment. Duncan and his friends were close, and they were going to find her. "Yes, please, I think I need some coffee."

∞∞∞∞

Julianne sat on the couch, watching the exchange between Steven and Ambrosia. The witch was giving him a pep talk of sorts, appealing to his pride and natural craving for power and control. And Julianne could see he was letting Ambrosia convince him. It had surprised Julianne when Steven had wanted her to love him as well as mate him, but it was most likely his pride telling him he deserved to be admired. The Steven she knew was ruled by his pride.

There was one question Julianne had forgotten to ask Duncan, and this was the time to find out. Her heart constricted in pain as she thought of the amazing man, but she quickly pushed all that to the back of her mind to deal with later. This wasn't the time. "Can one of you please tell me how mating is actually performed?"

Steven turned his head toward her and smiled. It wasn't a nice smile but one filled with triumph, like he had just won. "About time you realize who you belong to."

Rolling her eyes at his stupidity and pride, Julianne asked again. "How is a mating performed? I'm not a shifter, so I don't know. Can I please have the facts?" She made no attempt to hide the disgust and anger she was feeling.

Steven sneered at her before answering her question. "I fuck you and bite you."

Julianne was stunned. She had hoped that wasn't how mating happened, counting on it actually. Quite sure that something as permanent as mating would have to require more than sex and a bite. "And when you say bite, what exactly do you mean?"

Steven narrowed his eyes at her. "Why all the questions, Julianne? Afraid of the pain?" There was a glint of something vicious in his eyes.

Shaking her head slowly, she decided to appeal to his pride. "Sounds to me like you don't know the answer."

Snarling, Steven took a step toward her before Ambrosia put a hand on his arm to stop him.

"He will bite you hard enough to draw blood." The witch looked at Julianne with irritation visible in her expression. "Now. Enough questions. It's time."

Steven took a couple of steps toward Julianne as he ripped his shirt off.

Julianne didn't move, just kept her eyes on Ambrosia as she spoke. "In that case I'm already mated." Her heart was breaking as she let herself realize the truth of it, but she tried to keep any emotions from showing on her face.

"What?" Steven's eyes widened in shock as he stared at her.

Ambrosia's lips thinned as she was clearly fighting her anger at Julianne's words. "Steven would've smelled it on you if you were."

"Can you smell it within a few hours of it happening?" While she spoke, Julianne swiped her hair back from her shoulder and pulled down the collar of her shirt just enough to show the small cut on her collarbone.

"No." Steven was suddenly in front of her, still looking shocked. He leaned down and sniffed at her throat.

Julianne froze, afraid to move a muscle as his mouth and nose touched her skin. If he decided to attack her, there was nothing she could do about it. He would have her throat ripped out before she even knew what was happening.

A strange cry came out of Steven's mouth as he stumbled several steps back away from her. His expression was one of disbelief and, if she didn't know better, hurt.

The only reasonable explanation was that she was right. Julianne was mated. To Duncan. Who didn't love her, and would never love her. Because she wasn't the woman he really wanted. Even if Duncan came to care for her because she was his mate, it wouldn't be the same. In fact, it would be worse.

Julianne started as Ambrosia suddenly rushed across the living room, threw open one of the windows, and jumped out.

CHAPTER 19

Duncan was out of the car before it came to a stop, running at full speed into the small house. He would kill the fucking panther if he had laid a hand on Julianne.

After barreling into the kitchen, he came to a stop when he saw Julianne sitting on the couch, looking unharmed. Steven was standing a couple of yards from her but quickly moved farther away when Duncan stormed into the room. The panther was missing a shirt but was otherwise dressed.

Duncan tried to meet Julianne's gaze, but she looked away from him. And he understood why if she had heard what he thought she had, but it still hurt that she wouldn't acknowledge him.

Trevor stormed into the room followed closely by Michael. Both of them stopped next to Duncan and took in the scene in the room.

Duncan didn't know exactly what to say or do, but he couldn't just stand there. Julianne needed him, or at least he needed her. He had to clear up the misunderstanding and tell her what she meant to him. How important she was to him and how much he loved her.

"Julianne." He took a step toward her. "I'm sorry. I think we need to talk."

She sighed before lifting her gaze to his. There was so much pain in her eyes it almost floored him. "Yes, I think we do."

Duncan narrowed his eyes as he glanced at Steven, who had moved as far away from them into the living room as he could get. Swinging his gaze back to Julianne, he studied her more closely. "Did he hurt you?"

Before Julianne could reply, Steven spoke. "I haven't hurt her. I never touched your mate, I swear."

Duncan's eyes shot to the panther in surprise. He had called Julianne Duncan's mate. But why would he do that? Unless Julianne had claimed to be his mate to get away from the panther. But the panther could easily have verified that she wasn't. It didn't make sense.

Looking back at Julianne, he saw that she had closed her eyes and tipped her head a bit forward. Her shoulders sagged in defeat. But what had him closing the distance to her in three long strides was the tears that leaked down her cheeks.

"Julianne," he whispered as he kneeled before her and put his hands on her cheeks, wiping her tears away with his thumbs.

"Please don't," she whispered but didn't pull away from him.

Duncan didn't let her go. If she pulled away, he

would let her, but until she did, he would keep his hands on her, touching her. "You only heard a part of my conversation with Leith and Trevor, Julianne, and not the most important part. Please come with me back to Leith's house so we can talk. I'll explain everything."

Julianne nodded before opening her eyes. She pulled away from him, and he let his hands drop away from her. Pain settled in his chest, but he wouldn't push her.

She rose from the couch and walked around him toward the door. He got up and followed her. Trevor, Michael, and Steven were gone. He hadn't heard them leave the house, but they obviously had without him noticing.

When they exited the house, he saw Steven standing next to Trevor and Michael by Trevor's car. Jennie and Steph were standing a few yards away by Michael's rental.

"I won't, I promise." The panther's voice was laced with fear as he spoke.

Trevor's gaze moved from Steven to Duncan as Duncan moved toward them. "The panther has promised never to pester Julianne again. I'm not sure whether to believe him or not."

"I'll never even speak to her again." Steven turned to Duncan. "Please believe me. I didn't know she was your mate, or I would never—"

"Why do you keep calling her my mate?" Duncan frowned at the panther.

"What?" Steven looked confused. "Because she is. I realize you might not have had the chance to tell everyone yet since it's so recent, but—"

"No." Duncan felt his spine stiffen as the shock reverberated through his body. He hadn't broken her skin. He had checked. Her skin had been smooth and unbroken.

"You don't even know that you mated her?" Steven's voice was filled with anger and disbelief. "Did she even get a choice?"

"No." Duncan had whispered the word. If it was true that he had mated Julianne accidentally, that was unforgivable. He wanted her desperately but not like this. Never like this.

He spun and walked to Julianne, where she was standing on the other side of the car, facing away from him. Steven was raving about something behind him, but he didn't have time for the panther at the moment.

Walking up to stand in front of Julianne, he looked down into her face. She didn't meet his gaze, but at least she didn't turn away from him.

Studying her face, he asked the most difficult question he had ever asked in his life. "Did I break your skin when we had sex?"

Instead of answering him, she pulled the collar of her shirt down a little to reveal a small cut on her collarbone.

Duncan sucked in a breath at the sight of the small cut. His chest constricted as he realized what he had done. He had been so sure that he had been able to pull away in time, but his fang had nicked her without him noticing. And he hadn't seen it when he studied her, because she had been lying on her stomach, hiding the tiny wound from view. Even in the shower he hadn't noticed it, since it had been hidden by her hair at the time.

He looked down, not sure what to say. Nothing he could ever say or do could make up for what he had done to her. He had tied her to him without asking her if that was what she wanted. And there was no way back. No way to undo what he had done. He had condemned her to a life with him whether she wanted him or not. And if she didn't want him…

"I'm so sorry, Julianne. I didn't even know that… And that only makes it worse. I'm so sorry. So very, very sorry."

"Oh, stop apologizing and tell her that you love her." Trevor's loud voice made Duncan snap his head up to look at his friend.

Trevor rolled his eyes when Duncan just stared at him. "Duncan, you're hurting her. Tell her that she's your true mate and that you love her. That's what you set out to do when you left the kitchen, remember? Now, do it!"

"I…" Duncan moved his gaze to Julianne and was startled when their gazes locked.

"Is that true?" Julianne whispered as she stared up at him. Was there hope in her eyes? He thought there was.

"Yes." He'd breathed the word before repeating it more clearly. "Yes. I love you. You're mine, my true mate. I just didn't understand it until Leith and Trevor snapped me out of my old delusion. I've been so stupid, Julianne. I'm so sorry. I—"

His words were cut off when Julianne threw her arms around his neck and held on tightly. "I love you, Duncan. So much."

Enclosing her in his arms, Duncan held her tightly as he breathed in her scent. It was still her familiar scent of chocolate and cloves, but there was another scent woven into it. His own scent, marking her as his mate. His chest felt like it was going to explode with happiness and love. Julianne was his. Truly his forever.

∞∞∞∞

Julianne kept a tight hold on Duncan's hand as they walked into Leith's house together. She didn't want to let him go again. Not ever. She had been so sure that he loved someone else, and she still couldn't quite believe he loved her. They had only met a few days ago, and already they were mated. It was all a bit much really, but at the same time, she was deliriously happy. She was going to spend the rest of her life with this amazing man. Duncan was hers.

She had expected them to go to the kitchen, but instead Duncan pulled her down the hallway and into their bedroom, closing the door behind them. Before she had a chance to say anything, he was kissing her. Opening her mouth to his insistent tongue, she melted into the kiss. It felt so good being this close to him. So right. Like she had come home.

Duncan gently broke the kiss and lifted his head to look into her eyes. Caressing her cheeks with his hands, he leaned forward and kissed her forehead before gazing into her eyes again. "I thought I'd lost you, and I've never been so scared in my entire life. Don't be surprised if I don't let you out of my sight for a long time. I've got a strong need to keep you close and protected. You have to tell me if I get too overprotective and annoying, okay? I want you happy more than anything else."

Staring up into his warm black eyes, she smiled. "I thought I'd lost you too. That your heart belonged to someone else. Even though we had just met, and I shouldn't have been this attached to you, it still hurt so much. I'm sorry I ran, but I just had to get away. I needed some time to think and come to terms with you never being able to love me."

"I love you, Julianne." Duncan's eyes were filled with the emotion supporting his tenderly spoken words. "Leith understood it even though I didn't, and he helped me realize my infatuation with Sarah when I was seventeen was just that, a kid's stupid infatuation. I never loved her, and she was never my true mate. No wonder she thought I was immature and stupid when I told her. I was."

Julianne narrowed her eyes at him. If she ever met this Sarah, she would make her suffer for the way she had treated Duncan. Sure, it was a long time ago, but Sarah's behavior had caused him a lot of pain for many years.

"What?" Duncan stared at her. "You look angry."

"I am. I hope I never meet Sarah, because I'll make her suffer for what she put you through."

Duncan barked out a laugh. "My mate exacting revenge for my hurt feelings. I believe you, but it's not necessary." His expression sobered. "What Sarah did doesn't matter anymore. And if I'm going to be completely honest with you and myself, my pride is the real reason I thought Sarah was my true mate for so long. If I'd been man enough to talk to one of my friends about what happened back then, I probably would've realized my mistake many years ago. But I didn't want anyone to know that I had failed to secure my true mate. That I was a failure as a shifter. I was an idiot."

"No. You're not an idiot, but I think you're right about your pride." Julianne put her hand on his cheek. "But that's all over now. We're mated and are going to live happily ever after."

A smile spread across Duncan's face. "Happily ever after. That sounds good. Can we start now?"

Julianne laughed. "We've already started. Haven't you noticed?"

Staring into her eyes, he nodded. "Yeah, I think you're right." He leaned down and covered her lips with his.

The kiss was soft and tender, and Julianne felt like she could stay like this forever. Until a thought forced its way into her mind. Slowly breaking the kiss, she pulled away. "Before we get so wrapped up in each other that we forget where we are, I need to tell everyone what happened today."

Duncan frowned. "Everybody knows by now that Steven managed to find you even here in Fort Augustus. We'll get to the bottom of how he did that, but I don't think you need to worry about him pestering you anymore."

"I know, and I'm not talking about Steven. Well, not just Steven. I'm talking about Ambrosia."

"What?" Duncan took a step back, his eyes widening in shock. "You saw Ambrosia?"

Nodding, she put a hand on Duncan's arm to calm him. "Yes, and—"

Duncan didn't let her finish. "Did she hurt you?" His eyes studied her face before continuing down her body, obviously trying to find out if she had any injuries she hadn't told him about.

"No, you arrived before they could hurt me. And since I was already mated, they might've just left me alone. Steven had just sniffed my skin and confirmed my suspicion that I was mated to you, when Ambrosia suddenly ran across the room and jumped out of the window. She must've heard or sensed you somehow."

The color drained from Duncan's face as he stared at her. "Steven was going to mate you. With Ambrosia's help."

Julianne closed the distance between them and put her arms around his neck. Staring into his black eyes, she kept her voice calm as she spoke. "Yes, but it didn't happen. I'm fine, thanks to you. Because I was already your mate." Rising up on her toes, she put her lips on his before burying her hands in his curly brown hair, massaging his scalp with her fingers.

His body was rigid for several seconds until the tension gradually eased, and Duncan started kissing her back. A few seconds later he gently pulled away from her and studied her face. "I think you're right that we need to tell the others about this. If you feel up to it. But I don't want you pushing yourself. It can wait until you've rested."

Julianne smiled up into his face. Her mate. So kind and caring, and so strong and protective, all at the same time. She was unbelievably lucky. "I'm fine, Duncan. A lot has happened in the last few days, but I'm okay. And I've got you to lean on, giving me extra strength. Let's go talk to the others. I want to thank them. And I'd like to see Sabrina and thank her for what she did." During their drive back to Leith's house, Duncan had given Julianne a brief account of how they had found her.

He opened his mouth like he was going to argue his point, but then he closed it and sighed. "Okay, but if you feel tired, you tell me. Promise me."

Chuckling, she nodded. "I promise."

Taking her hand securely in his, Duncan opened the door and they headed to the kitchen.

Everyone was gathered in the kitchen when they walked in. Trevor, Jennie, Michael, and Steph were sitting at the kitchen table. Leith was standing by the coffee machine making coffee, and Sabrina was just placing two cups on the table in front of Michael and Steph. All heads turned in their direction, and Sabrina straightened and took a few steps toward them before stopping.

"Are you all right?" Sabrina's blue eyes scanned Julianne's face, probably understanding a lot of what had happened to Julianne just by studying her expression. It was part of her witchy powers.

Julianne gave her friend a big smile. "I'm fine. You found me in time, so nothing happened. I'm sorry that I left like that, causing so much trouble." She swung her gaze around to everyone in the room, meeting each person's eyes in turn.

"Well, you're not the first one to do that." Jennie smiled back at her. "First I went missing when I thought Trevor didn't want me, and then I gave him blue balls before I was able to finally accept his wolf. You have nothing on me. Although, I didn't have a possessive ex stalking me. That probably evens the score a bit."

"Don't remind me of all that. You almost gave me a heart attack." Trevor scowled at Jennie and pulled her chair closer until her hip was touching his. Putting his arm around her shoulder, he kissed the side of her head while Jennie smiled happily.

Julianne smiled at the obvious affection between the two mates. It reflected what she had with Duncan. Turning to him, she met his gaze. There was so much love in his eyes, and it was all for her. It probably would take her a while to get used to.

But there was something she needed to do. Turning back to look at the people in the room, she felt her smile disappear. "I have to tell you what happened when I left this house. You don't know all of it yet."

"Please have a seat first. Would you like some coffee or tea?" Leith moved to stand behind Sabrina as he talked, and Julianne noticed the way her friend's features stiffened a little. It was subtle, but Sabrina reacted to the man's presence. Julianne didn't know whether that was a good thing or a bad thing.

"Thank you, Leith. Coffee would be perfect." She smiled at him.

"For me too. Thanks." Duncan had spoken beside her.

They sat down by the table, Duncan pulling her close and putting an arm around her like he was trying to imitate Trevor's actions.

Julianne told them how she was offered a lift by Ambrosia, and how the woman had brought her to the small house just outside Fort Augustus. Judging by the shock on everybody's faces, none of them had considered the possibility that Ambrosia was helping Steven, or perhaps it was the other way around. When Julianne revealed how she had discovered she was already mated to Duncan, Sabrina narrowed her eyes at him. But her friend didn't look surprised at the revelation, indicating that somebody had already told Sabrina and Leith about their accidental mating.

Steph was the first one to speak. "That bitch. We have to find her before she tries again with someone else. For all we know she might have several other shifters lined up to be king of their shifter group. I don't like this one bit."

"I agree." Sabrina had taken a seat at the table. "You mentioned that it was a couple of weeks since Steven started calling and texting you. Do you remember the exact day?"

Julianne shook her head. "No, but I can check my phone later. I guess it doesn't matter if I turn it back on again now. He has no reason to contact me anymore."

"He'd better not. I'd kill him." The viciousness and power in Duncan's voice had her head snap around to look at him. There was something about the power in his voice that seemed to lick along her spine and cause her channel to clench in anticipation.

Duncan shrugged as he stared at Julianne. "I'm a shifter, Julianne. Anyone going after my mate is fair game. No regrets."

She just nodded slowly. Julianne didn't know a lot about shifter behavior yet and what mating really entailed. Duncan seemed to be serious about killing Steven if he contacted her again. It was both scary and strangely romantic.

"How have you been able to hide your power all these years?" Trevor's words made Julianne frown and turn to him. But he wasn't looking at her. His eyes were on Duncan.

"What do you mean?" There was a look of confusion on Duncan's face.

Trevor leaned forward in his seat, staring at Duncan. "You're clearly an alpha. How have you been able to hide your alpha power all these years?"

"I... I don't know. It's never crossed my mind that I could be an alpha. Although, I've never used my power much before."

"You have found your true mate." Leith was sitting next to Sabrina, and he seemed to be studying Duncan like he was seeing beyond his exterior. "The rejection of the woman you thought was your true mate when you were young may have subdued your power. Finding your true mate has healed you and allowed your body to attain its natural power level."

Duncan nodded slowly. "You're probably right." He was silent for a few seconds before he continued. "It's going to take some getting used to. I've never considered myself a leader."

Trevor chuckled. "I have. You'd be perfect as a pack master. I always thought it was such a shame that you weren't an alpha, because you have a way with people that is quite unique. You care about everyone around you, seeing and appreciating everyone for who they are. Adults and pups alike come to you for help and advice, and you give it freely. If anyone should be pack master in Fearolc, it's you."

"No, I..." Duncan stopped and turned to Julianne. "I want to spend more time with my mate before we even think about discussing what to do next. Whatever we decide to do, Julianne, we'll make that decision together. You're my life now."

Julianne felt tears well up in her eyes at his words.

He was the most incredible man she had ever met, and she already knew she wanted to spend the rest of her life with him. If that life was in Fearolc, it was okay with her. More than okay. She liked the serenity and beauty of the area, and Julianne knew she would be happy there.

EPILOGUE

Duncan closed the door to their bedroom behind them. They had all had dinner together and spent some time discussing the recent developments with Ambrosia and her plans to use shifters to gain power. Initially, they had thought Ambrosia's sole focus was alpha shifters, but since Steven wasn't an alpha, they would have to rethink their whole strategy. Their whole mission to prevent Ambrosia from gaining power and disrupting the shifter power structure had just become considerably more complex.

Turning to his mate, Duncan smiled when he saw she had already removed her shirt. Her hands moved to take off her shorts, but Duncan put his hands on hers to stop her. "Please, let me undress you. I would like to undress my mate and take my time doing it."

Julianne grinned up at him. "And how much time would that be? Five seconds?"

He narrowed his eyes at her, pretending to be offended. "Is that what you think of me? That I don't know how to undress a woman other than ripping her clothes off?"

Julianne laughed. "Well, I guess we'll see won't we."

His beautiful mate was teasing him, and he loved it. It was an aspect of a good relationship that he hadn't considered before witnessing the loving banter between Trevor and Jennie.

Looking down into Julianne's sparkling green eyes, Duncan smiled. "I look forward to sleeping with you. I've never slept next to someone before."

"You haven't?" Julianne's eyes widened in surprise. "You said you've never cuddled before. But you've never even slept beside a woman?"

"No." He shook his head. "So tonight will be two firsts for me."

"I like that. Being your first in something." Her smile was wide as she stared up at him. "You're the first man who's ever given me an orgasm without touching my clit. I've never experienced that before. I didn't even think it was possible for me."

Duncan felt himself grinning at his mate's words. "Good. I like that." He leaned down and captured her lips in a passionate kiss. Julianne's words about giving her an orgasm had his blood flow increasing to his already semierect cock. She was sore, and he completely respected that, but there were other options for giving each other pleasure that they could explore.

The taste of her sweet mouth was increasing his need for her. Reaching behind her back, he unclasped her bra before putting his hands on her hips. Caressing slowly up her sides, he continued until he cupped her soft breasts beneath her loose bra.

Julianne moaned into his mouth. She reached behind him and gripped his ass, pressing his hips tightly against hers.

Duncan rolled her nipples between his thumbs and index fingers, and Julianne squirmed against him. The friction against his cock had him breaking the kiss and growling in response.

When Julianne let go of his ass, he took a small step back. The friction between their bodies had felt amazing, but he wanted to do something for Julianne first before he was too far gone.

He wasn't prepared when her hand suddenly disappeared down into his shorts and gripped his shaft firmly. "Julianne." Her name sounded more like a growl, but he couldn't help it. Her hand moving up and down his straining cock made speaking difficult.

"I want you inside me." Julianne's voice was breathy.

Putting a hand on the one she had wrapped around his shaft to stop her movement, he stared down into her beautiful eyes. There was a glow in them showing her need.

"You're sore and I don't want to hurt you. But I can use my mouth on you."

She shook her head. "No, I don't feel sore anymore. I need you inside me, Duncan."

"Are you sure?" Just the thought of sliding into her tight, wet sheath again had his cock throbbing. But hurting her was unacceptable.

"I think so."

Duncan cupped her cheeks as he stared into her eyes. "Okay, but if you feel any discomfort, you'll tell me."

"I will." She stepped back from him and pushed her shorts and panties down at the same time, before shrugging out of her bra. So much for taking his time undressing his mate.

Duncan followed her example and stripped out of his clothes. He advanced on her, forcing her to back up until her legs hit the side of the bed.

He pushed her gently, until she landed on her back on the bed with a little squeak, and he quickly covered her body with his. Duncan supported some of his weight on his elbows as he crushed his lips to hers in a bruising kiss. He wanted her so badly his cock was throbbing where it was trapped between them.

Julianne's hands on him pushing him away made him lift his head and raise an eyebrow at her in question.

"It's my turn to be on top. I want to ride you." Julianne narrowed her eyes at him like she was expecting him to argue.

Duncan nodded. He liked the thought of having her sit on him. "But I want to make you come on my tongue first to make sure you're prepared for me." And it would allow him to verify that her soreness was gone before entering her.

"I want you inside me so much. I don't want to wait. And I think it will be all right if we take it slow."

Duncan nodded slowly. The determination in Julianne's eyes made him realize she had already made up her mind. "But if you feel any discomfort, you stop. Please."

Julianne smiled and nodded. "I will. Now get on your back and stop worrying about me."

He rolled over onto his back, and Julianne straddled

his hips, but before she could start lowering herself onto him, Duncan grabbed her hips to stop her. "Condom."

Her eyes widened as she froze. "I forgot again. What's wrong with me?"

"I'd like to think that you want me so much that you have trouble thinking about small things like protection." Duncan grinned up at her.

That made her laugh, which was his intention.

Getting off the bed, Julianne found the box of condoms and removed one package. Climbing onto the bed, she straddled his legs before opening the small package and taking out the condom.

"Ready, big boy?" Her eyes gleamed as she put a hand between his legs and fondled his balls. "Do you want me too?"

Duncan groaned and reached up to knead her breasts. "Yes, I'm getting desperate. I think you know by now the effect you have on me."

Julianne smoothed the condom down over his rock-hard shaft before rising up on her knees and moving to straddle his hips. Using her hands to position the head of his cock at her entrance, she slowly lowered her body to take him inside her.

Duncan fisted his hands in the sheets to prevent himself from gripping her hips. Just the sight of his cock disappearing inch by inch into Julianne's tight pussy had him already close to coming, and he gritted his teeth to hold on for her. He wanted her to come first.

"Duncan." The way she choked out his name had him looking at his mate. Her eyes were wide with what looked like a mixture of surprise and need. "Are you already close? It's like I can feel your pleasure building."

The last inch of his shaft vanished into her welcoming heat, and he groaned as Julianne sat down with him buried deep inside her.

Then he felt it too. Her body's response to him filling her. Like her pleasure resulting from having him inside her was somehow shared with him. It felt amazing, and even more so when she started moving up and down his length.

"Julianne. You feel so amazing I don't think I'll be able to hold on for much longer."

Duncan had intended to let Julianne be in full control, but feeling himself racing toward his climax, he reached between her legs and put his thumb on her clit. She gasped as his finger slid over her pleasure button, and he felt her pleasure build faster. Her movements became more erratic, and he put a hand on her hip to steady her as she increased her pace. Then she swirled her hips, and he felt himself tipping over the edge. Thrusting hard and burying himself deep inside her, his whole body jerked as he started coming hard. A couple of seconds later, he felt Julianne follow, and pleasure like he had never felt before flooded him. It erupted and spread through his body, taking his breath away.

"Holy fuck." Julianne's whispered words had him smiling. She was lying on his chest with his cock still inside her.

Duncan had no idea how long they had been wrapped in ecstasy together, but it must have been longer than he had ever experienced before. "I think that's an appropriate definition. I didn't expect us to be able to experience each other's feelings like that so soon after being mated. Apparently, it's quite common for true mates to be able to do that, and it's supposed to get stronger with time."

"Really?" Julianne raised her head and stared down at him. "Because that was out of this world. I think we should try it again to make sure it wasn't just a one off." A wicked smile spread across her face.

Laughing, Duncan gripped her hips and lifted her off him. "I'm up for that if you are. I just need to get rid of this condom and find a new one."

"You do that, big boy. I'll be waiting for you right here."

∞∞∞∞

Sabrina walked into her bedroom and closed the door behind her. Breathing out slowly, she rolled her shoulders to try to relieve some of the tension permeating her body. It felt like she had been on high alert continuously for most of the day. Some of the reason was what had happened to Julianne. But mostly it was because of Leith. She couldn't remember ever having been this attracted to a man. He was gorgeous beyond belief in an understated kind of way, with those dark-green eyes that could see directly into your soul. He was tall with the build of a swimmer, and Sabrina had trouble forgetting the image of his bare upper body.

But that was exactly what she needed to do. She had to forget him. Leith wasn't for her no matter how much she wanted that to be the case. He was too much of what she wanted, and that wasn't a good thing in her case. Sabrina had known for a long time that she would never be able to let herself fall for someone, and she had come to terms with that fact. Or so she had thought, until she met Leith. For the first time in her life, Sabrina regretted her situation, and she didn't want to be the one she was. For the first time in her life, she felt the weight of the sacrifices she had to make to be whom and what she was.

Sitting down heavily on the bed, Sabrina stared at the wall, not seeing Leith's beautiful paintings. At least Julianne had found a nice man. A fantastic man, actually. Someone who cared about her and cherished her for the woman she was. Sabrina was happy for her friend. Julianne deserved everything good that came her way.

Pulling in a deep breath, Sabrina narrowed her eyes in determination. So, life was a bit rough at the moment, but they would soon be leaving Leith's house, and she could forget about the man. It wouldn't be easy; she realized that. But it would happen with time. Soon everything would be back to normal.

Getting up and rummaging through her bag, she found her bikini and a towel. She hadn't been able to go for a swim earlier in the day, and even though it was close to midnight and dark outside, it would be nice to submerge herself in the water to clear her head. There was no way she was going to be able to go to sleep yet, anyway.

After opening her bedroom door carefully, she tiptoed down the hall to the lower level entrance. Sabrina didn't want to alert anyone to her plans. The door opened on silent hinges, and she stepped outside. Hopefully, nobody would lock the door while she was gone.

She hurried down the path to the small beach not far from the house, and after taking a quick look around, she stripped out of her clothes. A sliver of a moon was up, giving her just enough light to see the contours of the landscape around her. Eyeing her bikini, she considered putting it on, but then she decided against it. The beach and surrounding area were empty. Nobody was around to see her skinny-dipping.

Leaving everything on the beach, she walked into the water, careful not to make much sound. When the water reached her waist, she lowered the rest of her body into the dark liquid and started swimming parallel to the beach using long, silent strokes.

Sabrina didn't know what made her turn her head to gaze out across the loch. It wasn't a sound as much as a feeling. A feeling that there was someone there, or perhaps something. Not seeing anything unusual at first, she was about to turn her head back when she spotted it. The curve of a large body rose silently from the water for a few seconds before disappearing again as quietly as it had appeared.

Sabrina's feet found the lakebed, and she slowly stood as she stared at the spot where the creature had been visible. The water came up to just above her nipples, and she stood completely still as she silently prayed that the creature would surface again, to give her another glimpse of something unique and magnificent.

---THE END---

BOOKS BY CAROLINE S. HILLIARD

Highland Shifters

A Wolf's Unlikely Mate, Book 1
Taken by the Cat, Book 2
Wolf Mate Surprise, Book 3
Seduced by the Monster, Book 4
Tempted by the Wolf, Book 5
Pursued by the Panther, Book 6
True to the Wolf, Book 7 – May 2023
Book 8 – TBA

Troll Guardians

Captured by the Troll, Book 1
Saving the Troll, Book 2
Book 3 – TBA

ABOUT THE AUTHOR

Thank you for reading my book. I hope the story gave you a nice little break from normality.

I have always loved reading and immersing myself in different worlds. Recently I have discovered that I also love writing. Stories have been playing in my head for as long as I can remember, and now I'm taking the time to develop some of these stories and write them down. Spending time in a world of my own creation has been a surprising enjoyment, and I hope to spend as much time as possible writing in the years to come.

I'm an independent author, meaning that I can write what I want and when I want. I primarily write for myself, but hopefully my stories can brighten someone else's day as well. The characters I develop tend to take on a life of their own and push the story in the direction they want, which means that the stories do not follow a set structure or specific literary style. However, I'm a huge fan of happily ever after, so that is a guarantee.

I'm married and the mother of two teenagers. Life is busy with a fulltime job in addition to family life. Writing is something I enjoy in my spare time.

You can find me here:
caroline.s.hilliard@gmail.com
www.carolineshilliard.com
www.facebook.com/Author.CarolineS.Hilliard/
www.amazon.com/author/carolineshilliard/
www.goodreads.com/author/show/22044909.Caroline_S_Hilliard

Printed in Great Britain
by Amazon